High Crimes
and
Low Stakes

High Crimes
and
Low Stakes

Christopher
Worrad Payne

LIPA
PUBLISHING

First published by AuthorHouse Inc 2013
This paperback edition published by Lipa Publishing 2013

ISBN 978-971-9578-03-1(Paperback)
978-971-9578-07-9(eBook)

Lipa Publishing
Helen Street,
Base View Homes
Lipa City, Batangas
The Philippines 4217

http://lipapublishing.com

*To all my former colleagues at the
American University in Bulgaria,
this satire is respectfully dedicated*

High Crime

',,,,a crime of an infamous nature contrary to public morality but not technically constituting a felony;'

Webster's Dictionary

Low Stakes

From the quotation

'Academic politics is the most vicious and bitter form of politics because the stakes are so low.'

Wallace Stanley Stayre(1905-1972)
quoted in The Wall St. Journal
20th December 1973

This famous quotation is also attributed to many others, including Henry Kissinger, Woodrow Wilson, Richard Neustadt, C.P. Snow, Daniel Patrick Moynihan *et al*.

'War has rules, mud wrestling has rules - politics has no rules.'

Ross Perot
Businessman and Politician (1930 -

One

*F*riday night and I just got paid..' The music went round and round in Damon Dexter's head. Bored, he thought, I am definitely bored. What the hell am I going to do this weekend?

He had been at the American Embassy in this little corner of Southeastern Europe for four months now and life was becoming tedious. Every weekend the same pleasures or lack of them, in a country currently ranked where, well, fairly near the bottom that was for sure, of desirable and exciting places to live.

Why was he here, he wondered? His job title was 'Commercial Officer' but his actual job was collecting and arranging and reporting the scraps of intelligence which came his way either from what he picked up in casual conversations or from the newspaper or from some of his many stringers in a network of informants which he had inherited when he had first come to the country.

All these trivia were sorted into whatever order seemed appropriate and reported back to the Balkan Office chief at Central Intelligence Agency Headquarters in Langley, Virginia. Little of what he heard or read or saw ever seemed anything more than everyday gossip or small talk but presumably it was all of interest to his masters back at the CIA HQ who were responsible for constructing 'the big picture'.

Damon Dexter had been chosen for this particular position because he was fluent in many of the local languages of this part of the world. He was not just fluent in their formal versions, he could also understand the idioms, the slang and the nuances of the various peasant *patois*. This was because he was only second-generation American. His parents, Irina and Gregor Dettric, had retired knowing only basic American English, which had been little more than sufficient to get their surname changed to Dexter in an attempt to put their Balkan peasant upbringing behind them and to wear their new nationality with pride.

They were born and brought up near here, reflected their son, as he gazed out of the embassy window at a grey scene of concrete desolation, not yet modernized or developed more than twenty years after the ending of the socialist era.

Damon had had a difficult childhood. From a home where his parents would switch from Serbo-Croat to Albanian to Macedonian and several other tongues at will, he had started school with little English. As a result, his schoolmates were, as children are, cruel about his difficulties. They had taunted him for his lack of English and, when it began to improve, they taunted him for his accent.

But children learn languages quickly and by the seventh grade, he could speak demotic American teenager English perfectly and he was already soaring ahead of his contemporaries in all his academic subjects, even English.

After a *magna cum laude* bachelor's degree at the state university in Wyoming, he won a scholarship to work for a master's in international relations and modern languages at Georgetown University in Washington DC. From where it was just a matter of waiting for the CIA to make him an unrefusable offer.

He had been with the Company for ten years now, enjoying various postings around the world and an off-duty bachelor lifestyle of parties, fun and exotic women. He had been promoted twice, each time after he had been tested in the danger zones of Lagos and Beirut.

What he didn't know was that having done a good job in those two difficult cities, he was ready to be moved to

2

his ultimate posting in the southern Balkans where his familial knowledge of the local languages and customs would be of greatest value to his masters back home. The long, expensive apprenticeship in Nigeria and Lebanon, would, his seniors anticipated, soon be paying dividends.

He was a normal thirty-two year old single man and he needed the company of women. He wanted to continue, for as long as possible, the easy-going commitment-free way of life which he had enjoyed since he had left college for the CIA. He was aware that it was the Company policy to prefer married men when it came to promotion above Damon's present level, particularly men with non-American wives.

Thus, partly for career reasons, many of his seniors had Vietnamese or Korean or Hispanic wives whom they had married on one of their postings. The thinking was that a foreign wife will move to a different embassy in a new country more easily than an American, who will constantly be looking to go back stateside.

Damon was aware of the policy, and his ear was attuned to the regular heavy hints that he should get married soon before it was too late and the promotion bus had already left. Promotion, he thought, who needs it? Time for that later. *'Friday night and I just got paid...'*

When he had first arrived in this half-strange foreign capital, only half-strange because he had heard his parents talk about it often, he had soon found a fellow soul. Charlie Le Moine was another long-time CIA man, also unmarried and thirty-something. Together they had bemoaned the dearth of attractive ladies on the streets and the absence of decent places to eat, or, more importantly, to drink.

'What about the embassy wives?' Damon had asked

Charlie, shortly after he had arrived.

'It's very important that you stay away from the embassy wives,' Charlie had warned him.

'Why? There was a very hot scene in Beirut. The husbands were always away in lethal places like Iraq. It was a matter of 'enjoy yourself, it's later than you think' down there.'

'You will find, bro, that it is a lot different here. Just stay away from them.'

On his first weekend in the Balkans, Damon had made a once-only obligatory Saturday pilgrimage to his ancestral village in the hills. It was like stepping back in time. The hovels were still primitive – they reminded him of a survival course the CIA had sent him on, where they had to construct a shack from whatever materials they could forage and then live rough in it for 48 hours. The village's only street was a muddy lane which humans shared with pigs and geese. Damon couldn't get away fast enough.

That evening, he had gone back to his dormitory room on the US diplomatic compound. Senior personnel would get a housing allowance and could live, as they call it, 'on the economy'. But for newcomers and for junior staff, a comfortable apartment was provided in the gated compound, which was guarded by armed US Marines. That was fine for Charlie and Damon, who both had apartments there - the compound offered the advantage that they could live rent-free without needing to do any chores.

On most Friday and Saturday evenings, there was something of a party atmosphere in the compound's clubhouse where there was an American restaurant, a bar with drinks at subsidized prices and, most Fridays, a disco. The clubhouse was a regular haunt for most of those personnel without houses or apartments outside.

Actually, it was the only haunt because embassy staff were strongly advised not to socialize with the local people unless for strictly business reasons. Certain parts of the city, where the bars and brothels were located, were officially out of bounds. This was partly out of American prudishness but mainly because, over the years, there had been a steady stream of incidents.

These had usually taken the form of drunken fights between Americans and local men. Each incident had necessitated a public apology from the Ambassador to the Chief of Police or the Mayor. The apology followed automatically irrespective of the facts of the dispute or who had actually thrown the first punch or drawn the first knife. Or, for that matter, the level of personal damage sustained by any of the assailants. Very, very occasionally, the fights had led to serious bloodshed, even death.

After one such incident, the stabbing of an embassy clerk, the entire staff was ordered never to visit the dangerous areas after dark. They were also advised not to buy their own cars but to rely on a car pool where they could sign out a vehicle should they need it. When the compound had been built, the ambassador of the day had made sure that it was located in a quiet suburb far from the city center.

There being little else to do at the weekend, Damon and Charlie would sometimes spend time in the bar of the embassy's social club. On Saturdays there would be a movie. These minimal excitements, plus workouts in the gym, made it a boring and frustrating routine for a pair of single young men. By now, Damon fully understood what Charlie had meant by his warning to avoid the embassy wives.

When he had first appeared on the scene, Damon had quickly attracted the attention of some of them. On his first Friday night at the disco, the wives had looked

5

him up and down and, he surmised, they had liked what they had seen. He was, after all, a fit, good-looking presentable man with, crucially for the women who were appraising him so brazenly, no wedding ring.

Damon had ignored Charlie's advice at first. He was young, red-blooded and healthy and, when he made his first foray into the Friday night scene, he had had the effect he had been used to in his previous postings. It was only a few minutes after he had settled down with his drink before Karen came over to introduce herself.

Karen was one of those thirty-something Californian matrons who stays fit with constant workouts and remains tanned even in winter from long hours on the sun bed. Her inch-perfect figure was contained within a chic designer green cocktail dress which showed off, when she sat down, her tanned shapely legs and muscular thighs. She wore a single rope of pearls which had the intended effect of drawing attention to her perfect round cleavage. She was, she told Damon, tired of being left alone when her husband was off on one of his jaunts 'downrange', that is, to one of the world's warzones.

Soon Karen and Damon were drinking wine together and soon after that they were dancing closely. More wine and more dancing followed until Karen had become quite tipsy.

Damon, experienced in such matters, judged his moment carefully, while Karen was clinging tightly to him in a slow smoochy dance for which the disk jockey had turned down the lights.

'Shall we continue this upstairs?' Karen was instantly sober. 'No,' she said firmly, 'that's not a very good idea at all.' And with that she detached herself from him and strode purposefully over to the large round table where her friends had been waiting and watching, leaving Damon standing partnerless in middle of the dance floor, surrounded by couples still desperately wrapped around each other.

The last view Damon had had of Karen before he threw back his drink and went back to his apartment upstairs, was to see her in furious conversation with the other women who were casting angry glances at him.

The following Friday Damon had tried again. This time, he attracted the attentions of Maria, a Hispanic housewife married, she told him, to a very bad husband who was never home. Work, work, work, she complained. All he ever does is work unless he doesn't come home because he's screwing one of his secretaries.

'But,' she told him drunkenly, 'tonight is my night! Yes, Friday night is when I can be free!' Remembering his humiliation of the week before, Damon was especially careful with his timing of the shall-we-shan't-we critical question.

But Maria was willing, more than willing, it seemed, to go back to Damon's apartment. Once there, they began the dance of love. Damon even managed to unbutton Maria's blouse, unzip her skirt and remove her shoes. Before, that is, Maria came to her senses.

'No,' she cried, 'I can't. You got me drunk and now you just want to take advantage of me. It's not fair! It's sexual harassment! No, it's more than that, it's attempted rape! I've a good mind to make a complaint!'

With that, she put her shoes back on, zipped up her skirt and ran from the room, clutching her blouse. The door slammed shut in Damon's face.

On his third Friday visit to the disco, Damon tried one more time. This time his partner was a woman in her late twenties called Cherie-Anne, who was, she told Damon, fresh in from a training course stateside. She had, well, a sort of boyfriend, but he was in graduate school in New York, so she was now here pursuing her own career as a trainee diplomat. As the evening progressed, Damon found himself strongly attracted to this open, friendly young woman, who appeared to share none of the hang-ups of her older, married sisters.

When Damon asked her back to his bachelor apartment at the other end of the building, she had smiled and said, 'Yes, OK, why not?' and given him a little kiss on the cheek. Success at last, thought Damon. He escorted Cherie-Anne to the door of his apartment and briefly turned to put his key into the lock of the door. When he turned back to embrace the young woman, she pushed him away.

'I think you should know,' she told him, 'that I am not going in there. I have just been asked to be secretary of the sexual harassment ethics committee and what you are doing can get you fired! So leave it out, if you don't mind!' And she was gone.

Damon stopped going to the Friday night disco after that. Instead, Charlie and he would go to a safe bar near the embassy where they could eat and drink and commiserate with each other about sexual frustration and the neurotic mindset of the embassy women.

'What's wrong with them? asked Damon.

'I told you,' said Charlie. 'Leave the embassy wives alone.'

'It's not just the married ones though. It's all of them, single and married alike.'

'I agree,' said Charlie. 'It's like they've taken vows or something.'

'You, know,' said Damon, 'when you told me to lay off the embassy wives, I thought it was because of some order from above. Like it was some disciplinary thing, maybe embassy policy? But it's not. It's the women

8

themselves who are closing us down. They are leading us on and then refusing to put out.'

'Yes, they are all a bit too keen on political correctness and sexual harassment. It's probably because of that committee they set up. Spreading the word about male base desires and all that BS.'

'So,' said Damon,' it looks like our options are limited. Any ideas of just how two young fit guys are gonna get laid in this god-forsaken hole?'

'Embassy is a no-no, at least until the feminist storm-troopers go home. There are the local hookers, of course.' Charlie motioned towards two unsavory-looking women drinking beer and chain-smoking at the bar.

'They do say that you can become HIV positive just by entering this country's air space.' said Damon.

'You could try the local American University. Lots of nice girls from good families.'

'But aren't we barred from there by order from His Excellency himself.'

'That's true. It is probably not worth it. We would be in serious trouble if we went sniffing around there. Official line is that they are nothing to do with us and we are nothing to do with them.'

'In spite of the fact that half the faculty work for us.. Unofficially, of course,' said Damon.

'Unofficially. No point in having a so-called 'American' university in a place like this unless it's going to be useful for information.'

So the American University of the Southern Balkans or AUSB, was also eliminated from the list of potential sexual Eldorado's.

'I do have one idea, though,' said Charlie. 'I'll tell you what we could do.'

Charlie's plan was not the sort of thing that would have been approved of by His Excellency the United States

9

Ambassador. In fact, it was downright irregular, not to say dangerous. But desperate times drive men to desperate measures and they were certainly desperate, neither of them having been laid for months, whilst simultaneously having to endure the tantalizing provocation of the hair-trigger feminists who flaunted themselves at the Friday disco.

'What we will do,' explained Charlie, 'is to take one of the embassy cars and drive it over the border into Bulgaria. It's late spring now, so if we can get to Bansko, there are bound to be a lot of loose women down for the skiing. Book into a hotel.'

'That's perfect! A nice little bit of R 'n' R for two hungry boys!'

Damon found a hotel about four kilometers outside Bansko and Charlie arranged an embassy car. All would be wonderful on this little adventure and, feeling a little like naughty schoolboys playing truant from school, they took Friday afternoon off to travel over the mountains into Bulgaria. Their maps were good, the best that the CIA could provide and, when they showed their diplomatic passports at the border, they were waved through without being questioned. The distance on the map was only about 300 kilometers but over poor roads and mountain passes, they made slow progress and arrived at their hotel at eight pm after driving for nearly six hours.

'The night is yet young!'

'Yeah, and so are we! Let's party!'

Two

They got back into the embassy Mercedes and took the four kilometer trip into Bansko in search of any sex-starved female skiers who might be in need of American comforting. They finally wound up at the 'Miramar' Bar and Disco, which was exactly the sort of place they had been looking for. Once inside, they found themselves surrounded by young women.

'Hello American, you buy me drink?'

'Hi America! I love America. You sit by me? We make good time, yes?'

'These ain't your nice ski ladies, Charlie! These are hookers!'

'Relax! Enjoy yourself! You're only young once.'

The evening passed in a haze. The vodka came and went in an unending stream and the final bill, for the two completely drunk Americans, took every last cent of folding money they had been carrying. They were now both dead drunk and dead broke. Still, thought Damon, only three hundred dollars. Not too bad. ATM in the morning will put that right.

Being near incapable, they staggered outside to find that it had been snowing heavily while they had been in the Miramar and the Mercedes was indistinguishable from all the other snow-covered vehicles.

The cold also had the effect of sobering them up slightly but only as far as making them think, mistakenly, that they were fully sober when, actually, they were each about three times over most countries' legal blood alcohol level for driving. Beyond the lights of the Miramar's car park, the surrounding countryside was a dense impenetrable black.

They were already frozen by the time they found

their car and Damon had finally found his keys and opened it. They were both glad of the shelter and the promised imminent warmth. It had started snowing again..

'You take us, American.'

Charlie and Damon turned around in drunken surprise to see that somehow, they had no idea how, two of the hookers from the Bar Miramar had installed themselves on the back seats.

Neither girl looked older than about eighteen and they were certainly not dressed for the snow with their short skirts, bare midriffs, Lycra thigh-high boots and small zip-up jackets stretched tightly across their chests.

'You take us hotel, American. We go with you.'

'You can show us the way. It's the Hotel Aphrodite.'

'We know it good. Go there many times. No problem. Drive, American!'

Well under the influence, Damon and Charlie, with two teenage whores, called, possibly, Irina and Elitsa or maybe Elisaveta and Valentina, the men never learned their names, set off to drive the four kilometers in the dark and the snow to the Hotel Aphrodite. They turned down a lane on the right. Wasn't that the way they had come?

'No, wrong way, you take wrong. Now lost! Drive, American!'

Then, suddenly, ahead of them, they saw a light in the dark. They would be able to ask and get directions. When they got nearer though, they saw that the light was on one side of a road barrier which was being guarded by two Bulgarian policemen. This was a smugglers area, where contraband was smuggled nightly in and out of the European Union across the border with Bulgaria.

'Show them our diplomatic passports. They'll let us through. We can ask them where we are.'

'You forget, my friend, that we left our passports in the safe at the hotel as per orders.'

'So we have no ID?'

'Not unless we show them our Playboy Club membership cards.'

They stopped at the barrier.

'Papers!'

'We're sorry. They are back at Hotel Aphrodite.'

'No papers. This is very bad! You British?'

'No, American.'

The policeman then pushed his head right into the driver's side of the car. Damon could smell the policeman's stinking breath even though his senses were still dulled from the vast amount of booze he had consumed earlier. The policeman, a sergeant, was unwashed and unshaven and had bad, black teeth. Behind him cowered his colleague, a private. Not civilian police, military police.

'Hello American! You have dollar for me?' said the sergeant, waving his machine pistol in Damon's face. Then there was a click of the rear door as the two girls got out of the car and made a run for it.

'Your girls?' asked the sergeant. 'Let them go. Bad girls. Not nice. Find dollar for me!'

Damon felt under his seat. Always have at least two twenty dollar bills under the front seat in case you are stopped on the road, he had been advised on his training course. He felt again. Nothing there! The girls had taken it!

'I have no money!'

'So, American, this is very bad. You maybe got something in car. Get out! Give me keys!'

The sergeant and the private then made a large production number out of opening and slamming all the doors and the trunk. They even looked in the engine compartment. It was still snowing.

'You have no present for us? We good soldiers and so we let you go. What about watch? You have watch, maybe?'

'Yes,' said Charlie, 'we have watch.' He did indeed have a watch, a cheap Timex, and he handed it over to the sergeant.

'Now you,' said the sergeant, pointing to Damon. 'You have watch?' With that, he snatched Damon's prized Rolex, which had been a graduation present from his father.

'Thank you for watches. Very nice. Now you go.'

They both slumped down in the car and they were just about to switch on the ignition when they heard a shout from the other side of the road. The sergeant stopped lifting the barrier and let it drop again. Damon and Charlie got out their car once more, only to see a man in a major's uniform stooping under the barrier and making his way towards them. He was a short tubby man with slicked back black hair and a thin moustache. His car, an official BMW, was parked thirty meters away on the other side of the barrier. Standing beside it was the major's driver, a tough-looking corporal. The major addressed the sergeant tersely.

'These are smugglers you've caught?'

'No sir, American visitors.'

The major turned towards the pair and addressed them in English.

'Why you Americans come to my country? We don' want you. We hate all Americans.'

'I'm sorry, sir...' began Damon.

'You shut up! I speak! You listen! I hate your president! I hate your rock and roll! I hate your blue jeans! I hate your Kentucky Fried Chicken! I hate your Oprah Winfrey! All American all ver' bad! Now you come here and insult my country and our beloved president.

How you like it if I insult your American president?'

'Feel free. It's a democracy. You can insult him if....'

'You shut up! I speak. Only me. You shut up! You insult all Bulgaria! You go on trial! No, better, I kill you now!'

The major then turned to the sergeant and ordered, 'Sergeant, you shoot them! That is an order! You must shoot these two American smugglers now.'

'I'm sorry, sir. I can't do that,' said the sergeant in Bulgarian which both the Americans could understand but were pretending not to. 'We are only allowed to fire our weapons if we are fired on ourselves.'

'But I order you! You are defying a direct order!'

'Sorry sir. But these two Americans say they are diplomats from their embassy. If I shoot them there will be big trouble'

The major began struggling with his coat to reach his own sidearm.

'You are in mutiny, Sergeant! I will make a full report to your colonel! I will shoot them myself!'

The major's driver, who had been watching proceedings from a distance, now ran over and forced the major's hand away from his gun.

'Come along sir. No need to cause trouble over two stupid Americans,' the driver told the major as he dragged him back to the BMW. The major gave one parting order.

'Sergeant, if you want to keep your job, I order you. Keep the Americans waiting out in the cold until they can leave at daybreak! '

After the major had been driven away, still shouting, the sergeant turned to Damon and explained.

'The major, he very drunk. Not remember morning. I give back watch. Rolex, too expensive, cannot sell here. Your women here. They come back.'

And sure, Nadia and Sofia - or was it Polina and

Elena? - were, at that very moment, climbing into the back of the Mercedes.

'Here,' said one of them, handing over a wad of local currency in small bills, worth roughly half what they had just stolen from under the driver's seat, 'this for soldiers.'

It is probably better not to ask, thought Charlie as she handed over the cash, just how a pair of teenage Bulgarian hookers can raise lots of small bills in local money in the middle of the night outside an army barracks.

Charlie gave the wad to the sergeant.

'You are my friend,' he said. 'Americans very good men.'

The bedraggled quartet got back to the Hotel Aphrodite at five am, about two hours before sunrise. Damon and Charlie were completely exhausted but Josefina and Yulia still wanted to party. The first thing they did was to turn on the TV and locate some loud all-night popular music channel which they turned up to full volume.

'You have drink?' asked one of them. 'No? Then I call reception.' Before either man could stop her, she had rung reception and she was shouting over the top of the music for a bottle of vodka and four glasses.

'What do you mean, too late?' she shouted. 'We are guests. You must bring it now!'

'If you want a drink, there's a minibar. Over there,' said Charlie.

'Ah! minibar!! We drink!!' The girls then started on the range of miniatures, downing each in one.

'Now we show you,' said Elena or Sophia. 'We take clothes off for show! You like!'

The lights were still on and the curtains were not drawn but by now the sun was up. As indeed were all the other guests of the hotel who had been woken up by the

16

music and the shouting.

Many were standing at their windows watching the striptease being performed in full view by the two drunken women. They had just about finished taking off all their clothes and were dancing drunkenly nude on the bed to the loud music when the two men suddenly became aware of a loud banging on the hotel door.

Charlie staggered over to open it. Three civilian policemen rushed in, followed by the manager of the hotel. He was holding the two American passports.

'You leave! You go now! You all go! This is a good hotel! I report this! '

The leading policeman took one look at the diplomatic passports.

'Please leave Bulgaria today,' he said, and then after a pause, 'sir.'

Damon and Charlie packed quickly and put their luggage in the trunk of the Mercedes, all the while being assailed by screams from the two girls.

'What about our money?' they wailed. 'You owe us money! We good girls! We get you free from soldiers!'

They kept up this caterwauling until the three policemen wrapped them in hotel blankets and bundled them into the police van to be taken away. Damon and Charlie drove over the border and pulled into the side of the road for three hours sleep. While they were asleep, thieves relieved the Mercedes of its hub caps, radio aerial and radiator grill.

Joe Feldstein, the United States Ambassador, was not exactly overjoyed to find himself starting his Sunday with the unpleasant task of disciplining Dexter and Le Moine. He had convened early, at six am, a meeting of the senior diplomatic personnel with a video conference call to the

17

senior personnel directors of the CIA and the State Department in DC where it was still late Saturday night.

Neither the American nor the European halves of the meeting had been especially pleased at a meeting which, for both, was at an ungodly hour.

The meeting had been acrimonious, with the CIA anxious to protect its investments in expensive personnel. But as Feldstein insisted, he wanted the matter cleared up as soon as possible and certainly by the opening of embassy business on Monday morning.

Leave it any longer, he reasoned, and the rumor mill will get going. Then a clean, tidy, surgical solution to the problem would be impossible as more and more people poked their noses in. Better to dispense quick summary justice followed by a swift moving on.

Damon and Charlie had arrived back at the embassy compound late Saturday afternoon, tired and hung over. They had immediately been confined to quarters by the duty officer until the Sunday summons. The duty officer had then informed his boss, the embassy chief of staff, and the CIA station head. The ambassador was phoned at home to be informed of the problem by his deputy. Early morning conference call to DC, then a meeting at nine in the morning with Le Moine and Dexter, he had ordered.

Now the two men were sitting in front of him in Feldstein's large office, known informally as 'The Throne Room'.

'So, you two boys went on a little trip?' was the Ambassador's opening rhetorical question. 'You went on a little trip, over the border, which as you both know, you should not do without informing the duty officer. Which you did not do.'

The two culprits shifted uneasily in their seats.

'So,' His Excellency went on, 'you went on a little trip to Bansko, where you proceeded to get very drunk.

18

Am I right?'

The two nodded.

'And, then you drove your car, while dead drunk, through a Bulgarian military checkpoint, where you got into a fight with one Major Donkov, a serving officer in the Bulgarian Army. Yes?'

'No, sir, not at all, sir,' said Damon Dexter. 'There was no fight. In fact, the major threatened to shoot us before his bodyguard intervened. He, the major that is, sir, was drunk as well.'

'But,' went on the Ambassador, 'according to this report, from the three-star general to whom Donkov is answerable, you, and here I quote '.. became abusive and began to insult Bulgaria and the Bulgarian Army..' Then, and here again I am quoting General Tsankov, '..both Americans attacked Major Donkov and it was only by the heroic efforts of Sergeant Berisov and Private Malev, who were manning the checkpoint at the time, that Major Donkov was saved from serious injury..' Is that about right, gentlemen?'

'It was nothing like that, sir,' put in Le Moine. 'We were the ones who were being threatened.'

'Well,' said the Ambassador, 'the official record is that you attacked Donkov. Who knows what really happened and who cares? You just don't get it, do you? They are right and we, that is, you two, are definitely wrong. Look, this isn't about facts, or the truth. Facts don't matter.'

'If Donkov says you attacked him, then you attacked him and that is what is going to go in the official report and on your records. Got it? We are guests in their country and most of them don't like us. I've already written the official apology. My opposite number in Sofia is going to deliver it to the Bulgarian Defense Minister tomorrow morning. 'The United States regrets *et cetera, et cetera...*' Hopefully we can damp it all down before the story gets going.'

Damon and Charlie made to get up.

'Not so fast, boys, I haven't finished.'

'Sir?'

'After beating up the good major, you then turned your attention to trashing the Hotel Aphrodite in Bansko. According to the Chief of Police for the Blagoevgrad Region, one Brigadier Todorov, and here again I quote, you two

'...wrecked a hotel room during a long orgy of drunken violence and sexual misconduct with two underage Bulgarian schoolgirls. The police had to be called.'

Please explain yourselves, gentlemen.'

'Well, it was like this, sir,' began Damon Dexter before he realized that there was absolutely no point at all in putting his side of the story.

'Now this too, may be a fabrication, an exaggeration, just like the story of the attack on Major Donkov, and, strictly off the record, I don't believe you two idiots are actually violent idiots,' went on the ambassador, 'but sex with underage girls is a crime everywhere. If Brigadier Todorov is making it up then it's his word against ours and you did it in his country. And that makes it true. End of story.'

'Please sir,' began Charlie.

'Yes, Mister Le Moine, you wish to say something?'

'Well, sir, they looked eighteen at least. And they were working as hookers in the Bar, er,'

'The Bar Miramar,' the Ambassador completed the sentence for Charlie.

'And we never had sex with them, sir. We were all tuckered out by the time they started dancing in front of the windows. We never laid a finger on them, sir.'

'Yes,' answered the Ambassador. 'I believe you. I understand how these places work. But if you have been listening, you will have heard me say, quite clearly, that if Brigadier Todorov says that you had sex with two ninth grade students from the local high school then that is exactly what happened.'

'Our colleague in Sofia will therefore be making a second apology after he leaves the Defense Ministry. He will be going to the prime minister to apologize again for the attacks on young Bulgarian girls by American Embassy officials who do not have the sense they were born with. If he does it well enough, he may be able to make some arrangement with the girls' parents so that it doesn't become a major incident.'

'Don't count your chickens yet. If they're approached properly, they may be made to see the sense in not telling the world that their little darlings spend their weekends turning tricks at the Bar Miramar when they should be doing their homework.'

'Before I spell out to you two overgrown adolescents exactly what your future career path is likely to take, there is also the small matter of the damage to the embassy car which you took over the border without getting written permission. Repairs to a Mercedes come in a little expensive. The transport officer has an estimate of fifteen hundred dollars.'

"Now it is an embassy car and you two boys are CIA, so you can pay up out of your own pockets now, with a smile, or we can make it official with an invoice from State to the CIA including all the embarrassing details on the accompanying report of exactly how an expensive embassy automobile got vandalized while two CIA operatives were asleep inside. Better, I would have thought, to limit the damage, wouldn't you?'

'Finally, there is the little matter of your immediate

futures. Obviously you can't stay here. Even if this little mess does blow over, you are going to be open to blackmail. You've become liabilities and we need to be rid of you.'

'Colonel Sieghart wants a word with you and then you pack. You will take a Lufthansa flight to Frankfurt and then one of our military transports to DC. You report to Langley at nine am Tuesday. Get the details, tickets etc. from my secretary on your way out. It's all arranged. That is all.'

'Thank you, sir.'

'Thank you, sir.'

Colonel John Sieghart was the ranking CIA man in the region who had been with the Company since he had been recruited in Vietnam. He was a big powerful sixty-three year old with none of the ambassador's Ivy League refinement. Because of his plebeian upbringing and military experience he had the very useful camouflage of being able to hide a shrewd political intelligence behind a crude peasant exterior. He had always known he would never make general - he lacked the finesse and the right contacts. But he was still very proud of his record. Not bad, he often told himself, for an enlisted man from a slum neighborhood in Chicago. In spite of his manner, the inner circles knew better than to write him off as a buffoon, an image he found it useful to cultivate.

His official position at the embassy was military attaché and his official duties were NATO liaison. But his real job was to be *numero uno* for all CIA activities in the southern Balkans region. He was blunt when the two young men were told to go into his office. He did not invite them to sit.

'Well, you two clowns really fucked up this time!

You both got shit for brains or something? You go chasing underage tail in a foreign country, you beat up a serving officer, you wreck a hotel room! Jesus, who the fuck do you think you are - the fucking Rolling Stones?'

'And don't tell me you didn't do it. The official record says you did, which means you did. Tell me, where exactly did you two jerks learn to behave like morons? Was it at those fancy schools where they teach graduate courses in stupidity? I don't remember Georgetown University enrolling mental defectives. Or the London University School of Slavonic Studies, do they offer an elective in screwing schoolgirls?'

Colonel Sieghart had more to say.

'Have you any idea what it costs the good old American taxpayer to put two operatives in posts like yours? You both had ten years experience before you suddenly decided to go ape-shit.'

'You, Dexter, why do you think we sent you to Lagos and Beirut? Just for the fun of it, maybe? Did you never ask yourself why someone with a dozen Balkan languages was sweating it out in those shit-holes?'

'And you Le Moine, you've got a PhD in Bulgarian! Did you never wonder why you were in Berlin and Canberra, having a whale of a time at the taxpayer's expense? Did it never once occur to either of you that you were being trained in those places? Don't you realize you are here for a reason?'

' Don't ask me why, you'll be able to read about it in the papers or watch it on TV. This crummy hole in southern Europe is what your careers have been about, for Chrissakes! If I were a congressman, I'd ask for the money back, now you've gone and screwed up big time. Now we'll have to get two other suckers in to do what you should have been doing. Christ knows how long that will take. Oh shit!'

Colonel Sieghart took a moment to calm down.

'You're going back to Langley. They can do what the hell they like with you there, as far as I'm concerned. If they don't fire you, it'll certainly be a demotion and a posting somewhere where your screw-ups can be taken care of easier, Iowa, maybe or Nebraska. Now get out and don't come back.'

The colonel then turned his mind to his next task, preparing a formal request on behalf of the ambassador for two replacement commercial officers with fluency in Balkan languages. I wonder what lunatics they're gonna send me next, he mused.

Out of the office, Charlie was philosophical. 'You know what, bro? We may just have dumped our careers in the trash can, but look on the bright side! If they send us back to the good ole U S of A, at least we can get laid!'

Three

The President of the United States, O'Brien Bedford, known as 'O.B.' to his closest friends and on his campaign posters, was being briefed in the Oval Office. The Secretary of State, Alison Treadwell and the Secretary of Defense, George Zymanski, were there together with their deputies. Also present were the Director of the National Security Agency, Hubert Tuple, and the Director of the Central Intelligence Agency, Branwell McFall.

These six powerful men and one powerful woman, the seven most important people in the western world, were discussing a new think-tank idea dreamt up by some of those armchair warriors who frame grand schemes for men of consequence to decide upon and for men of action to kill or die for.

The president was a man of sharp intellect and extensive learning, not at all like the sort of political animal who usually gets to the top of the greasy pole. He had his political side, of course, but he preferred to project an image of calm cerebrality.

No-one could have come through the New York political machine and emerge triumphant from it without having left behind a few hostages to fortune in the form of favors still to be repaid. But if there were any dirt on his record, he had covered it well. He was, as far as the general public were concerned, a truly genuine honest man.

In spite of its early start - at seven am, straight after the president's workout in the White House gym - all seven were fully alert and they were discussing an interesting plan. There was a large map of the Balkans and the Caucasus on the wall at the end the conference table and each of the seven was equipped with microphone and laser pointer. Branwell McFall was in the process of outlining what was being proposed.

'Sir,' he began. 'This is a ten year plan - our suggested long term policy for this region,' – he indicated the map – 'following the Afghan drawdown. We are projecting that there will be no US forces on the ground within five years from now. We will still have our long term commitments to provide security for our NATO allies in the region.'

' And we will also have our oil interests, plus our need to provide a defensive shield against terrorists and insurgents. Our estimates are that the present sectarian conflict between the Shias and the Sunnis plus threats from Al Qaeda, will continue to spread from Iran and Syria into other nations around.'

'Maybe the South Caucasus, Turkey and possibly even to the European mainland, for example to Bulgaria, Romania and the nations of the former Yugoslavia, all of which have significant Islamist political groups, any one of which could be used as the base for extending the jihad.'

The president cut in.

'Thank you, Branwell, we all know about the level of the threat. Most of our NATO allies down there have cast-iron treaties with us. Many of them have US military on their soil and leave us a free hand. Some are so shit-scared of Islamic terrorism that they want us to increase our military presence. Take Bulgaria, for example. We have a garrison of about two and a half thousand, all air force. Their generals and their defense minister are always on at me to increase it.'

'But you can see the problem, can't you? Afghanistan and Iraq cost us - what, about two trillion? - and they are worse now than when we started. How the hell could I sell more of the same to the American taxpayer? Tell me that! We have forty million on food stamps! Eight million without a job! The national debt is going up by forty thousand dollars a second. A second! I think we can abandon any idea of more US peacekeepers on the ground. Cut to the chase, Branwell. What have the wonks at the Institution come up with this time?'

'Thank you, sir,' continued the Director of the CIA. 'What they are saying is that we remove all Army combat troops from Europe and Asia completely and move to a more aggressive remote, electronic warfare mode. That is, a higher level of cyber attacks from within the US with our propaganda efforts to be enhanced.'

'But, and here is where it becomes cost-effective, by creating a minimal new security infrastructure to replace all those boots on the ground. They are proposing that we build a defensive line across southern Europe, a chain of stations which combine listening functions with drone launch stations. It would stretch from here, Aviano in Italy, through Croatia, Macedonia, Bulgaria, Turkey, Moldova, *et cetera* right through to Kirgizstan, here.'

He pointed with his laser indicator.

'But, wouldn't they need to be defended?' asked the Deputy Secretary of State.

'No,' said Director McFall, 'that's the whole point. They can be completely unmanned. They will be situated a long way from centers of population and, as far as the citizens of those countries are concerned, well, they won't even know they exist.'

'Just how many of these stations will there be?' asked the president.

'Well, we are looking at up to a hundred. Plus backup from our air force base at Ramstein in Germany which would be the staging post for maintenance, repairs and so on.'

'The USAF bases in Western Europe will provide a fallback, a sort of final line of defense. But the automatic stations will cover each other, so if one base is under attack, then there will be sufficient fire power at the next station along the chain to destroy the attackers.'

'Tell me about the drones we'll be using. What's their range? How many will there be at any one station?'

'Well, Mister President,' continued the man from the CIA, 'range is not a problem. The Global Hawk drone, for example, has a range of at least eight thousand miles. But not just that type of long-distance machine, no, we will be using a variety of drones including small surveillance drones and medium range devices capable of taking out a single house or a single car. Or even a single human being.'

'And, of course, we are constantly developing new models. The longer the distance, the lighter the payload, of course, but we certainly have drones which can deliver a nuclear device from ten thousand miles away. As to numbers, there is no reason why each of the new stations shouldn't have as many as we need - hundreds, thousands, if you like.'

'Some will get shot down in a full-on shooting war, but mostly they fly under the radar like cruise missiles, so there should be a pretty good hit rate. The important thing is that no American lives need ever again be lost in combat.'

'And collateral damage, civilian lives?' asked the president.

'That's an unfortunate thing, sir. But more avoidable with good intelligence from the surveillance drones and the listening stations.'

The Secretary of Defense took up the theme. George Zymanski was an old cold war warrior who was as devout an American patriot as it was possible to be. He was dismissive of the fears of unnecessary civilian casualties.

'This is a war on terror and we are always

scrupulous. Yes, totally scrupulous only to target known terrorists or those who harbor terrorists. If they put their women and children in the firing line so that we will back off, then they are not just terrorists but cowards as well. Remember that they are also targeting our children. Remember nine-eleven? They didn't think about innocent civilians then.'

The president waved away this outburst.

'We will always take every precaution to avoid unnecessary death and injury to the civilian population. That's our line.'

Tell me,' he turned to Branwell McFall again, 'what is the control structure for operation of the drones?'

'Well, sir', said McFall, 'the listening post at each station will be the third tier of a network of electronic communications linked to our LEOs or Low Earth Orbit satellites and their GPS systems. There will be a back up via a separate satellite system to our communications center at Ramstein. The whole data mush is eventually processed by the USAF center at Fort Abelard in New Mexico. That is where the drones are controlled from.'

'So,' asked the president, 'if the US Intelligence Community agrees to all of this, how long before it's in place?'

'Well, sir, if everything went smoothly, we could probably be up and running with a complete blanket around all the troubled regions within five years. That is if there are no impediments.'

'But, there are impediments, or it would be installed by now?'

'Yes, sir' said Secretary of State Alison Treadwell. 'There are plenty of impediments, all of them political.'

'Go on.'

'Mostly, they are about getting agreements with the various countries involved. Many of them are afraid that the drones, carrying nuclear weapons, might lead to them being used against their own people. And almost all of them are afraid that having a drone site in their country will make them a target for the Islamic jihadists.'

'But some are with us, yes?'

'Indeed they are, but only at government level. Bulgaria, for example, would be greatly in favor, especially if we left a few American airmen on station. On the other hand, the Bulgarian people just voted sixty percent against a larger US military presence in the country. Not sure how reliable that is, sir. It was a private, unofficial poll for TV. But the main opposition parties are making a big noise about it.'

'If we go ahead in Bulgaria, we'd better do it now, before the present government gets kicked out.'

'And then there's Turkey, sometimes with us, sometimes not. Can't decide whether it's NATO, or Muslim Brotherhood or secular or European or Asian. If you could get the European Union to let them in, that would help. But that would be difficult. The Greeks have a veto.'

'Tell me the worst. Where's the biggest problem?' asked the president wearily.

'Here, sir,' said the man from the CIA, aiming his laser beam west of Bulgaria on the map.

'What can you tell us about the place, Alison,' the president asked the secretary of state.

'They have a large proportion of ethnic Turks, mostly Muslim. They are the second biggest group in their parliament, after Anastasia Makarovna's Catholic Conservatives who are the present government. The parliamentary opposition breaks down across religious lines as well, Muslims and Orthodox.'

' Yeah, I know, it's like something from a history book about the Crusades. The Muslims, as you might expect, are anti-US and they are threatening to secede from NATO if they ever get into power. The Catholic right may be the government now but the country is sick of them and their mishandling of the economy, not to mention the corruption. They're odds-on to be kicked out at the election which is due next year, unless they go sooner.'

'So what can you do about it?' asked the president.

'Well, sir, working through our embassy, we have set up an operation of intelligence collection and we are looking for subversive elements to - er, how shall we say? - er, leverage the electoral outcome.'

'Isn't Joe Feldstein our man there?'

'Yes, sir, he is.'

'He's a good man. You're working well with him? Who's the Company chief on the spot?'

'It's a Colonel Sieghart, sir, an old Vietnam vet.'

'Has this Sieghart, has he got it all covered?'

'We think so, sir.'

'Well, let me know how it goes. Update briefing in two weeks. Leave all your papers behind. Good morning, gentlemen, Alison'

'Good morning, sir.'

Soon after he first ascended to the most important job in the world, President Bill Clinton inaugurated a program of creating 'American' universities in some of those former communist bloc countries which had recently been liberated from the socialist yoke. Soon, many countries, newly freed from communism, found themselves with an 'American University of Wherever'.

The idea of American universities abroad was not new even then. The well-established American universities in Beirut and Paris, for example, had achieved not merely respectability, but eminence, in the mainstream of scholastic credibility. Others were very far from prestigious, or even academically respectable: some were little more than low-grade degree mills.

But academic respectability, while it is a useful by-product, is not the real point of the 'American' university. They serve, primarily, other functions.

First, they are excellent additional income generators for the home institution in the United States, usually a decent state university under whose aegis the 'American' university abroad can operate.

The benefits of the arrangement are mutual. The US institution can guarantee credibility for its upstart offspring via formal accreditation of the new university's courses and programs. In return there will be a lucrative source of tuition fees, plus State Department disbursements of various kinds, as well as a steady stream of future student applicants for the home school's graduate programs.

Then there are interesting visiting positions for American faculty on the lookout for a year abroad and lots of ego-boosting international travel for the senior officers of both organizations.

For while the American University of BlahDeBlah is providing its income stream for its American parent, there are even better, longer term reasons for its existence. The fees it charges are, if not quite at stateside levels, at least beyond the pockets of the ordinary citizens of the much poorer country in which it is located.

For example, it was usual to pay tuition fees of upwards of $10,000 a year to study at the American University of the Southern Balkans or AUSB. That does not sound much until you consider that the average professional salary in that country is only about $500 a month.

One does not need to travel very far from the

university building in a suburb of the capital before one comes across real third world poverty. But there is no shortage of students wishing to study there and to pay the fees. Some, of course, receive scholarships, but on the whole, most of the students are self-supported.

The presence of so many well-to-do young people in an emerging economy looks odd until you realize that these students, with their good clothes and strong white teeth and their fluency in two or three European languages, are not members of the local *hoi-polloi*.

They are, in fact, the children of a small wealthy élite, the sort of élite which always surfaces during times of economic changeover. Their fathers are often well-placed former party officials or freelance fixers and gangsters - the sort of people who do well under any regime and for whom political turmoil is nothing more than a business opportunity.

What is more, the canny Clinton doubtless realized, it is these children who will be forming the ruling class of the country a generation on. The students usually come to the American universities after an education in American or American-style high schools and after graduation they will proceed to study for master's degrees at a US graduate school, possibly even a top school like Yale or Stanford.

This total immersion in an American educational experience ensures that the civil servants, politicians, academics and businessmen who will be running Bulgaria or Bosnia or Moldova or Kazakhstan twenty years down the road will be as thoroughly Americanized as it is possible to be without actually holding the passport.

Now, while it is a sensible strategy, as any Jesuit will tell you, to capture the hearts and minds of the young if one expects to retain their loyalty in later life, it is always a good idea to add other strings to the bow of cultural and economic imperialism.

So these far-flung American universities have a third function. They also act as collection points for the gathering of low-level intelligence data and so they maintain a discreet connection with the CIA.

It is unlikely that much in the way of old-fashioned filmic cold-war espionage goes on. The methodology of today's computer-driven spookdom involves the systematic assembling of myriads of detailed small items of non-secret data.

Some American universities even employ special senior faculty without noticeable real work. Unless that is, one considers frequent trips to the US Embassy and fact-finding visits to Central Asian oil states qualify as full-time gainful employment.

A feature of all these places is the eagerness of the American senior staff to be seen to be deferring to local sensibilities. Due preference is always given to the employment of local nationals, sometimes even if they cannot speak English properly.

On the whole though, regular faculty jobs were always given to competent Anglophones and the top academic jobs of president and provost are always held by Americans. That's the way imperialism works.

The American University of the Southern Balkans, or AUSB, occupies a site just outside the capital, a long way from the tourist beaches of the Black Sea or the Adriatic. Its inauguration coincided with the start of the Clinton presidency in 1992 and the president himself was present at the opening ceremony in the first year of his reign.

The building chosen for AUSB was the old Worker's Palace of Culture, not much used given that it was not for the workers themselves but for the *apparatchiks* who ruled over them. Nor was it a palace, but more of an expensive office block surmounted by a gaudy sign in Cyrillic script.

The old regime had certainly made an effort to impress. The building was by far the largest building around and it was impressively sited at the top of the main street of the suburb, called, with unconscious irony, 'The Boulevard'. The whole layout had been intended to look like the view of the *Arc de Triomphe* from the *Champs Elysées* but the effect didn't quite come off.

As for 'culture', yes, there was some culture available in the form of a theatre nearby where plays were performed. It was popular with some of the citizenry if not with the American expatriates. But then, 'Waiting for Godot' in Albanian translation is probably an acquired taste.

The building had been the centerpiece of a pretentious development dating from the Soviet era. Its facade, on the other side from the boulevard, looked out over a large tree-lined plaza with fountains and terraces which led up to another square dominated by a pretentious opera house.

On one side of the plaza was the theatre and on the other was a multi-storey hotel, which had stood alone and unused since the top communists had morphed into gangsters and business leaders.

The official party line had been that the whole complex had been a munificent act of generosity to the citizens for the enhancement of their civic pride and for their cultural uplift.

In reality, the old party bosses were in the habit of visiting their generosity on each of the country's regions in turn when they held their annual party conference. In the months preceding the visit there would be a frantic building program in the chosen host district or city so that the comrades could be received in a setting appropriately sumptuous for the champions of the workers' struggle.

The main building of the University had first become vacant after the fall of the old order and no local could be found to take it on when the infrastructure of the country was being dismantled and the most valuable bits were being given to the commissars for their new careers in private enterprise.

So the American University had taken over the Palace of Culture while the luxury hotel next door, which none of the comrades had wanted for themselves when they had been given first pick of the national assets, was allowed to go derelict.

The ground floor was still in use – it had been converted into a bar for the *jeunesse d'orée* of the area. The basement was also saved and converted to a nightclub where the same gilded youth could spend their evenings under the proprietorial control of those heavy men with the bald heads and the black leather jackets from whom the bright young things might buy illegal substances, trade in which contributed so much of the local community's black economy.

Four

Professor Manuel Oliviera, Chairman of the Department of Business at AUSB, was preparing for his monthly departmental faculty meeting. All must attend.

They assembled, the teaching members of the Department of Business. Most were called 'Professor' but not all were equal, for under that umbrella title 'Professor' or 'Prof.' there existed a multitude of shades of social rank. There were 'full', 'associate' and 'assistant' professors who would be distinguished by being 'permanent', 'temporary with a three year contract', 'temporary with a one year contract' or just 'visiting' – those working at AUSB for one semester only. In addition, there were 'adjunct' professors, part-time teachers who could also be 'full', 'associate' or 'assistant' depending on their seniority.

To be a 'professor', of whatever rank, one needed to be in possession of the PhD degree. Otherwise the job title would be 'Instructor'. These fine class divisions were nuanced as finely and guarded as jealously as those of the famous English class system, where everyone knows, to within a millimeter, their exact position on the social ladder.

As the meeting began, the ruling elite of this tiny feudal state were taking their customary places in the front row. After all, they were the ones who would be doing most of the talking and taking all of the decisions. Second-class, third-class and untouchable-class teachers sat further back, each individual subconsciously aware of his or her place in the pecking order.

Manuel Oliviera brought the meeting to order. 'You all got the agenda by email. First item ....'

There was voice from halfway back.

'Point of order Mister Chairman. Who writes the agenda? Because I sent you a message asking you to include an item about approaching the president to find out why we had so many electricity blackouts last term and why there isn't a backup generator? I don't see it on the agenda.'

'No, it's not on the agenda. We thought it better not to include it?'

'Why? Who sets the agenda?'

'What I do is to consult with colleagues about what should go on the agenda and what should be left out.' said Oliviera.

'You didn't consult with me.'

'That's because you don't have a vote. Only professors with tenure have a vote. You know that. It is one of the rules of the department,' Oliviera answered.

Oliviera was saved from having to debate the logic of this regulation by the intercession of Hattie Reilly PhD, a long-tenured, full Professor of Hotel Management.

Hattie Reilly was of a type often met with in American university hierarchies. In appearance she was fifty- or sixty something, with grey curly hair cut short above a round, mean, tight little face. She invariably dressed badly, in pastel-colored suits with long skirts. Although she tried hard to exude a persona of care and concern, she could never completely disguise her inner sense of self-centered disappointment and contempt.

Her corpulence caused her to walk with a rolling seaman's gait as she bustled along in a wobbly waddle, rocking from side to side.

Her academic discipline, hotel management, was one of those semi-respectable subjects of university education which had grown up since the liberalization of curricula in the 1970's. As an academic subject, hotel management is up there with media studies, sports science and computer gaming – pseudo-disciplines which appeal to many of the new generation of students, especially those students not temperamentally attuned to traditional university study.

She did, nevertheless, consider herself well-blessed with great brain-power. She was never merely 'Hattie Reilly'. It was always, whenever she needed to write or speak her name, 'Professor Hattie Reilly PhD', with heavy emphasis on the last three syllables.

'The reason,' she slowly explained, thickly stressing each word, 'why only tenured professors have the vote is that tenured professors have been members of this department long enough to know what is good for the department and what is not. It is firmly stated in the departmental Standing Orders that only permanent faculty are permitted to vote on departmental matters. That does include some faculty, those who are on three year contracts and are associate and above. They also have the vote. Three year assistants do not have the vote and neither does anyone on any contract shorter than three years. I thought you knew that?'

'And does that extend to setting the agendas for the meetings?'

Professor Reilly PhD was now very angry. 'Setting the agenda is always done in the very best interests of the department. You have only been here five minutes. You will learn that this is the way we have always done it and we have always been a very well-run department. It makes no sense to change the rules now. That's all there is to it. Continue, Manuel, let's get on with the meeting.'

'Item one,' Oliviera began, 'the renewal of the SPSS contract. As some of you know, we are using SPSS in some of our courses. But now there has been change in the contract. We were using it on an educational-use license but it is, it seems, now owned by a new company and they are asking us to pay full commercial price.'

'Can't we get an educational discount to use it?' asked someone.

'No, that's not possible. We tried, but the new company wants to charge fifty thousand dollars for a new contract. That's a lot of money. The dean thinks it is too expensive. I think so too. What does anyone else say?'

'Why do we need SPSS at all?' The questioner was the same upstart who had just asked the impertinent question about the agenda.

Hattie Reilly PhD was quick to jump in. 'Because,' she expostulated, clearly annoyed at being questioned twice by one of the less important people present, 'SPSS is the standard statistical package for the entire hotel management profession. Every hotel chain in the world keeps its records on SPSS. You can't get by without it.'

The troublesome inferior, a computer scientist by training, had one last go. 'SPSS is a big old package and this new company can charge big fees because they have a lot of big clients with large amounts of data, clients who would find it too expensive to change to something else. But we are only a small department, with minute data sets. Microsoft Excel, which is on all the university's computers, can do the job just as well for us. It's not the job of a university to teach a particular software package. Any new employee in hotel management who needs to learn SPSS will be sent on a short training course.'

Professor Hattie Reilly PhD was quick in her response. 'You don't understand! You've only just been appointed! Other departments have the right software. So should we. Don't you agree, Manuel?'

'Right,' said Manuel, 'are we all agreed? We will ask the dean to sign the new contract to get SPSS for the next five years on the grounds that it is vital for courses in hotel management. Shall we take a vote?'

The one dissenting voice was the only 'no'. Professor Hattie Reilly PhD fixed him with a basilisk stare. 'You cannot vote, 'she said, loudly and forcefully.

'Carried unanimously,' said Chairman Oliviera.

The meeting had then been in progress for twenty five minutes and so far only the first agenda item had been resolved.

'Item two,' Oliviera began wearily, 'selection of members of the search committee for the new professorship in accountancy.'

'As you know,' he went on, 'we always have problems finding people for accountancy. We have put out some advertisements and we have a shortlist of four. Hattie was very kind to go through all the applications.'

'Three,' said Reilly. 'We didn't like one of them.'

'So, the Search Committee,' said Oliviera, 'any volunteers?'

Half a dozen hands went up. Oliviera pointed to a couple of teachers on the front row. 'Denis? Mark? Will you work with Hattie on this? You are both voting members. Obviously Hattie has to be on the search committee. You also have the experience.' He then turned to the rest of the department.

'Does everyone agree? Hattie will chair the search committee with Mark and Denis?'

There was no reply.

'Then it's carried unanimously. Item three, submission of proposals for revision of the final year course structure. Denis, you have something to say on this, I understand? '

Denis Denitsev was a local professor, who had not been appointed to AUSB for his subject excellence although he held the obligatory PhD. Nor was his teaching record exemplary. Students regularly complained of his absence from the classroom and his habitual lateness when he turn up.

But he did have one redeeming grace. He was very well-connected politically and many of his classroom absences were explained away by his needing to attend some important meeting at the Ministry of Education in the centre of the city.

Americans often feel, surprisingly, a sense of inferiority towards Europeans. The sly suave Europeans with their confidence and sense of history often appear to Americans to be devious, dissimulating tricksters. Consequently, Americans in Europe will give an exaggerated respect and attention to those European locals who appear to be able to bridge the two worlds.

Denitsev, for all his human shortcomings, was, therefore, held in high esteem by his American bosses as some sort of bilingual go-between, even if no-one else could ever quite put their finger on what other qualities this goateed, rat-faced, scurrying, ever-busy little man might have possessed.

'Yes, thank you, Chair,' said Denitsev. 'We need to make some changes to what courses we will be offering at the final year level. We are thinking of dropping mathematical economics. Poor Professor Petrova found the work too hard for her. We think the course is probably too difficult, so we will no longer be offering it. Strategic management is to be retained. Thank you, Morten, for teaching it.'

'Also, hospitality management which Hattie has been teaching for many years and is very popular with the students will also be on the new curriculum. Accountancy will no longer be offered at the upper level. The new professor will only be teaching at the freshman and sophomore levels. We are not sure about finance. It is a final year subject but we do not have any permanent faculty to teach it and we obviously can't give the course to someone on a temporary contract. Unless we are left with no choice, of course.'

'What about the accreditation?' asked one of the sans-culottes at the back of the room.

'Good question!' replied Denitsev. 'American accreditation is not due for three more years, so hopefully, we will have the right people in place by then.'

'And accreditation in this country?'

'Accreditation by our ministry? Oh, that is no problem!' said Denis brightly. That was why Denitsev was employed.

Oliviera's faculty meeting dragged on. Items three to six, on the rules for academic probation, election of a delegate to the university executive council (Professor Hattie Reilly PhD, elected unanimously), setting up a new course in entrepreneurship and the rules for sabbatical leave for tenured professors were all disposed of after long disquisitions from members of the front bench preceding the predetermined vote.

The front row had all their answers ready and, the decisions having already been made, the natural democratic process could follow without the unnecessary intrusion of unwanted opinions from the non-voting crowd at the back.

Oliviera had hoped that he could wrap the whole meeting up in less than four hours, which would have been a departmental record. Contribution to the debate was limited to those few whose experience entitled them to the holding of relevant opinions. Nevertheless, this restriction did not make for quick conclusive decision-making.

It was their interpretation of the democratic process that the automatic rubber-stamping of ready-made decisions is rendered somehow more valid if it is preceded by some lengthy, vaguely relevant, discussion.

Thus every resolution made by the front few on behalf of the whole department would need prior sanctification by an overture of aimless, time-wasting deliberation, also confined to the front row, as if 'we talked it through' would somehow render secret decision-making legitimate.

Each agenda item would therefore need to be introduced via a long speech before the voters would yawn and vote their meaningless vote and the majority present, the non-voters, would just yawn. From time to time, one of the unenfranchised would get up, mutter perfunctory excuses and escape.

By the end of the first two hours of this farrago of democracy, only the voters and a small rump, two or three, of the non-voters remained.

By item seven only a couple of non-voters were left to hear a proposal from Morten Nyborg, whose tenured full professorship of accountancy was not so much a mark of academic distinction as a long service medal. The chronic shortage of accountants, who could earn so much more in banking and finance or in private practice than they ever could in academia, meant that academic accountants could jump ship whenever they felt like it, knowing that they would quickly be snapped up by another university.

Nyborg was a large, silver-haired, confident and jovial man who exuded a manner of deceptive friendliness. His style was not in the slightest scholarly or intellectual – he had, for example, a vast fund of dirty jokes to go with an avuncular car-salesman's personality. Today he had a revolutionary idea to put forward to the meeting.

'These meetings are very time-consuming,' he

began, 'and we all have too much to do. So what I am suggesting is that we just hold electronic meetings from now on, by email.'

He then proceeded to elaborate his simple proposal via a ten minute speech which was approximately relevant, covering, as it did, everything from the heavy workload of accountancy professors to the benefits conferred on humankind by the Internet.

'I can't see anything wrong with that,' said Hattie Reilly PhD.

'Nor me,' agreed Denis Denitsev. 'It would save a lot of time.'

'OK, said Oliviera. 'Let's put it to the vote. All those in favor? Carried unanimously.'

'Wait a minute,' said one of the two remaining non-voting faculty members. 'I have a question.'

'The vote has been taken. It's official. Go on to the next item, Manuel,' said Reilly.

But the dissenter persisted. 'I only want to ask a question. I know I can't change the vote.'

'Go on then,' said Oliviera, wearily, 'ask your question.'

'It is this,' said the untouchable. 'How will those of us without a vote know there even was a vote? Will we be on the address list? Because what you are proposing doesn't sound very democratic to me. You could run your meetings without us second class citizens knowing you had even held a meeting.'

Hattie Reilly PhD turned on him. She was incandescent with rage.

'How dare you!! How dare you slight me like that!! I should never have appointed you in the first place.'

'I am just asking a civil question. I did not mention your name and I have certainly not slighted you. It is a very reasonable question. I think it deserves a fair and calm answer.'

'No!!' bellowed Hattie Reilly PhD. 'You are attacking my honesty. Suggesting that I am some kind of communist! I am an American. We Americans have always been the world's greatest defenders of democracy and fair elections! Don't you understand that? We invented democracy!'

'Well, I don't have a vote, fair or otherwise, so therefore I am a second class citizen.'

'You don't have a vote because you do not qualify because you do not have the length of service.'

'That's what I meant. I'm second class because I don't have a vote.'

'Why can't you get it into your thick head!' retorted Professor Reilly. 'You don't have a vote and that's that. That doesn't make you second class. It just means you don't have a vote.'

'So will we get details of the minutes and the agendas and the decisions, we second class citizens?'

'Of course, we will keep everyone fully informed. The whole department will be kept informed of whatever is appropriate,' said Reilly.

'Second class indeed,' she could be heard muttering, 'I've never been so insulted.'

Morten Nyborg came in. 'So that's it then. We replace these faculty meetings open to all by email meetings between voting members only? OK?'

'Final item,' said Oliviera at about the three hour mark. 'You will need a new chairman. I am leaving AUSB at the end of term. You will need to elect a new chairman for next semester.'

President O'Brien Bedford was once again in an early morning meeting with his small committee to discuss what had now been officially named 'Operation Warm Blanket', the plan to replace the network of USAF airbases by a line of unmanned drone stations. The plan had moved forward in the interim.

Branwell McFall of the CIA was explaining that the plan would require massive redundancy in the chain, so that if one base were attacked, there would be instant back-up from other bases. The participating nations would be all the NATO countries and several Asian countries which would, the thinking went, be happy to receive free American defense support.

The line of the bases would be roughly along what had once been part of the old Silk Road but which was now the route of the Trans-Asia oil pipeline, bringing today's vital fluid from central Asia all the way to the refineries of the Balkans and, ultimately, Western Europe.

Each country would be, McFall explained, in control, nominally at least, of that part of the high-tech war machine within its territory. In reality, though, the ultimate decision to deploy the vast fire power and the drones to deliver it, would be an American one only. The US would be responsible for maintaining each facility without any local involvement.

'The question is,' asked the president, 'how are we going to sell this idea to all these countries, particularly the non-NATO members? Any ideas about how we do that?'

'We could offer them full membership of NATO,' suggested Secretary of State Treadwell.

'We could but most of them wouldn't want it. Especially the Stans,' said President Bedford.

By 'Stans' he was referring to those countries in central Asia whose names ended in '.istan'. Most of them were suspicious of the North Atlantic Treaty Organization and its American domination, which had so recently been in conflict with their kith and kin in Iraq and Afghanistan.

Many of the Stans, though, did maintain an arms-length relationship with NATO via a loose alliance of traditionally uncommitted states called the Euro-Atlantic Partnership Council which also included traditionally neutral countries like Ireland, Finland and Austria. Some of them even had US facilities on their soil in the form of airbases for refueling and maintenance.

'Bear it in mind that we really need to do this quietly. Ideally, we don't want everyone to know about it, especially those guys in the countries which are not our friends.'

'Some of those places don't do democracy very well. A few of them are just old-fashioned dictatorships,' said Alison Treadwell.

'Those are usually the easiest to deal with. A little pot of money in a foreign bank account often does the trick,' said the CIA man.

'I didn't hear that,' said the president. 'Be careful.'

'Well,' interjected the Defense Secretary, 'we could always sell it as a natural scaling down of American power as well as bringing employment possibilities to remote, poor regions. Not to mention the countries where we've squared away whichever despot McFall's people have had to buy off.'

Hubert Tuple, the Director of the National Security Agency, then raised the question of which countries would get the nuclear weapons and which would not.

'We can't, obviously, put nuclear weapons into countries where they have never had them before . That's against the non-proliferation treaty. Or, for that matter, with those of our friends who are opposed to them anyway. But it does leave the core NATO members. Later on, when everyone gets used to the idea, we can re-negotiate the treaties. We have a pretty good record so far. Once a country sees the benefits of having American military in their country, they don't usually go back,' explained the president.

'France is the only one I can remember,' someone said.

'Damn Frogs!' said Zymanski. 'Cheese-eating surrender monkeys! '

'Our NATO allies, don't forget,' said President Bedford. 'Let's keep our eye on the ball, shall we? If this Operation Warm Blanket goes through, then it will be a great day for our country. We can bring a lot of our boys back from defending parts of Asia.'

'There are still a lot of people around who remember Vietnam and the way they reported it back then. There was day after day of TV footage of body bags and funerals. It did for Humphrey in sixty-eight and the US got Nixon.'

'Fortunately, we don't put that stuff out on TV anymore but the casualty count still matters. It can still swing elections. If we can bring back all the soldiers and just have air force, then we are half way there. We can then move over to replacing the air force in Europe and Asia with this line of drone bases.'

'That's brilliant, sir!'

'It's more than brilliant, Hubert, it's also economical. Even after set-up costs, and rent to the participating countries, what with a smaller Army and no expensive foreign bases.'

'Add in all those logistics savings, we may be talking as much as eight, ten percent off the annual defense bill. That's some dollars! And if it works in Asia, then who knows where else we could deploy it?'

'So this is the schedule. Next week I am going to Brussels to address NATO heads of government. They will be put in the picture. Meanwhile, I am looking to this group, and whoever you may need to co-opt, providing they have the clearance, of course, to start the implementation plan.'

'By our next meeting, we need a list of at least one hundred suitable sites for the bases plus an assessment of the political climate in all the countries who will be involved. Branwell, I guess you guys at Langley can do that? Another meeting in two weeks.'

'Yes sir.'

Five

In his high office on the third floor of the former Palace of Culture, now AUSB, Dean Mike Mulvaney, a long-standing expatriate, was in conference with Manuel Oliviera. Mulvaney was a patient man who was line manager to some sixty faculty members, ranging from journalists and musicians to computer scientists and mathematicians. He much preferred the quiet life – his usual accolade for a professor he approved of was to describe him as 'low maintenance'.

So worn down had Mulvaney become by fifteen years of listening to whines and moans, not to say anger and threats, from his charges, that he spent as much time as he could sequestered alone in his office, protected from the sudden intrusions of aggrieved teachers by his formidable secretary, Ramona, a kind, protective motherly woman who had seen too many confrontations between the Dean and some self-important, aggrieved teacher.

Oliviera was not low maintenance. He preferred the forceful approach. He was a Brazilian in an American environment and he was fluent in both temperaments, being both American loud and Brazilian hot-tempered.

Oliviera took his Brazilian-ness seriously. Throughout the year, even through the short, cold, Balkan winter, he always dressed as if for a day on Copacabana Beach, with his colored singlet, shorts and rubber sandals.

Maybe no one had ever told him that more somber attire might be more appropriate for a senior full professor. Or maybe that is just the way they do things in Rio de Janeiro.

'We need a new professor of psychology!!' he was shouting at Mulvaney.

'To take over Isabella Petrova's classes next term?'

'The stupid bitch!' shouted Manuel Oliviera. 'She just went! She just went! No warning!'

'Well, let's be fair. She did have a nervous breakdown,' said Mulvaney.

'And whose fault was that? Whose fault was that?' bellowed Oliviera. 'Not mine! Not mine!'

'As I understand it, you asked her to teach Mathematical Economics ME 444. She got a bit upset because she was hired to teach human psychology.'

'Psychology! Economics! All the same! All the same!! '

'No, I don't think they are,' said Mulvaney quietly. 'Look, I'll put out adverts for two professors. How about that? We need two people, one in psychology and one in mathematical economics. Can't say fairer than that, can I'

Over-excitable chairmen of the Business Department were a long-standing feature of Mulvaney's life. Indeed, the whole department had more than its share of neurotics. Oliviera was his fifth chairman since he had been appointed Dean and Manuel Oliviera was by no means the worst he had had to work with. It seemed to him, in his darker moments, that the whole department was a gusher of self-important academic *prima donnas*.

'Manuel, calm down. I am sure we can sort out this little problem. I'll put a notice in *The Chronicle of Higher Education.* We'll soon find someone.'

'That's good! We need someone good! Be sure to find someone good! This is a good place with top people! Find someone good!'

'Now, tell me,' inquired Mulvaney. 'What about Professor Petrova? How is she?'

'She cried a lot. She was very upset. We put her on a plane to Moscow. She'll be OK.'

'Who's going to cover her classes now?'

'Well, I think Sverdlov. He can teach the economics.

He doesn't know it well but that's no problem. He'll do it OK.'

'And her human resources courses, what about them?'

'It's no problem, Dean. We'll find someone. Anyone can teach human resources. It's just simple personnel management. A child can do it. It's just a matter of staying one page ahead of the class. The students never notice.'

'Is that all?' asked Mulvaney.

'Not quite, my good friend. You know my contract finishes at the end of the semester. I am not going to renew.'

'Why not? You haven't screwed up.'

'No, I've not screwed up. I teach well. But being chairman of the department is very difficult. I need to go home. Get my bearings. Find my feet again.'

Mulvaney knew that Oliviera was right. The average length of a chairman's office was something around nine months and Oliviera was now well into his second year.

'Any ideas about who we should ask to do the job next?'

'Well, Dean, all I can say is that it will have to be one of the usual suspects. So the choice is limited to just Hattie Reilly, Morten Nyborg, Denis Denitsev and maybe Mark Kowalski. What about the new guy? What's his name? Balfour?'

'Don't know much about him. We could ask him, I suppose.'

The President of the United States was also in a one-to-one meeting - with Secretary of State Alison Treadwell.

'The way I see it, Alison, 'explained President Bedford, 'is that the core NATO countries in Europe will probably go along with the plan. They will let us quietly dismantle our bases and replace them with automated drone stations. They are not the problem. The problem is going to be selling the idea to the others, those countries which just have minimal USAF cover at present.'

'Well, sir,' said Secretary of State Treadwell, 'we could always explain to them that we are withdrawing all our ground troops and, in return, we will be extending our defensive air cover over their territories. We don't have to tell them what form the new air cover will take.'

'I can't see that working,' said O.B. 'They are sure to ask the details. There's been a lot of talk about drone warfare these last few years. They are bound to guess what we have in mind.'

'Look, sir,' replied Alison Treadwell, 'why not set up a treaty for Warm Blanket which doesn't mention drones at all? Make it look like we are simply building a few more regular conventional bases. We could sell the idea as a strengthening of American commitment to the defense of the region. Then, over the next few years, we can gradually change the plan. The regular bases will take at least five years to construct. We should be able to twist a few arms in that time. If we do it carefully, we could have the whole drone network in place by then.'

'That's sounds feasible. Maybe it's the easiest way. But what you are proposing is highly questionable. Can we get away with it, do you think?'

'I think we have a good chance, Mister President. When the treaty is published all it will say is that we are proposing an increase in regular aircraft in all those countries where we already have a presence. That should be our line for the time being. We can introduce the drone idea to each of them separately over time, quietly. Right now, we are so far ahead with drone technology, it must be the obvious way forward. The drones are getting faster and bigger. We don't really need men in planes anymore.

Technically, we are at least ten years ahead of the Chinese or anyone else.'

'We need to get American service personnel out of Europe and Asia as soon as possible, while things are relatively quiet. They are costing the American taxpayer far too much.'

'They sure are, sir.'

'What about all those countries that want drones outlawed under international law? Are any of them on our list?'

'No, sir, the core NATO members and most of the Euro-Atlantic Partnership are neutral.'

'There's a general feeling with most people that drones are, well, a little unfair. Too many civilians get in the way. As George Zymanski said at the meeting, it's the Osama Bin Laden's of this world who hide in civilian areas and use the ordinary people as shields.'

'So, those countries shouldn't complain,' said Treadwell,

'They are saying that it turns armed conflict into a video game. The controllers back in New Mexico are never put at risk themselves.'

'But surely that's the whole point, isn't it, sir' replied the Secretary of State. 'We are the good guys, the peacekeepers. We only ever use force in defense of peace. Like a cop. The cops have to have better weapons, better body armor *et cetera* because that is the price of world peace. The cops do not have to be put at risk. And that's what we want, a world where our troops are not in harm's way.'

'OK, Alison, 'continued the president, 'I've read all the position papers from McFall's boys and Zymanski sent me a whole bunch of stuff. I just need to go through it with you before the Brussels meeting.'

'First, why do we need to build extra bases for these

drones? Can't we just replace our manned planes with the drones in the regular bases we have now?'

'Well, sir, we could but it would defeat the whole point of the exercise. Drone bases are a lot different. They are unmanned until needed. Just regular overhauls by technicians who can be flown in from Ramstein or Lakenheath in England as needed The drone base needs only a short runway for the service plane, no more than a couple of hundred meters, which also doubles up for the drones themselves. They can be virtually hidden away in a hangar, a sort of large cave in the side of a mountain. Drone bases can be made more or less invisible if they are camouflaged well enough.'

'But we could still do that from the bases we have now, surely?' asked President Bedford.

'Yes, we could,' answered Alison Treadwell, 'but that ignores the extra cost of running an old-fashioned base like Ramstein – all the logistics, family housing, utilities, all the contracts with local suppliers, a helluva lot of dollars going out, plus the fact that a regular base is obviously there for all to see. You can't hide it like you can a drone station. Planes taking off, large runways, lots of people in and out. The local economy likes them, of course, for obvious reasons. Drone stations are invisible. No one will know they are there. Not to mention that our regular bases attract terrorists, like in Afghanistan.'

'That's right, Alison. Now that we have the technology, we ought to be using it. I don't see any down side to the plan. It saves American lives and it saves money.'

'I agree, sir. However we do it, we have to go over to a completely unmanned air force sooner or later. It's just a matter of stepping carefully and not upsetting any of our allies. They might not see the advantages it has for them as well as for us.'

'Advantages for them? I don't see too many of those.'

'Well, maybe not, sir, but it's the future and they'd better get used to it.'

Colonel Sieghart composed his request to the Human Resources Office of the CIA at Langley Virginia and took it to the Ambassador's office. The Ambassador checked it over and made a couple of small corrections before nodding his head.

'Let us hope they send us some intelligent ones this time,' said Feldstein.

'Yeah, let's hope, although I'm not confident.'

'Why not John, if you can tell me?'

'Well, sir, I am not confident because you just don't click your fingers and get two well-trained people like those two. How many people do we have here who can speak street Macedonian, for example, or both varieties of Albanian?'

'Albanian comes in two flavors?'

'Sure, apparently they're called Gheg and Tosk. That idiot Dexter could speak 'em both.'

'People like that must be hard to find.'

'You're telling me - especially if they have full Company training and ten years in the field.'

'Why is it so important, John, can you tell me that?'

'Sir, all I can tell you is that this part of the world is coming under close scrutiny. There may be something happening soon. We need two good agents in place and soon, just in case the storm breaks, which it could at any time.'

'Come on John, the Balkans have always been like that, ever since they shot that archduke at Sarajevo a century back. Ten different countries, four or five religions, a hundred different dialects, even three or four different alphabets. And all banged up together only a few hundred miles from each other. There was only ever any stability when Tito was alive.'

'True. That is why we need proper intelligence about the place. Those two bozos could merge in with the crowd and pick up useful bits of gossip. They also knew how to collect information from their networks without the sources realizing they were just a small cog in the machine.'

'What will happen to them?'

'Knowing the Company, there will be no forgiveness, ever. First they will be demoted. Then maybe sent to some safe but hellish place like Liberia or Togo. Could be fired, or retired at the first sniff of financial cutbacks. They'll be lucky if they end their working lives as untenured assistant professors at some community college in South Dakota.'

'It's as bad as that?'

'Yeah, it's as bad as that. It's a real waste. One thing's for sure. They can't ever come back here. The local secret police here will have tabs on them if they do. They won't be able to move without the local spooks watching their every move.'

'OK, John, I'll send it now.'

He called to his secretary, 'Mary, would you send this classified, coded. Langley.'

'Yes sir.'

Two days later the Ambassador got the reply. He called John Sieghart. 'John, can you step into my office, please? '

'John, you're not going to like this. Back from Langley – no replacements available. Current Balkan trainees do not graduate for three months yet. Then they need the field craft course. They have no experienced

58

people. They suggest that we use local personnel until the new officers are ready. So, four months at least and then they could be just rookies. Sorry, John. Do you know what you are going to do?'

'Off the top of my head, sir, I've no idea.'

'Do you know any local people who could take over quickly?'

'I'll have to think about that. We do have some people here, low level operatives. They are reliable enough but only for the basics - nothing too dangerous or sensitive.'

'Maybe you'll have to use them for the time being and hope nothing breaks before Langley can send us decent replacements.'

'Thank you, sir. I'll look through the files and see if there's a stop-gap.'

'Good luck, John.'

'Thank you, sir'.

For the next few days, John Sieghart scratched his head about just how he was going to find some experienced field operatives to fill in the gaps left by the enforced departure of Dexter and Le Moine. It was by chance, over drinks with some of the senior people at AUSB, that he picked up the interesting news that there was a vacancy at the university for a provost, a new number two to President Alaric Potts. He knew just the man, and, after he had spoken to Ambassador Feldstein and after Ambassador Feldstein had spoken to Potts, who owed Feldstein a favor or two, and after Alaric Potts had made his recommendation to the AUSB Board of Regents, the right provost was appointed. His name was Darius Galpin.

Every year since its inception in 1949, the North Atlantic Treaty Organization, NATO, has held a meeting of all of its members, usually attended by each country's head of government who might also be the head of state. They were usually accompanied by other senior ministers, usually the country's defense and foreign ministers.

Until the ending of the Cold War and the falling of the Berlin Wall in 1989, the main business of the Organization had been to provide security in Europe, which had meant that its primary objective had been to stand ready to throw back the Bolshevik hordes should they take it on themselves to invade the west across the North German plain. Now that the Soviet Empire was history, NATO's remit had been extended further east, to the oil-rich states of Asia, to counter the new threats of terrorism.

This year's meeting in Brussels was enhanced by the attendance of representatives of all 22 members of the Euro-Atlantic Partnership Council , which included most of the new states of the old Yugoslavia and most of the 'Stans' from Central Asia. They were something like associate members of NATO.

Prime Minister Anastasia Makarovna and Defense Minister Alexei Alexandrov were sitting at their table before a small national flag - red, blue and black stripes, symbolizing the three main ethnic and religious groupings of their country.

They were awaiting the start of a closed session which was to include a debate to be opened by US President Bedford. All the non-political people present, the secretaries and aides, the reporters and the photographers, even the stenographers, were banished from the room. The doors were locked and two guards were posted outside. The hundred or so delegates listened expectantly.

'Fellow members of NATO and the Euro-Atlantic

Partnership,' began the American President, 'we have come to a significant turning point in the history of both our organizations. I want to take you with me on a journey into the future.'

He then went on to explain that it would no longer be practical for NATO and its sister Partnership to engage in wars which involved NATO troops on the ground. Armed conflict involving NATO soldiers was, after Afghanistan and Iraq, no longer militarily feasible. Future Asian conflicts would attract humanitarian support only. NATO would no longer get involved as a participant.

'However,' he went on, 'this does not mean that NATO will withdraw from Europe and Asia. The Organization still has a major role to play in defending any of its members who might be attacked by rogue states or by terrorist groups. And we in the west still have to defend our trade interests, especially those in Central Asia, whose energy supplies form a vital trade link between Asia, Europe and North America.'

'So, what we in the United States are proposing is a new defense treaty, provisionally called Operation Warm Blanket. First, there will be a withdrawal of all US ground forces from the entire region. We are asking our NATO allies to repatriate all of their regular soldiers also. We see ground-based troops based abroad as an anachronism in the twenty first century when the nature of conflict is undergoing significant technological change.

Second, we see a doubling of NATO air power in all the countries of our two great organizations. This will mean additional airbases in all the countries whose representatives are present here today, so that we can have the air power in place to meet any threat immediately and effectively.

Third, the United States government will place additional funds at the disposal of NATO and the

Partnership to underwrite the infrastructural changes which the new plan will entail in participating countries.

And fourth, all new NATO airborne garrisons will continue, as at present, to be under local operational control, including all construction, supply and personnel where appropriate.'

'The North Atlantic Treaty Organization has now been a successful force for world peace for the last seventy years. Its form may change, but its ideals, to keep all of us safe and a world at peace will continue for many more years to come! I hope that tomorrow, all fifty of us can sign the treaty authorizing Operation Warm Blanket as the first step on that mission of peace! '

He sat down to excited and prolonged applause.

In her private face-to-face meeting with O'Brien Bedford, Anastasia Makarovna was blunt.

'Tell me, Mister President, what are the benefits of this Operation Warm Blanket for my country?'

'Your country is in the front line for the defense of the oil pipeline from Central Asia. I am advised that a second NATO airbase plus missiles and electronic defenses will need to be constructed. All construction work and non-military personnel will be sourced locally. The military personnel will be multi-national NATO airmen and women. In addition, NATO will double its financial support to your country.'

'Thank you, Mister President, thank you very much!'

The following day, there was a grand signing ceremony when the heads of government of all fifty countries, trouped up, one after the other, to shake the hand of the NATO Secretary-General and to sign a treaty document between NATO and each country in turn, which signified the legality and imminent implementation of Operation Warm Blanket.

Six

Professor Oliviera, having resigned the Chairmanship of the Department of Business at AUSB, had gone back to his beach hut in Rio. Meanwhile the Business Department went back to one of its periodic interregnums – those frequent occasions when it did not have an official chair. Mulvaney took over nominal chairmanship of the department, as he so often had had to do in the past as one chair after another had thrown down the poisoned chalice after only a few months in the job. As soon as he could, Mulvaney would pick it up and offer it around to any likely, or gullible, candidate.

The regulars in the department, the old-stagers - Denis Denitsev, Professor Hattie Reilly PhD, Morten Nyborg, Marcus Kowalski and others, were frequently asked to take on the role and they had always refused. They were far too experienced in the ways of the department to want the public exposure or the extra work. No, they all unconsciously realized, the power to control the department without the responsibility for their actions, suited them so much better, especially since, this being a university, management responsibility came with a hefty dollop of clerical make-work, dressed up as 'administration'.

Already, in the corridors of power in this unexceptional university department, the tongues were wagging about the possible candidates. The little cabal of Denitsev, Reilly and Nyborg were determined that they would need someone who could be easily controlled. It was an exercise which they had gone through several times already. Their criteria were well-defined. They did not want someone who would create upheavals in their well-worn schedules by demanding curriculum changes.

They especially did not want someone who would give them new classes to teach in place of those they had been teaching for many years. The outgoing chair, Oliviera, had been ideal in this regard, being content not to disturb the *status quo* with curriculum innovations, or much else for that matter.

His relaxed approach to his chairmanly duties had been perfect for the little gang. Even so, ignoring the old dictum about not speaking ill of the dead, they nevertheless felt justified, after he had retired to his southern sun, in criticizing him for his faults, both real and imagined. Having little else to do with their time, they were able to devote a fair proportion of it to gratuitous complaints about their now departed former boss.

'Not a good chair...'

'I never liked him...'

'Why was he ever appointed?'

'We must get someone different this time...'

And so on, and so on, they would prattle their malice.

General Alexei Alexandrov, as his country's Defense Minister, was an old hand at playing the politics of his small country, politics which were even less stable than those of its larger neighbor, Bulgaria. He had been there when the country had liberated itself from the socialist tyranny and he had played a part in the *putsch* which had brought the head of state, President Leonid Balashirov, to power sixteen years previously. Since then Alexandrov had divided his time between running the country's small armed forces and making himself immensely rich.

It is a country where the electorate votes along strictly religious lines and given that the population of the country is divided roughly a third each Catholic, Orthodox and Muslim, it meant that no single party could govern without help from one of the other two. Alexandrov himself was an oddity, an Orthodox Christian in a Catholic Party, the Conservatives, the party which had formed a minority government for most of the country's short history.

That is why the wily General had deserted his religious roots and joined them. Makarovna's government was forever on the brink of collapse but, as in so many countries where the ruling party is in a permanent minority, the actual governance of the country was achieved by cronyism, continuous favor-trading and the periodic setting of one opposition faction against the other.

The Conservatives were in favor of the American military presence and they would be happy to see it enhanced. They had signed up to NATO and had even supplied a token force for the war in Afghanistan.

The country's main NATO contribution took the form of a small remote airbase, Altameda, some ten miles from the nearest town and way up in the inhospitable northern mountains. Few people knew of its existence or of the two and a half thousand US airmen and their families who lived there. The base was not marked on any map and the only road to it was a winding two-lane highway, also unmarked. Local workers at the base were bussed in from surrounding villages. Europe, since the end of the Second World War, has many such places.

Inside the base, which was provisioned by air from USAF bases at Ramstein in Germany and Aviano in Italy, one could be excused for thinking one might be in a village in Michigan or Maine. It contained everything necessary to support American small town life - roads on which to drive American SUV's, a movie theater, a church, a football stadium and shops. Since going off-base was difficult, a posting here was, in reality, little more than a comfortable prison sentence but the USAF had made the experience of service at Altameda as much like going to one's home town as it could.

The personnel who lived and worked there were happy with their enforced seclusion. They mostly showed little curiosity about the country they were living in. They knew rightly enough that they were keeping the world free and peaceful and they were sure that the natives, if they had ever met any, would rejoice in the liberating American presence and the benefits it conferred, the benefits of democracy and civilization.

And when, at the end of their tour of duty, they returned home to a small town in the mid-west, they would be greeted as sophisticated world travelers, even if they had not learned a single word of any foreign language nor used any other currency than US dollars nor, in some cases, ever spoken to a single non-American.

Altameda was not enough for the Catholic Conservatives. They wanted a much bigger, better-known and more visible American military deployment. They wanted more bases and the jobs the bases brought. They wanted also for the country to look stronger to its many unfriendly neighbors. Most of all, they wanted the country to be locked ever more securely inside the profitable NATO embrace.

Prime Minster Anastasia Makarovna met with Alexandrov straight after they had returned from Brussels and her private meeting with O.B., as the President had invited her to call him.

'So, they have agreed that we shall have more Americans here in our country. They finally saw our point of view and they will begin construction soon on a second base. It should be located far from their present base, on the other side of the country, maybe at Nyo Brutske, near the Greek border. The Americans will use our local labor for the construction and there will be permanent jobs for our people! It will bring great benefits. But, Alexei, I left out the best bit of what O.B. told me. The Americans will pay us rent of double what they are paying now while the base is on our territory! Isn't that wonderful? We are sure to win the election now!'

'It sounds very good news, indeed, Madame Prime Minister. But can we trust the Americans? Will they keep their word? What will they want in return? '

'It seems that the Americans need to consolidate their forces in the Balkans, to protect small NATO countries like ours from terrorist threats, especially to the long pipeline which goes through here. After Afghanistan is fully closed down, we will become vulnerable, or so he said. So there will be new bases in all the countries along a line from Europe to central Asia, including us.'

'If this doesn't win us the election, whatever will?'

'Now, Alexei, right now, only you and I know the full details. So it will have to be explained very carefully to our friends. They must be brought onside. When we are sure we are all together, it will be your job to announce it in the chamber. You can expect some dissent. But the prize is worth fighting for!'

'Quite true, Prime Minister. There will be a lot of resistance from the Orthodox Party and the Red Crescent Group. There's not much affection for the Americans there.'

'I will talk to the leaders. This is for the whole country, not just one party. I will appeal to the people's patriotism and isolate any dissenters as unpatriotic.'

'Let us hope that it works, Prime Minister.'

Shortly before the start of the fall semester, Dean Mulvaney called his first departmental faculty meeting. He began by introducing the four new professors recruited over the summer. Three of the newcomers were on short, one-semester contracts, the fourth was the new three-year appointment in accountancy, lately of a college in South Korea.

Mulvaney moved swiftly to the first agenda item. 'Item one, I hope you have all read my submission to the university executive council about the timing of midterm examinations? '

There were a few nods.

'Right then,' said Mulvaney, 'would anyone like to propose that we accept this new timing schedule?'

Morten Nyborg broke in. 'I'm sorry, Mike,' he said, 'but I think we need to discuss this before it's put to a vote. For example, you have said that we should start afternoon exams at two pm.'

'Well?' asked Mulvaney.

'Well, Mike, we have always started the afternoon exams at two fifteen, not two o'clock. I just wonder why you are making this change now?'

'Well, 'said Mike Mulvaney, 'my thinking was that we should hold three hour exams from two until five and then two hour exams from two until four.'

'Ah!' said Nyborg, warming to his theme, 'but if we bring the start time forward from two fifteen to two o'clock, then the students will not have enough time to get to main building from the dormitories. A lot of the students take lunch in the dorms.'

'I don't see that as a big problem,' said Mulvaney. 'The morning exams finish at twelve noon. The students still have two hours to get their lunch.'

'I don't think you understand,' said Morten Nyborg. 'The start time for afternoon exams was set way back. You won't remember, it was before your time. But the two fifteen time was agreed so that students could get their lunch and get back in time for an afternoon exam. It's in the record.'

'What does the meeting think?' asked Mulvaney.

'Speaking on behalf of the long-term faculty,' said Hattie Reilly PhD, 'I think we should stick with two fifteen. It's the way we've always done it. I don't see the point of changing it now. What do the rest of you think?' She looked around at the rest of the assembled professors.

'I'm quite happy with two o'clock,' said one of the new members.

Hattie Reilly PhD glared at him. 'You've not been here long enough! You don't know! We fought long and hard to get two fifteen and we don't want to give it up now! It's always been two fifteen!' she declared with a flourish.

The poor fellow persisted. 'I'm sorry,' he said,' but I just don't see that it's very important. It's only fifteen minutes.'

Hattie Reilly PhD was becoming very angry.

'Only fifteen minutes!' she hissed. 'Only fifteen minutes! It was a long battle to get those fifteen minutes! It was long before your time. You don't understand. You've only been here fifteen minutes yourself!' She said this last phrase with a sarcastic smirk, as if she had just made a brilliant witticism.

'Anyway,' she said, as she made her clinching argument, 'you don't have a vote on departmental matters. I told you at the last meeting. You don't have a vote because you are not tenured.'

With that, she turned to the Dean, who had been sitting back watching this display of middle-aged petulance. 'So, it's agreed,' she told him. 'Two o'clock is to be cancelled and two fifteen reinstated. Let's take a vote.'

'Right,' said the Dean, 'a vote. All those in favor of changing the schedule back to two fifteen, please show.' Five people out of the assembled twenty or so put their hands up.

'Against?' asked the Dean. Eight hands went up.

'That's it,' said Hattie, 'passed unanimously. We stick with two fifteen.'

'But, I made the vote eight to five for two o'clock,' said a quiet middle-aged man from the back.

'You don't understand,' Hattie corrected him. 'None of those eight are entitled to vote. They've not been here long enough or they are only on short contracts.'

'But nobody gets a long-term contract anymore. All new contracts are short-term. Does that mean that only you four or five people can vote because you got your jobs before they stopped awarding long contracts?'

'What's wrong with that?' riposted Hattie Reilly PhD. 'We will still be here after you are gone. So it's only fair that we are the ones voting on important policy matters. Passed unanimously. Dean?'

'Passed unanimously,' said Dean Mulvaney, struggling to keep the weariness out of his voice. 'I will delete two o'clock and restore two fifteen.'

'Item two,' he continued, 'research seminars. President Potts has asked me to nominate a maximum of three faculty members to give short talks on their research work on the new program of research seminars he wants to promote. Is anybody interested?'

Here, Richard Smalley cut in. Smalley was a new recruit to the ruling inner circle. He was a young, thin, self-important, emotionally-repressed young man who fancied himself as the department intellectual. A wiry crop of black hair sprouted above his coarse, gormless face on which, perched above the acne, he wore a pair of heavy-framed glasses. It was the uniform of the look-at-me-I'm-so-clever college lecturer, *circa* 1964.

His subject was business strategy, which he claimed to have studied to doctoral level at the University of Alice Springs in Australia. He considered himself to be especially clever on account of his having earned a degree, *summa cum laude*, from that august institution.

He even styled himself on his office door, with his full academic CV - *Richard Smalley BA (Summa cum Laude), PhD (University of Alice Springs)*.

'Well,' he told the gathering, 'as you know, I do research myself and I am certainly going to be contributing to this program, me. I think it is very important, myself, for a university to be involved in real scholarship as I myself am, me. I regard work of this kind to be very, very vital and I will be giving at least one talk myself, me.'

'As I understand it, the president is hoping to set up a series of international meetings and inviting famous scholars such as Nobel Prize winners and other well-known people to contribute. I, myself, will certainly want to be associated with that.'

Who does he have in mind?' asked the same man who had earlier raised the question of voting rights.

'I think he's got in mind people like Al Gore, Henry Kissinger, Paul Krugman, Tim Berners-Lee, people of that caliber,' answered Richard Smalley,

'People like that? Coming here?' the quiet man was incredulous.

'Why not? I am sure they will be perfectly happy to take part in our seminars.'

Again, Hattie Reilly PhD took up the theme. 'I would be very happy to take part. Like many of you, I would love to have the time to do original work. Do research. But we just don't have the time. There is always too much else to do. It would be nice to have the luxury of being able to sit down and do some research. But there it is. Sorry.'

'So, anyone else?' asked Dean Mulvaney. There was no response. 'Right then, it's just Richard. I'll pass that on to President Potts.'

'So, item three, election of a departmental faculty member to the university executive council. Do I have any nominations?'

'It has to be a permanent staff member, not a short-term contractor,' interposed Hattie Reilly PhD.

'So, any ideas?' asked Mulvaney.

'I propose Denis Denitsev,' said Reilly. 'He has all the right experience and all the right connections. And he's already doing the job. I propose Denis.'

'Seconded,' said Morten Nyborg.

'Does anyone want to nominate anyone else?' asked Mulvaney.

'Must be full-time,' said Hattie Reilly PhD.

'OK, then Denis Denitsev it is,' said Mulvaney. 'Unanimous.'

'Item four,' said Mulvaney. 'Now is this the biggie, the selection of a new department chair. Remember, I am just acting chair. I don't, or rather, I can't, do the job much longer. I've been chair since Oliviera left before the summer, but I have enough to do with my full-time day job. So I'm looking for nominations. Before I do that, I have asked Hattie Reilly... '

'Professor Hattie Reilly PhD,' she corrected Dean Mulvaney.

'Sorry Hattie. I have asked Professor Hattie Reilly PhD, as a long-standing professor, if she is willing to do it but she feels, if I am quoting you correctly, Hattie, too busy to take it on.'

'It really needs someone who can take the job on full-time – there's a lot of work involved. I just can't spare the time to do it properly,' said Hattie Reilly PhD.

'So, I have asked Dave Balfour if he is willing to do it,' said Mulvaney.

'This is a huge job, and I am new here. I think someone else might have better experience. It's probably down to Morten or Denis if Hattie can't do it,' said Dave Balfour. Balfour was an old-school full professor with a respectable provenance going back more than forty years. He had been born in the week of the attack on Pearl Harbor and now he had become a wiry, careful, white-haired old pro, suspicious of unasked for job offers.

'Look, Dave,' said Mulvaney, 'you and I have talked about this before. I understand that you are reluctant to take it on so early in your time here. But I think you could do it.'

'Actually,' said Balfour, 'what we talked about was how I would be compensated for doing the job. Anyone who takes on this job will be doubling or even tripling their workload, so I would need to be paid the right compensation for the extra work involved.'

'I hear what you're saying,' said Mulvaney in reply, 'but I've spoken to the new provost and it is not university policy to pay a supplement to professors who take on the job of departmental chair.'

'Well,' said Balfour, 'I have to tell you that it is my policy not to work for nothing. And even if you did pay me the going rate, I would also need some guarantees about freedom of action about my duties as chair.'

'You know I can't make those guarantees,' said Mulvaney. 'Policy will continue to be made by this faculty committee. As for extra pay, I promise I will speak to the provost again.'

The departmental meeting had now been going on for two hours and little had been resolved. Mulvaney came wearily to the final agenda item.

'Item five,' he announced. 'It is proposed by Morten

73

Nyborg that the format of these departmental meetings be changed to electronic meetings only. '

Morten Nyborg explained his idea. 'I brought this up at the last meeting with Manuel Oliviera and it wasn't taken up. But I still think it's a good idea. First, as a modern university department we should be keeping up to date with trends and using electronic media for our communications. I am proposing that we hold our meetings by email. It would mean that we wouldn't need to fix a time and place when everyone could get here. The meeting could take place over a longer period without interrupting classes. Second, the circulation could be arranged so that we only received notice of agenda items we are interested in. Voting could be done online. Does anybody have any ideas?'

'Well, I, for one, think it's a great idea,' said Hattie. 'It means that if you don't have an interest in something and you can't vote on it, then you don't have to hear about it.'

'Me too,' added Denis Denitsev.

'Wait a minute,' said one of the temporaries,' does that mean that us non-voting members will not even know what's being talked about, even if it concerns us?'

'That's true,' said Morten. 'If you don't have a vote and the item doesn't concern you, then you don't need to know about it.'

'I think,' said Dean Mulvaney, intervening,' that we can postpone this discussion until next time. As I recall, university regulations require face-to-face meetings for each department, at least once per semester. Let's put Morten's idea on the back burner. Is there any other business? No? Right, meeting adjourned.'

Whereupon those members of the faculty of the Department of Business who had stayed to the bitter end of a meeting which had resolved almost nothing, got up and left.

Seven

Defense Minister Alexandrov had taken his seat in the Chamber of Deputies for what promised to be a difficult session. The chamber was full. The government would be making a major announcement about the Brussels talks and Operation Warm Blanket and no deputy wanted to miss it. The leaders of the two opposition parties, Mehmet Caradescu of Muslim Red Crescent and Mikhail Simonov of the Orthodox Liberals were already in their seats at the front and by their body language, it was obvious that they were spoiling for a fight. The Minister of Defense got up.

'Mister Speaker, Honorable Deputies,' he began, 'Madame Prime Minister and I have just returned from the NATO meeting of heads of government in Brussels. I am privileged to be able to report a significant development in the defense capabilities of our country and the economic advantages it will bring.'

'The prime minister has signed an agreement with our NATO allies for a doubling of NATO bases in this country. A second base will be established at Nyo Brutske in the south-west of the country. The construction of this new facility will create a large number of new jobs in a poor region. It will have a permanent NATO garrison including some of our own military personnel and there will be some three hundred new civilian jobs.

The construction work will begin in two years time and it will be completed within five years at the latest when the base will become fully functional. The United States will base its G34 fighter wing there and will pay this country an annual rental.' There was a noticeable angry murmuring but the minister pressed on.

'All our NATO allies and several non-NATO

countries will also be extending their involvement in a defensive wall of airbases stretching from Aviano in Italy to Almaty in Kazakhstan. It is to be known as Operation Warm Blanket. The...'

He got no further before one deputy at the back of the Orthodox Party seats shouted, 'YOU'VE SOLD US OUT TO THE AMERICANS FOR MONEY!'

'Don't be ridiculous!' retorted Alexandrov. 'This is vital for our country. It protects us and brings in much needed income. It will create at least a thousand construction jobs in the short term and maybe three hundred permanent jobs when the new base is opened. Maybe the member is ignorant of the economic facts of life as they apply to this country!'

The member who had spoken jumped to his feet. He was just about to protest at being so sharply put down when his party leader, Mikhail Simonov, cut in with his own question.

'Has the Minister of Defense not considered that any new bases will be under the exclusive control of the Americans? Just like our present base at Altameda? Once it is here it will be here forever with no chance of ever getting rid of it - and for what? Is the Minister too stupid to realize that the more American troops we have on our soil, the more we become a target for terrorists and crazy people!'

'No, no!' the Minister shouted above the rising anger. 'The United States is our friend. We are in an alliance with them. That is what NATO is, a joint defensive alliance of equal partners.'

'The Minister is treating us like children,' snorted Mehmet Caradescu. 'Does he really think we can trust the Americans? Equal partners? Does the Minister think we are simpletons?'

'How dare you talk to me like that!' shouted

Minister Alexandrov. 'This is an excellent deal for our country!'

'You mean an excellent deal for you, don't you?' someone shouted.

'How much are the Americans paying you?' shouted someone else, as tempers rose.

Soon both sides of the chamber were shouting at each other. The Speaker was trying to keep order by banging his gavel and shouting. His voice was not heard as the deputies kept up a barrage of insult and counter-insult.

'You're in the pay of the Americans!'

'You don't care for this country. Just so long as you can win the election and carry on looting the country!'

The shouting went on for about five minutes as various deputies took their opportunities to air old grievances and settle old scores.

'Still taking bribes for building contracts, eh, Dmitri?'

'What about you? You old lecher, still screwing teenagers, are you, Stoyan?'

'Miroslav, how did you come by the new yacht? Russian money, was it?'

'Fuck you! You thieving bastard!'

'Don't talk to me like that, you lying scumbag!'

'What did you call me?'

'I called you a lying scumbag. That's what you are! Fuck off!'

'Are you still paying off the hush money for staying out of jail on that tax charge, you thief?'

'Don't talk to me like that, you filthy little pedophile! Screwing kids! Your sort needs putting down.'

'Your wife is a whore!'

'Your son is a drug addict!'

That was the end of civilized parliamentary

discussion and, tiring of the frustrations of mere debate, Mehmet Caradescu walked across the chamber to punch Defense Minister Alexei Alexandrov squarely on the nose. It was the sign for the entire chamber to erupt into a brawl.

The armed guards who had been waiting outside came to the door of the chamber and watched. It is a cardinal rule of security personnel everywhere that when a pitched battle of this type breaks out, it is best to let the participants exhaust themselves before taking control.

So when the combatants were seen to be starting to tire, the guards quickly took over. With the help of their truncheons and a few well-aimed kicks, a sort of order was restored. Ambulances were called for the twenty or so deputies who had sustained minor damage.

Unfortunately, the whole scene had been recorded on national television and within minutes it was an instant success on every news channel around the world where it mostly featured as a humorous item to close the show, accompanied by snide comments from jokey presenters.

President Leonid Balashirov was waiting in his Palace. He was expecting the call any minute. Eventually, his secretary came through.

'Sir, the prime minister is requesting a meeting?'

'Is it official or social?'

'Official, I'm sorry, sir.'

'Yes, I've been expecting to hear from her. Tell her to come right away. No calls for two hours.'

It was an open national secret which no one mentioned, that Leonid Balashirov, fourth term president of the republic and Prime Minister Anastasia Makarovna were long-time lovers. The president's secretary would hold all calls when they were in conference together, which was at least twice a week. Before each meeting, Irina Lomonosova, who had been Balashirov's secretary for the sixteen years since he had first come to power, would discreetly inquire 'official or social'.

Madame Makarovna had been instantly attracted to this handsome, powerful, intelligent man. She was a fine-looking woman of nearly fifty, a late entrant to the profession of politics after a lucrative career in banking. She had first caught the president's eye when she had been a rising star of the Conservative faction. His behind-the-scenes string-pulling had advanced her career rapidly and from humble deputy she had moved to the government and then to the premiership within five years. Nothing is for nothing, she had warned herself, but in spite of her initial reluctance to get emotionally involved with Balashirov, she was now glad she had allowed herself to become the president's official mistress.

He greeted her warmly when she arrived. They embraced passionately and then broke off.

'I'm sorry, Leonid. We have a crisis.'

'Yes, I was just watching those clowns in the chamber. Don't worry, Tasha.'

'We'll have to call an election. Our ticket will have to be support for the American plan.'

'Then you'll lose. And one of those two idiots, Simonov or Caradescu, will form the next government.'

'We are committed to the new base. I signed the treaty. They will just tear it up.'

'How important is the treaty to you, Tasha?'

'I would rather the treaty was ratified by the Chamber and I would prefer to keep my job. If either of those two becomes prime minister, the treaty is lost and with it all the jobs and the American money. But if that's what they call democracy then we will just have to live with it.'

'Let's not talk of defeat, my dear. You can still win, Tasha. There is still everything to play for. Maybe the Americans will lend a hand? There is a lot a sitting prime minister can do. Especially if she doesn't mind getting her hands a little dirty.'

'I'd rather not do anything illegal. It would be good if this were a fair election.'

'If you play fair, then you will lose. Winning is the only rule. If you have to break the law here and there to win, then that is what you must do. The laws are only there to control those people who don't have any power or ambition. How do you think I stayed in power all these years - by obeying rules and laws invented by someone else?'

'You are so wise, Leonid. I don't know what I would do without you.'

'So, my darling Tasha, let us find a way to win. Honestly and legally if possible. If not, then by some other means.'

'What about us, Leonid? You will not have anyone in the government to be your little mole.'

'I would prefer you to win. You're a very good prime minister. Those other two will not be nearly so useful or competent.'

'Or so sexy eh, Leonid?'

'Or so sexy. Look, Tasha, don't worry. If you should happen to lose the election, we can always find you a nice job. How would you like to be president of the state bank? It's not as interesting as politics but it's an easy way to become rich.'

'There's time for that later. I'm enjoying being prime minister. The state bank can wait.'

'Don't leave it too long. I am not going to be living in the presidential palace forever.'

'Let's not think about losing, my darling. Maybe if I win, we could alter the constitution to make you president for life?'

'Not so easy, love. You need two thirds majority in the Chamber of Deputies if you want to change the constitution, and you'll not get that. Anyway, our American friends tend to get a little fastidious about that sort of arrangement.'

'Maybe we can try to change the constitution after the new base is built?'

'Yes, maybe we could try to do it then. Look, I'll issue the decree for the election at six pm this evening. What if I set it for mid-September, about six weeks from now?'

'Thank you, Leonid.'

'Well, Tasha, we still have an hour before Irina starts putting calls through again.'

'So we have, darling,' murmured the prime minister, as she slipped off her jacket and began to unbutton her blouse.

Ambassador Feldstein and Colonel Sieghart watched the fight in the Chamber of Deputies on CNN in the TV lounge at the American Embassy.

'That's democracy in action, John,' said Joe Feldstein.

'Makes you wonder why we liberated 'em in the first place. You never saw democracy like that when the Russians ran the country.'

'It's their country and it's a gangsterocracy. If they choose those hoodlums for politicians, what can you expect?'

'Quite right, sir! It serves 'em right.'

'But, John, let us not get too superior too soon, just because we don't solve our political differences on Capitol Hill with fisticuffs and billy clubs. It still leaves us with a big problem. This new thing, this, er, Operation Warm Blanket, it's not going to be easy to sell to the politicos here. Do you have orders about it?'

'Well, sir, I can't go into details, but we have been told to load the dice a bit - so that the lovely Anastasia gets a little discreet help.'

'Any idea of how you're going to do that? You're a bit short-handed at the moment.'

'Well, sir, we are going to be putting Darius Galpin to work right away. We also have one or two other people we can use in an emergency. And this looks like it's going to be an emergency.'

Later that evening, Ambassador Feldstein was watching the expected presidential statement that fresh elections would be held in September. He also heard the claims of the other two party leaders that each was confident of winning and they would take the country in a new direction free of external domination. Confident and forward looking, blah de blah de blah...

He picked up his cell phone and phoned John Sieghart. 'Come and see me ASAP. I can't talk on the phone.'

'Did you watch it?' asked Sieghart when he was seated in the ambassador's office.

'Yeah! Not much Madame PM could do really except resign after that shambles in the Chamber this morning.'

'She might be a bitch but her heart's in the right place. I won't miss Alexei though, if she loses.'

'Even if Anastasia wins, which she probably won't, I think he will be out, whatever happens. Too many people are asking where he gets all his money from.'

'Amen to that. He hasn't been too careful about hiding it.'

'Look, John, your work starts right now. I'm not going to ask how you are going to handle things. Just remember, I don't want any nasty surprises. A little warning, if you can, please, so I don't have to go apologizing to Alison Treadwell for some screw-up we could have foreseen.'

'I hear you, sir. I understand the Secretary of State is one fearsome lady.'

'She is that!' the Ambassador laughed. 'Let's just be sure we come up smelling of roses when the waste material goes fanwards. Regular reports and if you are thinking of planning anything special, please let me know, if you can.'

'You got it, sir.'

Balfour was a small, intense man who had none of Oliviera's laid-back casualness, nor was he the sort of sloppy liberal who would pay much heed to sentimental notions of treating ordinary teachers as anything other than employees, paid to do a job. He was definitely one of the old school, with a firm belief in hierarchies, management structures, clearly defined job descriptions, clear demarcations of management responsibility and an understanding that responsibility and authority are not separable.

On speaking to him for the first time after Hattie Reilly PhD's search committee had appointed him, Dean Mulvaney had smiled an inward smile. Perfect, he thought, just what we need.

Dave Balfour, in possession of all the right experience and qualifications was, had they but known it, everything anathema to the little clique which ran the Business Department. However did he manage to get past their finely-honed sense of danger, their vigilance lest they admit to their exclusive club someone who might upset their carefully tended cozy little setup? How had he done it? How did he fool them into thinking that he was one of them, a clapped-out, time-serving, academic wastrel with no interest in his career save that there be no surprises?

He had done it by guile and by a superior understanding of the way academia works, as befits someone who had been attending interviews, on both sides of the table, since the late 1950's. That was long before any of his three Search Committee interrogators, Professors Denis Denitsev, Hattie Reilly PhD and Morten Nyborg, had even started high school. Because David Balfour knew the game and he could play it better than his interviewers.

With the long experience of age, he knew that their accusatorial interview style, learned no doubt from old courtroom movies, was merely self-display. He knew that he would need to flatter them, but without laying on the flattery with too heavy a trowel. He knew that they would not be listening to his answers so it mattered little that he could be inconsistent here and there provided that the right tone of answer was forthcoming.

He knew also that they had already made their minds up about whom they were going to appoint and the interview was just a time-filler. When it came to academic politics, he could run rings around them, so he was ultra-careful to appear humble, grateful and respectful, for nothing warms the cockles of the interviewers' hearts more than supplicatory self-deprecation.

What mattered were not his scholarly credentials or his cleverness or his achievements as an academic and an intellectual. All that mattered was that his face would fit - that and nothing else. And over a forty year career, during which he had come by this basic truth from numerous painful lessons, he was able to make sure that, whatever other sterling qualities he might or might not possess, he knew how to make his face fit.

When he had been asked about whether he would make any curriculum changes, he had his bland answer ready. 'From time to time, we need to modify student offerings. Even in what I teach, there are periodic changes in the subject material.' The interview panel nodded at this politicianly response.

When they asked him about departmental management structure - 'Tell us please, Professor Balfour, what is your opinion about the effectiveness of faculty participation in departmental decisions?'- he spotted the elephant trap as if it had been neon-sign-posted.

His answer was perfect. 'I think that good faculty participation is crucial to the efficient working of a successful department as you have here. But there are limits, of course. Sometimes confidentiality is vital, such as, for example, when it comes to faculty appointments.'

A few more answers like that and he had got the job. The search committee had been very impressed that he had shown absolutely zero independence of mind to add to his almost slavish subservience. Because that is how you get jobs in universities and Balfour knew the rules.

So, Denis and Morten and Hattie Reilly PhD had been most happy to welcome Dave Balfour into their gang. They believed that he would, for they did not possess the imagination to see otherwise, be someone who could be relied upon to see out the final phase of his career placidly and quietly, as befits an old man.

What they had failed to understand was that old men are not, if they are still employed, in search of peace and quiet. They will shortly have all the peace and quiet they will ever need.

Old men are in a hurry and they are not afraid of the consequences of giving offence or of speaking their minds. Old men are liberated from the need to bite their tongues when they need to speak unwelcome truths. Old men, with promising futures behind them, have little left to lose.

The esteemed Business Department Search Committee ought to have known that. But they did not possess that level of understanding of human psychology and how age changes it.

Nor were they aware of Dean Mulvaney's hidden agenda to promote Balfour to a management position as Chair of the Business Department with a brief to destroy, once and for all, the insidious influence of the corrupt system of running it by self-appointed clique.

When Denitsev had taken the news to Mulvaney that Balfour had been appointed Senior Professor of Management, Mulvaney felt a warm glow of self-satisfaction..

Soon, he thought, those weekly confrontations when Hattie Reilly PhD would berate him for not carrying out the orders of the faculty, would be over. But let's not rush things. He isn't in post for another two months yet, after which he will need a few weeks before I can spring the chairmanship on to him. Still, I can wait, Mulvaney told himself.

Eight

Balfour had duly taken up his place in the Department of Business and had begun his work as a regular professor. He proved to be disconcertingly energetic and he was soon involved in various initiatives such as helping to develop the research interests of junior professors so that they could join the career paper chase - the publishing of academic papers which would be read by few but the output of which is a harmless part of the promotion game.

He also organized student field trips, gave extra classes after hours and involved himself in that pastoral care of students which is expected of all full-time teachers, even in universities.

His real personality was also slowly emerging. One of the first signs of it occurred when he was asked to join the search committee for a new associate professor of strategic management.

'Why are we teaching strategic management?' he asked pointedly as the *ad hoc* committee sat down to consider the several dozen applications they had received.

'Well,' replied Denitsev, 'strategic management is a capstone course for the whole business program. It is always taught as a senior year course, just before the class graduates.'

'Yes,' said Balfour, 'but just because we do it does not mean that it should be done. In this day and age, mathematical economics, which you have just removed from the course offerings, will be much more useful to the students.'

Denitsev was nonplussed by this simple argument. 'Much more useful, what are you talking about?'

Balfour persisted. 'Look, our students, most, if not

all of them, will become strategic managers one day, but not for at least fifteen or twenty years. They're not going to be senior managers the moment they leave college. By the time they do become strategic managers, they will have forgotten everything we ever taught them.'

'Strategic management,' he went on, 'would be OK for thirty-something MBA students who are about to move into senior positions, but frankly, it is wasted on the young. Another point as well - by the time our students get into senior management, the whole thinking about strategic management will probably have changed anyway. So what we tell them now will no longer be relevant.'

'That's wrong! We've always taught it. Are you suggesting we change the program?'

'Well' went on Balfour, 'if the program needs changing, then we should change it. Strategic management is a good place to start. It should not be a core course. Maybe an elective for those students who want to take it, but making it a graduation requirement is ignoring the facts of life.'

Hattie Reilly PhD broke in. She was obviously getting angry. 'We can't just change the program willy-nilly, just like that! We have to get approvals, go to the provost, the Executive Council. You can't just come in here and tell us to change the way we've been doing it for years!'

'Yes,' said Balfour, 'I am aware that we have to go through channels but you don't seem to have a master plan of what we should be offering the students. The world changes quickly and we have to keep up with it and make the changes to the curriculum as needed. I don't see any logic to the way things are structured at the moment.'

'You might well say that,' riposted Hattie Reilly PhD, 'but I can tell you, because you obviously haven't read it, that the last accreditation have us 'excellent' for our program.'

'Yes,' said Balfour. 'That's probably because it's like all the others. In my experience, most business programs are out of date and need constant refreshing, which we are not doing here.'

'Yes, OK' said Denitsev. 'Are you saying we should not employ this new professor of strategic management?'

'It takes time to change things, granted. If you ask my opinion, we should offer the job to someone who can also offer some other, more relevant subject,' said Balfour.

'You mean like mathematical economics?' sneered Reilly.

'That would certainly make sense, if you could find someone. None of our students is going to become a strategic manager straight after graduation, but a fair number of them are going to go into the finance industry, probably as 'quants' - those people who use computer models.'

'Let's move on,' Reilly replied. 'I suggest we choose this one, this one, this one and this one for the shortlist. They all have strong majors in strategic management. I'll give their names to Human Resources, if that's all right with the rest of you.'

She then put the four shortlisted applications on one side and gathered up the others into a black plastic sack,

'We'll keep these on file, just in case.'

Balfour could see that this casual selection process, while it may or may not have unjustly bypassed the best candidate, did guarantee considerable unnecessary expense for AUSB, given that the committee had just committed the university to paying interview expenses for candidates from Alaska, Iraq, Japan and Australia. Whether there might have been the perfect candidate living just across the street was never considered. But that is the nature of what the guardians of the soul of the Business Department considered to be their right to 'academic freedom'.

The next day, Balfour reported back the conversation of the search committee to Dean Mulvaney.

'I suppose you heard that we had a little difference of opinion,' Balfour asked Mulvaney.

'No not a word. They never tell me the details, just the decisions. They think I have no right to know how they make their minds up. You don't need to tell me unless you want to.'

'I'm not bound by any confidentiality agreement. I'll tell you all about it.'

Balfour gave Mulvaney all the details of the little spat with Denitsev and Reilly..

'It was,' he said, 'a travesty - against all professional standards.'

'So,' said Mulvaney, 'would you like to be chair of the department? Shake them up a bit?'

'It certainly needs it,' agreed Balfour, 'but I would need some guarantees that I would not have to put up with all that pseudo-democratic bullshit. I would need the authority to overrule them when they get above themselves. And, I would need a hike in pay. I am not in this business for the good of my health.'

'I'm not sure about the pay. I would need to speak to the provost about that.'

'But the rest? Would I have the authority to go with the responsibility if I am going to turn things around?'

'You know I can't be seen to be anything other than completely impartial but you would have my full support.'

'No guarantees that you will back me in any dispute because I am bound to ruffle a few feathers? A little cosmetic change here and there isn't going to cut it. It's going to have to be major surgery – a new enhanced curriculum, different, fairer, recruitment procedures, the odd contract not renewed. Are you willing to give me the sort of guarantees that you will support me? No namby-pamby even-handedness. If you want a business department fit for the twenty first century, I will need guarantees.'

'Come on, Dave,' said Mulvaney. 'You know I can't do that.'

'Well, in that case,' answered Dave Balfour, 'thanks for your kind offer, but no thanks.'

Provost Darius Galpin had been appointed to AUSB over the summer after a tumultuous couple of years at the American College in Libya. No one was exactly sure what a provost was for except to be in charge of all matters academic and those Galpin invariably devolved to Dean Mulvaney anyway. He had also been provost in Libya and before that he had been provost at the American University in Prague. He was one of those people whose career path had begun at a senior level with no apparent apprenticeship to learn the trade, no promotion through the ranks. Right now he was visiting his old friend Colonel John Sieghart at the American Embassy.

'Well, Darius,' Sieghart told him, 'we have one helluva problem. I don't need to tell you that we have an election coming up in a few weeks time and our girl is not likely to win it.'

'Yeah, I heard.'

'Darius, this is big. What do you know about Operation Warm Blanket?'

'Not a lot. Isn't it a new line of US bases across a line from Italy to near China?'

'It's something like that. We, sorry, NATO, in the

91

form of local personnel, supported by the US, are there to defend the oil pipeline. It's a great idea. The US will withdraw all its ground forces from the various Middle Eastern hell holes, so that American soldiers' lives will not be in danger.'

'Where do I come in?' asked Provost Galpin.

'Where you come in, my friend,' said Sieghart, 'is that you are now the highest ranking CIA field operative in this shithole of a country - after me, of course. And you have clearance. You did a helluva job in Tripoli when you got rid of those guys who took over after Gaddafi and the way you neutralized that Al Qaeda cell in Prague was beautiful. The Company is very grateful. But now, we have a new job for you here. Not too difficult for a man of your talents.'

'I thought you had full-time staffers for field work?'

'Yeah, well, that went wrong. We had a coupla guys we should have used but they got recalled to Langley and, it seems, the Company doesn't have any replacements. So it's your baby.'

'My baby?'

'What we want you to do is just a few dirty tricks. Nothing you haven't done before. Just a matter of making sure our side wins the election.'

'I'll need help. I haven't been in the country long enough to build up my own network.'

'No problem. We debriefed the two guys we sent back to DC. There is a ready-made network. You need to contact this man, Konstantin Zonkov. He's expecting you. He's our contact with some, shall we say, useful people.' Sieghart passed over a small note.

'How far do you want me to go?'

'For the moment stick to regular things like screwing up election meetings, blacking out political TV broadcasts, ballot papers with names missing, a bit of blackmail. You know the routine. Remember, we want this government to win. It's vital for democracy. We'll see how it's going about two weeks from now. We'll decide then what more needs to be done.'

Provost Galpin, now in his accustomed role as a CIA senior field operative, wasted no time in setting up a meeting with Zonkov who turned out to be a standard Identikit Balkan gangster.

Zonkov was in his mid-thirties, large and corpulent. He wore blue jeans, black T-shirt and the obligatory black leather jacket. His head was shaved bald but he sported a three day beard.

They met in Zonkov's 4x4 in a side street two miles from the embassy where Zonkov described the services he would be able to offer.

'Printing wrong dates on the posters, that's no problem. We can do that. The same with ballot papers. No problem. I know a lot of good people in all the print shops. Same with TV blackout. We have people in the power stations. Newspapers, we can speak to writers in the papers. They will do what we tell them.' said Zonkov confidently.

'Also starting fights at meetings. Easy, no problem. A few people might get hurt. It doesn't matter. You tell me what you want. I can do it.'

'What is your price for all this?' asked Galpin.

'Not expensive. I have small problem with my shipments from South America. Your police stop my supplies from Columbia. I lose a lot of money from your Drug Enforcement Agency. They are bad for my business. My price is that you stop all these problems for three months, OK?'

'I am sure that can be arranged, Mr Zonkov.'

'You are a good man, American! I like you!'

In spite of Balfour's protestations over his compensation and his misgivings about exactly how much authority he would have if he were to make the necessary changes, Dave Balfour did indeed pick up the poisoned chalice and drink deeply from it. All the teachers received a memo from the Dean, confirming Balfour's appointment as Chair of the Business Department with immediate effect. Some deal, some off-stage horse-trading had been cobbled together and Balfour had become the chosen one - or the fall guy, depending how you looked at it.

Balfour promised, because he was a civilized and experienced man, a sympathetic new regime without any of the casual insouciance of his Brazilian predecessor. He was also intending to create, although he was careful to keep these ideas to himself, a more ambitious and disciplined atmosphere within the department. Balfour knew the dangers of complacency, of sitting back and doing nothing and allowing the ruling clique to regain the initiative.

He began his chairmanship by interviewing all the professors, of whatever rank, one by one, to gauge the prevailing attitudes and to try to get a sense of the political forces at work in this microcosm. Sensibly, he deferred his first open faculty meeting until he was sure he had a good sense of which way the political wind was blowing. What he found out from his interviewees had confirmed his deepest suspicions.

The majority of the departmental faculty members were fearful for their short-term contracts but they were unable to speak out for a different way of making faculty appointments because they would not be rehired. The hiring process was firmly in the hands of the permanent tenured professors, Reilly, Denitsev and Nyborg, a group now increased to four in number, after Richard Smalley had been recruited to the group. To argue, or even to disagree in any way, with any of the gang of four would result in certain non-renewal.

He also noted that many of the students going on to graduate studies in Europe or the UK or the USA were taking longer than they should have to complete their master's degrees because they had had to make up certain basic courses which AUSB, because of its faculty shortage, was no longer offering, such as entrepreneurship, decision science and mathematical economics.

After the interviews with the faculty, he drew up the list of changes which he would try to bring in and then he prepared an agenda for his inaugural faculty meeting.

First, he would reinstate all the missing courses Then he would seek a change to faculty standing orders to extend voting rights to all professors regardless of status. He would also extend membership eligibility of the faculty search committees to all business faculty. Finally, he would simplify the elaborate process of making faculty appointments.

Before publishing it, he took the precaution of showing it to Dean Mulvaney. The dean was unimpressed.

'I wouldn't upset the apple cart if I were you,' he said.

'But these are essential changes if AUSB is to stay competitive,' said Balfour. 'We must offer a full range of courses which means that we need good professors to teach them. One of the reasons why we can't attract good people is that the selection process is down to the same three or four people and is too long and convoluted. One way to bring more people into the decision-making would be to allow all working professors to serve on search committees and to let them vote in faculty meetings irrespective of rank or the length of their contracts.'

'You are going to find it hard getting that one past Hattie Reilly,' replied Mulvaney. 'She practically invented the faculty recruitment and evaluation procedures single-handed.'

'But changes have to be made, or this department is going nowhere,' Balfour insisted.

Mike Mulvaney was now starting to wonder whether he had been right to ask this energetic revolutionary to be business department chair.

'I hope you can make the changes you think are necessary, but you will meet a lot of opposition,' warned Dean Mulvaney. Be sure to present your plan to the provost before you throw it to the faculty.'

'And, by the way,' Mulvaney added, 'you do know, don't you, that the AUSB constitution for faculty meetings says that the rules can only be changed by a two-thirds majority of voting members? You may find it difficult to get around that.'

'So, who came up with that rule?'

'I'll give you three guesses.'

Dave Balfour left his proposals with the provost's secretary.

'Professor Galpin is going to be out for at least a week,' she told him.

Nine

In fact, Darius Galpin was spending a lot of time at the embassy. He had even been found an apartment in the compound. His main day job was now CIA operative - being provost was, at least for the time being, until after the election, just a part-time occupation.

Since no one had any idea what was on his AUSB job description anyway, he was not much missed there. It was noticed that he was absent for a couple of meetings which he should have chaired but Dean Mulvaney ably sat in for him and whatever decisions they had made would not have been affected by the provost's absence.

After a couple of weeks in his new role, he found himself ordered to a high-level embassy meeting. Sieghart was there with a new man he had not met before, called Norman Bland.

Bland had the appearance of a typical CIA operative - fit, fortyish, well-groomed with hair cut short and slicked down. He wore a good suit, rimless glasses and expensive English shoes. His watch was an Omega Seamaster.

'He probably also has a Burberry trench coat and a trilby,' thought Galpin. 'No, not a trilby, they went out years ago. But he would probably have smoked a thin briarwood pipe, if smoking hadn't become politically incorrect since the stereotype had been cast.'

'Bland by name and bland by nature,' thought the provost.

Norman Bland obviously outranked Sieghart because he took the chair and opened the meeting.

'Galpin, it's good you could come. How's the dirty trick business these days?'

'We're making some progress, sir. A couple of TV broadcasts shot down from electricity failure, a few election meetings screwed up. False ballot papers ready to go on polling day. Power workers will arrange power cuts when the votes are being counted so that the boxes can be switched.'

'Yeah, yeah,' said Bland. 'That's all textbook stuff. Any results?'

'Some. The polls are moving in the government's favor.'

'But not fast enough. We don't think it's likely to work. Our computer predictions are that the Orthodox party will get in with a small majority after some defections from Red Crescent. That means that we may need to redouble our efforts. We need something more decisive.'

'We have a couple of demos organized,' said Galpin, 'protest marches by the opposition which will turn violent, bravely controlled by riot police led by the Interior Minister. It should be worth a few percentage points.'

'It's unlikely to be helpful,' said Bland. 'Just as many people will see it as police repression. It could easily backfire. No, what we are thinking about is something more creative. The theory back in Langley is that we need to divide and rule, to set the two opposition parties against each other. Something that looks very ugly on TV - ideally a pitched battle in the main square. Although there are other ways, as well you know, if you get my drift.'

Darius Galpin did indeed get Bland's drift. What it meant did not need to be spelled out to him.

'Yes, well, and here this is highly, very highly classified,' said Bland, 'but we all have the clearance.'

'The thinking now, said Bland, 'is that our government, or rather Madame Makarovna's, to be precise, must be re-elected or the entire Operation Warm Blanket will fall through. If we can't sell it to her, then we will have no chance in selling it further east. That is why we are working on this country first. It is vital that she wins this election. You have a free hand. Just make sure that we get the right result.'

Galpin was about to ask a question about why the election was so different than any other but Bland gestured him to listen as he continued.

'O.B. is not being completely frank about the nature of the bases. Even the fragrant Anastasia hasn't been told everything. I can't say more than that. That is why she must be re-elected for a few years, so that we can start work on the new facilities and have the whole project up and running before they have another election.'

'Can't you just buy off Simonov and Caradescu in case they win? They seem to be nice and corruptible.'

'I wish it were that simple. Unfortunately they both have links to some groups we don't actually approve of. The project will never get off the ground if either of them forms the next government. Let me have your ideas by nine am tomorrow. We will have one more meeting then and after that it will be down to you, Galpin, and your team.'

'Speaking of which....'

'Oh yes,' said Bland, 'your little payment in kind. We've had a word with the DEA and doubtful shipments to this part of the world will not be searched for three months from today.'

'Thank you,' said Galpin.

'Third item,' went on Bland, 'is what we do about strengthening the CIA coverage in this country now that we lost two key operatives? You can't do it all alone, Galpin, and you are going to be missed at the university. If you are away too much, they'll start asking questions.'

Bland wasn't finished.

'First, we need to change your AUSB president. Your

man, Potts, is OK as a figurehead but he isn't CIA. We need to put that right. Then consolidate all the senior people with our own guys. I'm sorry, Galpin, the top job isn't for you. We'll bring someone in.'

Alaric Potts was a three-star general who had made the transition from the United States Army to a top job in academia, courtesy of some useful contacts in the Washington corridors of power. He had needed a well-paid sinecure to boost his retirement pay and favors had been called in.

It would have been difficult to find someone less suited to running a university than Lieutenant General Potts. He had achieved his college diploma via a sports scholarship and he could not even remember what he had majored in. All he could remember from his college days was that he had played a lot of basketball, a skill which had helped project his college, a minor state college in Kentucky, to the top rank of lucrative college basketball.

In spite of his limited intellectual abilities he was a voracious reader. He could claim to have read every single book on military strategy which he could find, as well as any war novel he could get his hands on. But his main talent, that which had taken him near to the top of the military tree, was a single-minded attention to the need always to obey orders without question. Obedience, reliability, promotability - those were the words he had always lived by.

In his tenure of the top job at AUSB, he had made what he thought were certain necessary changes to the way things were done. For example, he had changed the format of the Commencement, the diploma-awarding ceremony, to make it more military. So there was now a detachment of US Marines to present the colors and to mount the guard with an impressive display of close-order drill. A military band was brought in to play 'The

Star Spangled Banner'.

And that was about it. His real job description seemed to consist of little more than collecting his salary. His days were spent reading the sports pages of the newspaper and reflecting on his past glories. He would stay cloistered in his office until 5 pm when he would leave with his office staff, mainly young women, to whom he paid extra special attention. As a result of his paternal attention, many of the AUSB ladies - his hand-picked group of special favorites on whom he lavished the most affection - went on to secure well-paid jobs in the offices of Potts' old Washington friends.

'I'm sure you don't need me to tell you that General Potts is not the best man to be president at a sensitive time like this. We need a CIA man at the top.'

'I agree' said Galpin, 'but he does have a contract for two more years.'

'He needs to go soon,' said Bland, 'this month, no later. Do you have any ideas?'

'If it's going to be that quick, the only way, apart from sudden death, is sexual harassment.'

'OK, find a woman to make a complaint.'

'Will any woman do?'

'Unless she's old enough to be his mother and if she's not an obvious lesbian, then yes, any woman will do. A little casual threat should do it. I'll square the Board of Regents back stateside.'

Sexual harassment is definitely the quick way to remove someone from an American university. As would be the case for Potts, there would never need to be any due process because sexual harassment is the one crime which does not have any defense. In puritan America, an accusation is all it takes to be sure of a conviction.

Potts knew this, which is why members of his harem were carefully chosen and well looked after. They

101

were always protected from dismissal, whatever their failings. Misdeeds they committed, misdeeds which would see most people out of the door without their feet touching the ground, were openly tolerated.

In one famous instance, Annabella Markova-Casillias, Assistant Professor of Economics, had tired of one of her lovers, a junior clerk at the embassy. She had asked the ambassador, by email, to send the man home.

Ambassador Feldstein, not knowing that Professor Markova-Casillias was a bedfellow of General Potts, had replied with a furious refusal. He had complained bitterly to Potts and he had even threatened to take the matter up with Alison Treadwell herself. There had been a long angry exchange of messages between Potts and Feldstein before Feldstein had caved in and had sent the poor fellow packing.

Potts ordered the then provost that Assistant Professor Markova-Casillias be made up to Associate Professor immediately and that she would be exempt from any future faculty evaluations. Indeed, he was already using his contacts at Georgetown University to secure her a tenured professorship there, should she ever move to the US. He would need a close warm personal friend in the DC area when he himself eventually retired.

But not all the faculty women had been so favored. Galpin sought out one of the neglected ones. 'Tell me, Professor Sarplova, how long have you been an assistant professor?'

'Well, sir,' she began.

'Call me Darius. We are colleagues, aren't we?'

'Well, Darius, about fifteen years. I've applied for promotion three times, but I really haven't published enough.'

'Your record looks good enough to me,' said Galpin,

leafing through her file, 'and there's a new evaluation coming up soon. I am sure you are going to pass that one with flying colors.'

'I hope so, er, Darius.'

'But if you didn't get approval this time, there would be no more chances. You would have to leave. Be 'demised', as they say.'

'Yes, fingers crossed. I need this job for at least another five years until my children graduate from college.'

'I think you will be OK. I will be chairing the evaluation committee. But tell me, how do you get on with President Potts? He could still overturn my decision.'

'I don't know him,' replied Angela Sarplova. 'I've never had much to do with him.'

'Unlike some of the women here?' asked Galpin.

'Well, I've heard stories.'

'Yes, they're all too true, unfortunately. Strictly off the record, of course, but he's getting the university something of a bad name. Just between you and me, only his girlfriends are ever likely to get promoted.'

'Like Annabella Markova-Casillias?'

'Yes, like Annabella Markova-Casillias. Has Potts ever approached you to join his little band of groupies.'

'I don't want to be one of his whores!' answered Ms Sarplova. 'He did once ask me to stay behind for a private meeting but I told him I had to get back home.'

'Didn't you consider that sexual harassment?'

'Not really, no. I just took it as a normal try-on.'

'But it was sexual harassment really, wasn't it, an unwanted sexual advance, as defined in the university statutes? When was it?'

'Oh about five years ago.'

'What if I told you that Potts has vetoed your promotion once more since then, even after you had passed the evaluation? I will recommend you for promotion this next time but, if he is still here, then he will block it again. If you fail next time you will be out. And you can't afford that, now, can you?'

'I know. I'm desperate. But what can I do?'

'Look, what I suggest you do is this. You write down all the details of that first time when he propositioned you, and how you have missed out on your promotion as a result. I will make sure it gets to the right people on the Board of Regents. I am sure that this time you will get your much-deserved promotion.'

'I am not going to lie about this.'

'No, Angela, there's no need to lie. Stick to the truth, which is that since he asked you to stay behind after work and you refused, your career has been blocked and that you are now in danger of losing your job. Just email me the message and I will take care of things.'

'Thank you, provost, thank you so much.'

And Potts was out within the week, to be replaced by a safe Company man, President Curtley Spring, temporarily recalled from retirement.

A good job well done, said Galpin to himself after Angela Sarplova had left his office and he could go back to going over in his mind what Bland had said at the meeting. Whatever could it mean - '...O.B .is not being completely frank about the nature of the bases. Even the fragrant Anastasia hasn't been told everything...'?

Something important was afoot and there was a gap in his information. Right now, though, he had his orders and there was work to be done. He called Konstantin Zonkov, his connection with the country's criminal classes, to set up another meeting.

Ten

Galpin and Zonkov met that evening in a quiet lane some four kilometers from the embassy compound. Galpin took a taxi from the university and, there being people around, gave loud directions to a place in the opposite direction. Once inside the cab, he corrected his instructions and gave the driver directions to the Winter Park, a well-known landmark from where he would walk to Zonkov's car. The cab driver gave him a knowing leer – the Winter Park is the local equivalent of Paris's *Bois de Boulogne*, an after-dark *rendezvous* for prostitutes, wife-swappers, orgiasts and every other possible kind of sexual libertarian.

'Yes, Winter Park! Very good! Nice time! Nice place, Winter Park!' the driver was saying.

Once dropped off at the iron gates, where, for a small tip, the night creatures would be admitted by the gateman, Galpin instead turned away and walked left, right and left again into a small lane where Zonkov was waiting in his large people carrier.

'Good news first,' said Galpin. 'The DEA have agreed your shipment request. No inspections for three months from this week.'

'That's good! Very good! I like do business with American. Honest! Stick to bargain!'

'Right,' Galpin went on, 'the posters? Is everything fixed?'

'Posters are no problem. We change the dates for meetings by Caradescu and Simonov. No one will show up for some. Other meetings will be on the same day, at the same time. There will be big confusion, I promise. Who knows, maybe big fight? Very good! '

'What about the ballot papers?'

'You will like! We print three, maybe four hundred thousand extra papers. Maybe a million, who knows? Same as the real ones! I have a big team. Big team of ver', ver' good people! They are writing them now! Fill in X, just like real! Then we take boxes and change them when electricity go out!'

'Yes, that's good!'

'Also, my boys, they will join meetings for Caradescu and Simonov. Make big trouble. Throw petrol bombs, start riots. Get on TV.'

'I hope they don't get hurt.'

'No problem! My boys, they like it ver' much. Hit bad people! Good time for them!'

'Well,' said Galpin, 'we have got something a little more serious for you.'

'You think that what we do not good enough, maybe?' Zonkov asked suspiciously.

'No, it's good, it's very good. The problem is that it doesn't make it absolutely certain that Anastasia Makarovna will win. We have to be one hundred percent sure. Nothing left to chance. This is very, very important.'

'I am very interested. This business good for me so far. Tell me. What do you want me to do?'

'Well, what we had in mind was a little political elimination. Can you arrange the removal of Caradescu - permanently? '

Zonkov's eyed narrowed. 'You want me to kill him?'

'Can you make it look like Simonov's boys did it?'

'That is no problem. I can do a good job. But this is murder!'

'Yes, it is. Does that scare you? It's in a very good cause.'

'Black out TV, no problem. Print false posters, OK. Change ballot papers, no problem. A bit fighting, some tear gas, petrol bombs. We can do all this. But to kill big man like Caradescu is different. Caradescu has his own men guarding him. Then there is a big problem for me. Maybe I get killed too.'

'You have good protection, don't you?'

'Of course! The very best! Good boys! '

'It doesn't have to be Caradescu, it could just as easily be Simonov - either of them, just as long as the other gets blamed for it. With luck, one will be dead and the other will be arrested.'

'I can do it. OK, I rub out one man. No problem. But expensive.'

'What do you mean, 'expensive'?'

'Yes, expensive. If I kill Caradescu then I need get Caradescu's men work for me after. They lose jobs, so they must come to work for Zonkov. I need to pay them. Like Manchester United! Big transfer fees!' he laughed.

'So, it's a deal?' asked Galpin.

'OK, deal if I get six months free shipments, not three. I have big expenses.'

'I'll talk to my people. I'm sure we can work something out.'

'Six months. We do business, American! '

'I'll call you tomorrow at midday. We'll arrange a new meeting.'

Galpin then walked back the way he had come from the Winter Park. The same taxi driver was waiting. Was he being followed? He got in the cab.

'You have nice time in Park? You find very nice girls, yes? Or you like boys better, eh?'

'No, I like girls. I met my two favorites. We had a very nice three together in a tent.'

'You are very fast. But I think you are not away long enough for two women.'

'I have to get back to work.'

'I take you back to the embassy. I see you there

often. You like our girls, eh? Better than Amerikanski girls, no? '

Galpin would need to change the place for tomorrow's meeting. Who was this cab driver working for? Had he been followed to his meeting with Zonkov?

Dave Balfour now had his plan for the Business Department. He would broaden the curriculum to take in all those subjects which should have been taught but weren't and ask the university authorities, which meant the president, the provost and the dean, to appoint some new professors to teach them. He would also ask the business faculty to agree to allowing all the members of the department an equal vote, if only on those matters which applied to them. He called a faculty meeting for the start of the fall semester.

It was to be held in a classroom which had tiers of desks. By the time he arrived, five minutes before the scheduled time, the front row was already occupied by the four departmental stalwarts, Denitsev, Reilly, Nyborg and Smalley. Behind them were the seats for the lower orders, the *sans-culottes*, the second class citizens, the voteless temporaries, the unenfranchised part-timers and those visiting professors, who, however eminent they might be, could never be admitted to the golden circle of the decision-making established front-row professoriat.

Balfour went straight to item one of the printed agenda. 'What I am suggesting is that we do some work on expanding the curriculum for our students so that they are better placed for graduate studies.'

'Last year, sixty eight percent of our graduation class went on to master's programs in the west, including Oxford, Yale, the LSE, Stanford, MIT and several more. I have had twenty five messages back from them saying that they were all missing vital courses. So I suggest that between us we decide what is missing from our programs and plug some gaps.'

Hattie Reilly PhD cut in. 'Are you saying that our program is not good enough? I have to tell you, before you go any further, that our business education program is the best in the region. Why do you think all those top Brit and American schools would take our students if they aren't good enough?'

'I never said anything of the kind,' said Balfour in reply. 'It's just that we need to be giving them a wider and more relevant set of courses to prepare them for graduate studies.'

'I beg your pardon,' expostulated Hattie Reilly PhD, 'but we are not here just as a feeder college for those expensive schools in the UK or back home. We can set our own program. And we have been doing that very successfully for twenty years.'

'Don't you think that we should be continuously reviewing what we are teaching our students?'

'Obviously yes, and that's why we have the five-year curriculum review,' said Reilly, with an angry edge to her voice. 'We will be reviewing the course structure in two years time.'

'That's a very long way off,' said Balfour, suddenly realizing the reaction he was up against.

'Well, that's when it will happen,' retorted Hattie Reilly PhD. 'Not before.'

'Well,' said Balfour, 'I am suggesting that we start a course review now. I think we should remove Strategic Management One and Strategic Management Two from the list of options and replace them with ...' He got no further.

'You can't do that!' shouted Morten Nyborg. 'Those are core courses! We've been teaching them since nineteen ninety seven! They are vital to the program!'

'You mean, because you teach them?'

'And damned well I teach them too!' answered Nyborg. 'The students like them. There's always a big sign-up.'

'That's because you give the grades away,' came an unidentifiable voice from the back.

'But they are hardly relevant for our students, are they?' answered Balfour. 'By the time your average twenty two year old gets into strategic management, twenty years have passed, the subject has changed, his old textbooks are out of date and he's forgotten everything we ever taught him.'

'Calm down everyone,' said Denitsev. 'Let's hear what else the chair has to say.'

'Thank you. Denis. To continue, I think we should offer quantitative methods, a second course in IT, entrepreneurship and financial operations. I have draft outlines of the syllabi here. Also, we should make operations management and decision science core courses instead of electives.'

'Do you have any reasons for doing this, or are you just trying to give us a lot of extra work and trouble?' sneered Hattie Reilly PhD.

'Of course I have reasons,' Balfour snorted back.

'Oh yes? What are they?'

'If you look at the employment patterns of our graduates, they generally end up in some branch of finance or banking. A few go into information technology and operations. About five per cent of them start their own businesses. None of them goes straight from here or their masters programs into strategic management or human resources. But we offer double courses of those two. I am just saying that we need to trim the curriculum to what our students need. Here is a position paper I have written.' He passed out twenty or so copies of a one-page paper.

'You want to wipe out twenty years of very good work by some fine people. That's what you are trying to do,' said Hattie Reilly PhD.

'Don't be silly,' said Balfour. 'I am simply trying to drag our offerings kicking and screaming into the twentieth century.'

'It's the twenty first century now,' said a voice at the back.

'One step at a time,' muttered Balfour.

'Right,' said Hattie Reilly PhD, 'I don't think we should accept the chair's proposals.'

'You must put down a proper motion,' said Balfour, 'according to procedure. It must be properly proposed and seconded. Do I have a proposal?'

'Yes,' said Nyborg, 'I propose that the chairman's proposals are not accepted and that we retain the current course structure for the next two years.'

'I second that,' said Hattie Reilly PhD.

'Before we put it to a vote, does anyone else want to say anything?' Balfour looked up at the rows further back.

'Yes,' one of the temporaries said, 'I think the proposals in the paper are not particularly revolutionary. Most undergraduate business schools do offer similar things. What is more, the proposed new courses match with our students' employment patterns.'

He was about to say something more when Hattie Reilly PhD fixed him with a poisonous glare and addressed him in her most sarcastic tone.

'What would you know? You've only been here five minutes and everyone knows you got in through the back door, without going through the formal evaluation procedures. Some of us have been here for a lot longer than that and we have built up a very successful

111

department. By our own efforts! Now you want to destroy all that we created!'

'I don't want to....'

'That's enough! We've heard enough! That is why people like you aren't allowed a vote. You just want to destroy years and years of very good work! Chair, put it to the vote.'

'All those in favor of the motion not to accept the proposed changes please show.'

The four professors on the front row all raised their hands.

'All those against?'

This time seven of the people at the back raised their hands.

'Those seven don't have a vote, so it's carried unanimously,' said Nyborg.

'Well,' said Balfour, 'I won't leave it there. This is not very democratic.'

'Of course it's democratic. We had a fair vote,' said Denitsev.

'No,' said Balfour, 'it's the very opposite of democratic. Only you four at the front get to say anything and vote on it. What about all those people at the back. Don't they count? Look, what I am going to do is to take my proposals to the university executive council. I'll see if they are more democratic.'

'So, you are going over our heads?' asked Nyborg. 'That's certainly not democratic. You are asking faculty in other departments to make decisions affecting us.'

'If necessary, yes.'

'So,' retorted Nyborg, 'you are not going to include us in your decisions. You are just going to treat the department as your own little fiefdom, is that right?'

'No, it's not. You four have all the power and will block anything I come up with!'

'That's because we have the interests of the department at heart and you have just come in and started to run your own little fiefdom. I don't like fiefdoms!' And with that, he got up and stalked out of the room.

The rest of the meeting passed in acrimonious quiet after Nyborg's little tantrum. Everything on Dave Balfour's agenda was voted down by the gang of four, now reduced to three. Unfortunately, none of the assembled visiting professors, short term contract holders or part-timers was permitted to speak and even if they had spoken, it would not have made any difference to the decisions, or rather, the non-decisions.

Later in the evening after his meeting with Konstantin Zonkov, Darius Galpin called John Sieghart at the embassy. It was near midnight when they met.

'So your man is getting greedy,' began Sieghart.

'Yeah, well, he's not exactly Saint Francis of Assisi. Can we do it?'

'I'll have to ask Bland. What's he offering in return for the six month layoff?'

'He reckons he can erase either Caradescu or Simonov and make it look like the other ordered it. Plus, of course all the usual dirty tricks with the election.'

'Rubbing one of them out and blaming the other should certainly do the trick for the lovely Tasha. But six months! Jeeze! He could smuggle half of Columbia into Europe in that time.'

'He's ambitious. Whoever he takes out, he'll have to take over their little army. He reckons his wage bill will go up.'

'Wage bill, my ass! With six months uninterrupted supply he'll practically own the whole economy!'

'Maybe he wants to become the next Balashirov?'

Sieghart picked up the secure line. 'Mr Bland? Look sir, your plan as discussed yesterday. Yes sir, that one. Well our man wants the time the DEA looks away to be extended from three months to six. Can we do it? OK. Gotcha! Thank you, sir.'

'He's talking to the DEA. He'll get back in ten minutes.' Sieghart said to Galpin. A few minutes later, Sieghart picked up the phone again.

'Yes, sir......yes, sir... very good, sir... full removal... Thank you, sir.'

'Bland says go ahead,' said Sieghart to Galpin, who, once out of Sieghart's office, phoned Zonkov.

'No, we'll meet at a different place. Bar Whiskey at eleven. It's on,' Galpin told Zonkov.

Galpin had chosen the Bar Whiskey, a cheap bar near the bus station because it was somewhere he would not need to go to by taxi, he could get there by bus. He drove to a little-used car park a mile from the embassy and changed into workman's clothes inside his BMW with the tinted windows. As soon as he could be reasonably sure no one was watching him, he got out of his car, looking like any other working man.

He locked the car and walked across the street to the bus stop. When he arrived at the Bar Whiskey, he saw Zonkov sitting at a table alone. Galpin sat down at the next table with his back to him.

'We agree your price,' said Galpin quietly, out of the side of his mouth.

'Good,' said Zonkov and got up and left. Galpin picked up the empty cigarette packet from the table and put it in the pocket of his jacket. Then he too, left. He read the message on the bus. It said only 'SUMO'. The job would be Sunday next with a meeting on Monday.

Galpin got off the bus and retraced his steps to

where he had parked his car. He got inside and changed out of the workman's clothes. He took off the jacket and cap and put on his necktie. Then he changed his cheap glasses for designer spectacles. Next he took off his boots and blue jeans, replacing them with the other half of the Armani suit and Lobb shoes. The disguise was bundled up in a canvas sack for next time. Then he drove back to the embassy. As he parked, he noticed a familiar taxi.

'Hello sir! You remember me? Maybe you will go to the Winter Park again tonight? I pick you up!! You meet very nice girls?'

'No thank you, not today.'

'OK, tomorrow? No problem! I am Malik! I fix you nice girls!'

At just about at the same time, Dave Balfour was reporting back to Dean Mike Mulvaney on his abortive attempts to bring the Business Department into line. Mulvaney was not completely unsympathetic.

'I agree with you, Dave,' he said, 'the courses we teach in business are out of date. The rules that only the top four professors get to vote are unfair. The way your department appoints people is long-winded and over-complicated. But what can we do?'

'You have the power to impose reforms,' countered Balfour, 'or at the very least support me when I bring the matter up at the Executive Council.'

'I don't think I can do that,' said Mulvaney, in reply, 'I must be seen to be completely impartial at all times. I can't be seen to be favoring one side over the other. It would look like I'm interfering in faculty decision-making. That would never do.'

'So you are not prepared to support me, even when it is blindingly obvious that what I am proposing is only commonsense and for the good of the university.'

'But, that's the problem, Dave,' said the Dean, 'it's wheels within wheels.'

Dave Balfour looked puzzled. Whatever was the Dean talking about?

'I don't understand, sorry,' said Balfour.

'Not necessary,' said Dean Mulvaney.

'Look,' persisted Balfour, 'why appoint me to the departmental chair, if you can't support me?'

'But I am supporting you!' said Mulvaney. 'You have my hundred and ten per cent support all the way. You can rely on it! You are doing a great job!'

'It doesn't seem that way to me. I have the responsibility to update the Business Department but without the authority to do it properly.'

'Of course you have the authority. What more do you want?'

'Well, maybe if you will give me the power to change the standing orders so that everyone in the department, not just the old guard, gets a vote. Then you could actually say that the decisions were made by the entire faculty, not just the same few faces every time.'

'Look, Dave, you know I can't do that. Any changes have to come from within the department after a full consultation.'

'But that's impossible with the present set-up.'

'Sorry, Dave, but that's the way it is, it's wheels within wheels.'

There, he'd said it again. What was the fellow getting at?

'Look, Dean, I know I have your full support but changes need to be made. Maybe if you won't give me the necessary authority, would you mind if I asked the provost?'

'It's a free country. Mind you, the provost is out of

the office a lot these days.'

'I'll try to catch him.'

'I don't think you'll get very far with the provost. He's a very strong believer in faculty consultation, even more than me.'

'But I have your agreement?'

'Sure, good luck. But remember, wheels within wheels.'

Dean Mulvaney had now said that three times. Whatever am I being warned about, wondered Balfour?

As the election approached, all three party leaders, Makarovna, Caradescu and Simonov, spent every day addressing big meetings of their supporters. This Saturday afternoon, late in August, there was to be a big rally of Simonov's supporters in Revolution Square. It was a hot sunny day and Mikhail Simonov was surprised to find at least twice as many present as he had been expecting.

After the playing of the national anthem and some patriotic singing from a troop of young girls dressed in the old peasant national costume, the PA system announced the top of the bill.

'Comrades! Citizens! Our next prime minister, Deputy Mikhail Simonov!'

There was some unease in the crowd and someone shouted.

'Where's Caradescu? We came to hear Caradescu!' Someone else shouted, 'No we didn't! This is our meeting!! Simonov!! Simonov!!'

'CA-RA-DES-CU!!   CA-RA-DES-CU!!' There was chanting and the stamping of feet.

'SI-MON-OV!! SI-MON-OV!!' The liberal faction took up the chant.

The point and counterpoint of the two mobs rose to a fever pitch as Mikhail Simonov tried to calm things from behind the microphone on the stage.

'Fellow citizens!!' he yelled in vain. 'Please calm down! The world is watching us!' His hand pointed to the cluster of TV cameras busy taking in every moment. The TV companies had been quietly tipped off that something would be happening similar to the scenes in the Chamber of Deputies a few weeks previously.

But the crowd would not be stilled and the chanting was now being accompanied by the rhythmical stamping of hundreds of boots. Most of them were now standing and some were banging the chairs on the ground in time with the chanting.

'SI-MON-OV!! SI-MON-OV!!'

'CA-RA-DES-CU!! CA-RA-DES-CU!!'

The only missiles at hand to throw at the opposition were the chairs and pretty soon the world's TV audiences were treated to pictures of salvoes of flying chairs. Then came the hand-to-hand fighting. As the number of casualties grew, the National Guard was called in to try to restore order. They were not over gentle in their approach and in the process of preventing further injury, they obviously found it necessary to create a few injuries of their own by using the traditional methods of state peace-keepers everywhere – clubs, tear gas, water cannon and rubber bullets.

After half an hour or so, the National Guard seemed to be getting the upper hand but a few carefully aimed petrol bombs from Zonkov's boys soon restored the balance of power on the battlefield. It took another forty-five minutes after that for the three sides to wear each other out and for peace to be restored.

Eleven

President Leonid Balashirov, masterly politician that he was, instantly recognized the riot as a heaven-sent opportunity to assist his mistress. He went on television immediately after the six o'clock news bulletin to make a non-party presidential broadcast.

'Fellow citizens, we have all just witnessed the dreadful scenes in Revolution Square this afternoon. I join with all of you who deplore the violence and the disgraceful behavior of some who claim to be supporters of our two main opposition parties. Our thoughts and condolences go out to the families and friends of the innocent victims of this criminal action, which must never again be repeated. There is no place in a fair and democratic election for disorder of any kind. Anyone found guilty of criminal behavior and taking part in this afternoon's dreadful scenes will, I promise you, be brought to trial. Anyone found guilty will be punished severely.'

' I also want to praise the professionalism and bravery of our National Guard who were able to bring the fighting to a peaceful end and restore order. They acted magnificently on behalf of our country. I also join with the government and with acting Prime Minister Makarovna in condemning all violence. We promise all our citizens that the government will be ever more vigilant in its maintenance of law and order. Scenes of this sort must never be seen on our streets again. Thank you and may God bless you all.'

Galpin, Sieghart and Bland, each in his own office, smiled separately at the CIA-inspired handiwork. They had watched the riots on all the TV news channels where the scenes were repeated hour after hour in full gory detail. Two killed, forty-three injured. Bland immediately phoned Sieghart to congratulate him.

Then Sieghart phoned Galpin. 'Darius, that's great work! Come over for a drink!'

'Thank you, John.'

John Sieghart poured them both rye whiskey on the rocks.

'Can you tell me anything, Darius?'

'There will be something tomorrow - the big one, then feedback Monday. That should just about do it. The ballot boxes will be stuffed in time for the election.'

'Not going for overkill, are you?'

'I don't think so. You can never overdo it in my experience.'

'The ambassador will be making a speech of condolence about this afternoon's events and O.B. himself will also be putting something out.'

'The usual stuff about how the United States will always support peaceful democracy and violence will never be tolerated *et cetera..*?'

'That's the one. You've heard it before? Let me fill your glass.'

'Tell me, John,' said Darius Galpin. 'What's all this about?'

'What do you mean?'

'It must be pretty big if we are going to all this trouble of rigging elections, organizing riots, making the whole country look stupid in the eyes the world. We usually keep our hands off the election and wait for the new guy to get elected before we tell him the facts of life.'

'Yeah, that was always the way we used to do it in the past. Let someone win and then tell him he's working for Uncle Sam.'

'So why change it now?'

'I dunno, Darius. All I do know is that it is something to do with this new Operation Warm Blanket.'

'But why should a few more bases make any difference? We have plenty of bases and no one objects to a few more, just as long as they're nicely hidden away where no one can see them.'

'Maybe the thinking is that Caradescu and Simonov might close the present base up in the hills if either gets in. Maybe that's why our masters back in DC want Makarovna,' said John Sieghart.

'I can see the point. Better the devil you know. And she's definitely our woman.'

'By the way, you did a great job on the video of her with Balashirov.'

'The one round the pool? Yep, I was quite proud of that.'

'So, Darius, your guess is as good as mine. No idea what it's all about?'

'You've not heard whispers?' asked Galpin.

'Not much. A lot of technical info comes across my desk about electronics. I just pass that on to the geeky boys. The military business has sure changed a helluva lot since my day. Now it's all automatic planes, computers. I'm just an old-fashioned station man. It's not like it was back in 'Nam. These days you need a diploma from MIT just to fire back.'

Sieghart was getting expansive after his second drink. 'You know something,' he said. 'Some fella from the geeky group was telling me that the next war will not have any human casualties at all. It'll all be done from a bunker in the Utah Desert. Groups of unmanned drones taking out ground targets. Just like a computer video game!'

'Wow!!' said Darius Galpin. 'Wouldn't that be something? No more American boys lost in action!'

In a revelation, Darius Galpin suddenly started to get the glimmer of an idea of exactly what Operation Warm Blanket might be all about and why it was that he had had to order the assassination of a high-ranking politician the following day.

But all he said to Sieghart was, 'well, it's all too darned high-falutin' for me. Thank you, John, yes, I will have another drink.'

After the calamitous end of Balfour's departmental meeting, Nyborg and Denitsev met in Hattie Reilly's office.

'That was a disgrace!' began Hattie Reilly PhD.

'Yes, it was,' agreed Denitsev. 'We can't let things go on like this.'

'He wants to bring in more finance and economics. We have enough already. I've been teaching bookkeeping for twenty years. What more does the man want?' said Nyborg.

'And, he wants...he wants...' Hattie Reilly PhD was struggling with anger, '...he wants to replace my office operations specialty with something called 'business policy', whatever that is. We have been teaching office operations here for as long as I can remember. We even had a conference with the local chamber of trade, what, just five years ago. It was very successful. He's worse than Mubarak, Gaddafi, Saddam Hussein, any of those.'

'He ought to go back to Oklahoma where he belongs.'

'What was that he was saying about bringing our curriculum into line with the Bologna Process?'

'What's the Bologna Process?' asked Professor

Morten Nyborg.

'The Bologna Process,' explained Denitsev, 'is an initiative by the European Union to bring all university teaching programs up to a common standard.'

'Oh, right,' said Professor Hattie Reilly PhD, who had not been concentrating on Balfour's explanation. 'If it's from the European Union, then it's not going to work. This is an American university run on American lines. What do we want with the EU?'

'Well,' pointed out Denitsev, 'we are located in Europe. Our students are European and we do have to get accreditation from the national government.'

'So? So?' replied Reilly, indignantly. 'We are an American institution. We were opened by President Clinton himself. The aim of this place has always been to bring American education to Europe. It is for the Europeans to adjust, not us Americans. They invited us here.'

'Actually,' put in Nyborg, 'we invited ourselves. Although they must be damned glad we came.'

'Right!' replied Hattie Reilly PhD. 'They should be damned grateful. We have been a godsend to the economy of this country. Have you any idea what Europe was like before the Americans started putting it straight? And now they want to tell us how we should be educating their students! After all we've done for them!'

'That's right,' said Nyborg, 'democracy and civilization. If they don't want us Americans over here, we can always go home and leave the place just how we found it. Which was a helluva mess, I can tell you.'

'What do you mean?' asked Denitsev.

'The Second World War. We won it. My father flew bombers. Flattened Berlin almost single-handed. The Europeans weren't so high and mighty then. And it was us who had to put it all back together again.'

123

'Can we get back to the main point? What are we going to do about Balfour and his god-damned Bologna Process?' asked Hattie Reilly PhD.

'Fight him tooth and nail. Outvote him at the next meeting?'

'The damage may already be done by then. What he's going to do is to try to persuade the provost to back him at the executive council. If he can get them to allow all the temporaries and part-timers a say-so then who knows what they are going to be able to push through.'

'We can put up a counter proposal. What about proposing a sub-committee to review the proposal? That would sound sensible and in the meantime we could work on Galpin. We have the votes, so we can get it through.'

'Ideally, we really need to get rid of the cocksucker altogether.'

'Difficult. But definitely desirable.'

'By the law of averages, he won't last long. What's the average time for a chairman of this department, a year, a year and a half? He already sounds pissed off with the job.'

'Average is about nine months,' replied Hattie Reilly PhD. 'We've had six in five years.'

'You're right! There was Pietersen, Dimitrov, Nguyen Thu. Then came, let me see, Oliviera, Dean Mulvaney and now Balfour. Statistically, he can't last much longer. He's already been doing the job for three months.'

'One of us could do it instead. What about you, Hattie?' asked Nyborg.

'No, I don't think so,' she replied, 'I already have far too much on my plate. What about you, Morten?'

'I don't think I can spare the time,' Morten Nyborg said. 'I always have a full class load. You could do it, Denis. You'd be good at it, with all your contacts at the Ministry.'

'Not for me, sorry,' answered Denis Denitsev. 'I haven't got enough time as it is.'

'So, we are against any more work on this - what do you call it? – process.' asked Hattie Reilly PhD.

'The Bologna Process.'

'So we stop any more time-wasting on the Bologna Process,' put in Morten Nyborg.

'Right!' said Reilly. 'Stop it dead. Plus the damn stupid idea to give votes to all the here-today-gone-tomorrow temps and adjuncts.'

'I don't think we can stop it dead for the whole university,' said Denis Denitsev. 'It's actually mandated by the government and the Ministry of Education. All my friends there are very enthusiastic.'

'Enthusiastic?' echoed Hattie Reilly PhD incredulously. 'Enthusiastic about something from the European Union? I thought your government wasn't a full member yet?'

'Well,' explained Denitsev, 'we are not yet full members, but the policy is that we join Bologna because it might just raise the profile of our universities as a whole. Oxford, Cambridge, the Sorbonne, they've all joined Bologna. All the universities in the region – Romania, Bulgaria, Greece, Serbia, they're all in favor. We can't really stay out.'

'But we're not an EU institution. WE ARE AMERICAN!' Hattie Reilly PhD was shouting now. 'You won't find Harvard having to ask permission about what to teach from no 'Bologna Process'!'

'Well,' said Nyborg, in an effort to calm her down, 'let's face it, we're not Harvard.'

'No but we are American and that still matters!' she riposted.

'All I am saying is that top schools in the US like MIT or Harvard don't have to ask permission from no

125

government department before they write their syllabi.'

'I didn't know you went to Harvard,' asked Denis, innocently.

'Well, no I didn't,' said Hattie Reilly PhD, now a little calmer, 'but I could have! I was good enough!'

'So why didn't you?'

'I didn't think the Harvard program was right for me! Simple as that! '

'So, where did you study?'

'If you must know, I went to Florida State College, Tampa. I majored in office supply management. I made the Dean's List every semester.'

'Never mind that,' said Nyborg. 'What are we going to do about Balfour? Obviously we can't let him push through this Bologna thing. Who knows what it might lead to?'

'But,' said Nyborg, 'these things take time and, who knows, they might just get scrapped. We don't want to take on a whole load of extra work for something that might not happen.'

'Look, whether we are working on this Bolivia thing or not, we still have to get rid of Balfour,' said Reilly.

'Why?' asked Denitsev. 'So far it's only the Bologna Process that he wants to push that's upsetting everyone.'

'Everyone?'

'Yes, everyone - you, me, Hattie. Everyone.'

'I think you have to include Richard Smalley. He hates Balfour as well, plus one or two others. There are quite a few don't like him.'

'Remember, we only have to get the support of those with voting rights. Which is only us three, plus Richard and two, no, three, others. We already have a majority, if you count Smalley.'

'We could put a vote of no confidence at the next departmental meeting.'

'On what grounds? Why don't we have confidence in Dave Balfour?'

'Oh, I think we all know the answer to that one. Because he's an obnoxious, bad-tempered, Okie little shit. Isn't that enough? Even the provost doesn't like him.'

'He's got some important backs up, that's for sure. But we still need a reason or we'll just look like spoilt kids,' said Nyborg.

'You haven't had to fight your corner against him,' said Hattie Reilly PhD. 'He just doesn't see sense.'

'He beat you in an argument and you're pissed about it. Is that right?' asked Morten Nyborg.

'He did not beat me in an argument! I've had one or two differences over strictly academic matters but he does not seem to respond to reason. He's quite unfit to be chair of this department.'

'So, none of us likes him,' said Nyborg, 'but we don't have a good reason to get rid of him. Except that he wants to bring in this Bologna Process and we don't think we need it.'

'Look,' said Denitsev, 'suppose we organize a petition of the whole department and take it to the president?'

'That might work,' said Reilly. 'But can we be sure that we will get the right result?'

'It could rebound badly. A lot of the non-voting faculty actually like Balfour. He appointed some of them without consulting us. If they ever get the vote, they're not going to vote against him,' said Nyborg.

'Quite the opposite, I'd have thought,' said Hattie Reilly PhD. 'He's been threatening to change the standing orders to allow all of them to vote at departmental meetings.'

'And we could never allow that. It would mean that we would be outnumbered by a bunch of part-timers. It

127

would be impossible to develop proper policies and maintain decent academic standards and continuity.'

'So, a petition is out,' concluded Denitsev.

'We could try approaching the Dean,' suggested Lucia.

'That's not going to work. Dean Mulvaney only appointed him three months ago. He's going to look silly if he gets rid of Balfour now,' replied Denitsev.

'What about going to the provost?' asked Nyborg.

Hattie Reilly PhD said, 'No one sees anything of Galpin these days. He's always out. He just passes everything over to Mulvaney.'

'The provost has the power and he doesn't like Balfour. So that is where we should be aiming.'

'Does the provost care about things like that? I know he recommends the contracts on Mulvaney's say-so but he isn't much involved, is he?' said Nyborg.

'The hiring and firing is down to the president who is new anyway. The provost just passes the hiring and firing decisions from Mulvaney's desk to the president's. Potts always rubber stamped them. Good chance the new president, what's he called – Spring? - will just do the same.'

'So what does the provost actually do?'

'He seems to spend a lot of time at the embassy and in DC.'

'You mean Langley, Virginia don't you?'

'Shsh! Don't say that too loud.'

'So we're back with the problem. We have to get rid of Balfour somehow, but how?'

'Pity we can't just call up some private hitman?'

'That would be the best solution all around. There must be plenty of guys out there on the local economy. All those heavy men in the SUV's with their bald heads and leather jackets and fat stomachs. There must be one of them could do it.'

'I'm sure there is. But how do you find one? I think those fellows are just for domestic consumption - the local drug industry.'

'So, it looks like we're stuck with the bastard. We can't vote him out because it would look too bad. We can't get a petition because we might not win it and our credibility would be damaged. We can't go to the dean because the dean won't fire him after just appointing him. The provost is never here. The president hasn't found his feet yet and we don't know how to hire a hitman. We're stymied. Do you have any other ideas?'

'We could push him off the roof! Sorry, only a joke!!'

'We all know your jokes, Morten,' said Hattie. 'This is a serious matter. We don't want to be stuck with him. So we have to think of something. Denis, are any of your government friends in immigration? Could you get his visa revoked?'

'It's possible,' replied Denis Denitsev, 'but it takes time. His papers are probably in order. They will be if Elitsa in Human Resources got them for him. He could appeal. I could ask. Maybe there are some people who could just put him on a plane, but there might be problems. My friends might not think it's worth it, now that we are trying to look respectable before full EU membership.'

'Oh shit,' said Nyborg, 'that means we are stuck with him.'

'Oh, I don't know,' said Denis, 'I think I have an idea.'

Konstantin Zonkov was nothing if not reckless. It was his best quality. Together with two of his most psychopathic colleagues, he drove to the headquarters of Caradescu's party at exactly the moment when he calculated Mehmet

Caradescu would be leaving for his daily round of meetings and election rallies. They parked around the corner until they could see Caradescu exit from his office to make a fast dash from the safety of the building to the bullet-proof car.

In those few seconds he was vulnerable, even though he was surrounded by his well-paid bodyguards, there to take a bullet for him. A bullet might have worked, but Zonkov had thought more ambitiously than that. Spraying the street with bullets from a Kalashnikov AK-47 was too imprecise, he reasoned. He might hit all the guards and miss Caradescu.

No, he had a much better idea. The driver put his foot down and the car sped up alongside Caradescu's while it was just on the point of pulling away. Zonkov's car stopped alongside Caradescu's just long enough for one of his underlings to attach a magnetic bomb to the driver's door. A quick burst on the accelerator took them out of danger before the bomb was detonated by cellphone. All the occupants - Caradescu, his driver and a bodyguard were killed instantly.

The car Zonkov had used for the assassination was deliberately traceable. He had had it stolen from Mikhail Simonov's car park the previous evening. Away from the city, the three occupants changed cars in an empty piece of waste land hidden from the main road by trees. Gasoline was taken from the trunk of the escape car and poured over it. Then Zonkov torched the Simonov's old vehicle so that it would look like a botched job of hiding the evidence. He was careful to leave the number plates and the engine number intact so that the car could be easily identified as belonging to Mikhail Simonov.

Twelve

Any detective worth his salary would see instantly that Simonov was being framed for the attack. If Simonov had really wanted to murder Caradescu, he would have done a much better job of covering his tracks. The Chief of Police knew that and so did acting Prime Minister Anastasia Makarovna. But they both, for their different reasons, needed to arrest someone quickly and Simonov was the obvious choice. They fully understood that it was contract killing by person or persons unknown but the opportunity for political advantage to the ruling party was just too good to pass up. As were the kudos of a quick arrest for the Chief of Police.

As soon as he heard of the murder, Simonov knew too that he would be soon arrested for Caradescu's death. But a trial would not take place until well after the election which he would now have to watch on prison television. He was in the middle of making a statement to the media deploring the use of violence in a democratic process when the police came to arrest him, an arrest which had been precisely timed for his televised press conference.

He was dragged away pleading, in English for the media's benefit, his innocence of anything to do with the assassination. He also knew that, since he had not been responsible for the assassination, whoever had done it was probably working for Makarovna, which meant that he could easily have been the victim himself. He wondered if the choice of Caradescu and not him had been made on the toss of a coin. He wouldn't, he told himself, put it past the bitch.

Anastasia Makarovna was, at that very moment, watching Simonov's public arrest from the bed of

President Balashirov. She had caught the president watching events on CNN. One thing had led to another and they had both decided it would be better to watch Simonov's performance from a more comfortable horizotal position.

'So, Leonid,' said Anastasia, 'it's an ill-wind. Simonov didn't do it, of course.'

'Of course not, Simonov is innocent. He would have to be very stupid if he left his fingerprints all over the crime scene like that. Using his own car! Ha, ha! No, it's someone else.'

'I wonder who, cherie?'

'For the time being, my dear, it doesn't matter. Now you will win the election and we will have Simonov released in a week or two for lack of evidence or just plain clemency – a generous gesture to make you look good. The point is, you will be in office for four more years! Then another few years at the State Bank and you can retire to a nice dacha with your earnings.'

'I do love you, Leonid. You are so thoughtful and so kind and so generous.'

'It's a good job the Minister of the Interior knows how to run a decent police force. Arresting Simonov is obviously in the national interest. If there is some hitman out there killing our finest, it is probably safer for Simonov in jail. Are you ready for your press conference?'

'Yes, my dear. Let's give them a good show. Time to get dressed. Duty calls.'

Anastasia Makarovna handled her press conference well. She used the complete range of emotions from sadness at the use of violence, to maternal sympathy for the dead men's families, to indignation that she might benefit from it. But then she was a natural, expert politician.

'Tell me, Prime Minister,' asked one journalist, 'how do you think the murder of Mister Caradescu and the arrest of Mikhail Simonov will affect the outcome of next weekend's election?'

'I am only acting prime minister right now,' she answered smoothly. 'I am just a candidate running for the privilege of being prime minister of our beloved country. But to answer your question, I am hopeful that these dreadful events will not affect the way people will vote. It's a free vote and each elector must choose the deputy he or she thinks will do the best job.'

'Is it true that you and President Balashirov are quite close and that he is secretly backing you?' The audience tittered gently at this provocative question. But Anastasia was ready with her answer.

'It is impossible not to admire a fine president who has led this country with distinction for sixteen years. While I have been prime minister I am pleased to say that I have enjoyed his full confidence.'

'That's not only full thing of Balashirov's she's enjoyed,' whispered one reporter to another.

'Ms Makarovna,' another journalist was asking, 'now that both your main opponents are out of the contest, doesn't that clear the way for you? Aren't the killing of Caradescu and the arrest of Simonov exactly what you needed to ensure victory next weekend?'

'Certainly not,' Anastasia Makarovna was indignant, 'today's tragedy marks a low point in our domestic politics! If I am re-elected I will not rest until the evil-doers are brought to justice.'

'So, why arrest Mikhail Simonov?'

'The police have detained Mikhail Simonov for questioning. If they think he is guilty of this terrible act, then he will face a trial. If not, then he will be freed. That is our way.'

'But he will not be able to take any further part in this election. And surely that is to your advantage.'

'You, as an American, with your country's strong belief in the legal process,' she answered the impertinent reporter, 'surely you should understand that the law must take its course. Thank you, ladies and gentlemen.'

'One last question, Ms Makarovna, please, please?'

'OK, final question,' said Anastasia.

'Is it true that this election is all about the new US airbase and Operation Warm Blanket? Isn't it true that Simonov and Caradescu were against it and with them out of the way, you will be able to push it through unopposed?'

'I believe that Operation Warm Blanket will bring much needed economic benefits to our country and will enhance our security in a world where, as we have seen, terrorism and disorder are all too frequent.'

'Are the rumors true, Madame Prime Minister?'

'What rumors? What rumors are you talking about?'

Anastasia Makarovna was gathering up her papers and turning to go but the reporter persisted.

'The rumors that the new base will be completely unmanned and no local nationals will be employed there.'

'I am sorry, I have no such information. I think you are wrong. No more questions. Sorry.'

Back in her office, she was furious.

'What the hell was that last question all about?' she screamed at her secretary. 'Is there something I should have known?'

'Sorry, Ma'am, I've heard nothing.'

'Get me Alexandrov! NOW!'

'Alexei,' she shouted when he called. 'Do you have any information about the American plans to make the new base completely unmanned, with none of our people employed there?'

'I've heard nothing. Do you want me to ask around? It will be difficult now that we aren't fully in charge anymore. It will be easier to extract the required information from likely sources once we are actually back in power after the election. If we win, of course.'

'Thanks to whoever kindly eliminated Caradescu, I think there's a very good chance we'll be safe.'

'But if those rumors are true, we would be in trouble.'

'Yes, we would.'

Are they true, wondered Anastasia Makarovna? Is it possible the Americans were lying to her? No, she decided, it was just some troublemaker of a reporter trying to stir things up. She had met O.B. many times and he had always struck her as a fairly straight kinda guy, as he regularly described himself.

At AUSB, Denis Denitsev was explaining his idea. 'Look, why don't we just go to the provost and present a petition from all the faculty of the department expressing our total lack of confidence in our chair,' he told them.

'We've already been there,' said Hattie Reilly PhD. 'Most of the faculty, the part-timers and adjuncts and temps, they think Balfour's OK. Especially now he is planning to give them voting rights.'

'But, Hattie, that's the whole point. We can't wait until they get the vote. It would mean that we would never get a fair result. We have to move now. I like Morten's idea that we don't hold open faculty meetings any more. We just have email meetings of voting members only. The non-voting people will never even know if a decision has been taken. Or even if we have had a meeting.'

'So, we could have an email meeting now and make

the decision to present a petition.'

'But won't the provost notice if there are only four names on it.'

'I've thought about that. As voting members we can pass a resolution to stand proxy for all those faculty members who don't have votes. That way, we can get the majority of the department behind us. The non-voters will never know that we have written them into the petition and the provost will never check because he spends more time at the embassy than he does here.'

'Is it legal?' asked Nyborg.

'According to statute, we have all the voting rights and all the power. It might be construed as bending the rules slightly but think of the good it will do! It will get rid of Balfour once and for all!' Denitsev assured them.

'I don't know,' said Hattie Reilly PhD. 'I think I have to draw the line at forging someone else's signature.'

'No need to do that,' Denitsev reassured her. 'The provost is not Balfour's friend either, so we can just give the impression that we have the whole department behind us.'

'But Balfour's just signed a new three-year contract, so he must be safe.'

'Means nothing,' said Denis Denitsev. 'The provost will tear it up if he wants to, and let Balfour sue, if he can afford a legal action against a major American university.'

'I'll draft something,' said Hattie Reilly PhD.

The next day the little group met again to finalize Reilly's petition. She read it out to them.

'To Dr Darius Galpin, Provost of the American University of the Southern Balkans.

We, the undersigned, the longest serving tenured members of the Department of Business have taken soundings amongst all our colleagues

136

and we present the following complaints regarding the conduct of the present chair, Dr. David Balfour.

1. Dr. Balfour intends, unilaterally and without faculty consultation, to change the standing orders of the department to extend voting rights on matters of departmental policy at faculty meetings to unqualified AUSB employees viz. those without tenure, including adjunct professors and temporary or visiting professors.

2. Dr. Balfour wishes to change unilaterally the course structure of our established and successful programs without proper mandate from the faculty. He intends to do this also without reference to the University Executive Council and its ordinances.

3. Dr. Balfour has instituted a dictatorial regime on the Business Department which is inimical to the basic precepts of academic freedom.

We therefore request that Professor Balfour's appointment as Chair of the Department of Business be terminated in the interests of academic integrity and departmental harmony.

Signed
  Professor Denis Denitsev PhD
 Professor Morten Nyborg CPA
 Professor Hattie Reilly PhD
 *Professor Richard Smalley BA(Summa cum
        Laude), PhD (University of Alice Springs)
 on behalf of the entire faculty of
 the Department of Business.*

'What do you think?' Hattie Reilly PhD asked them.

'It looks good,' said Nyborg,' but who's going to deliver it?'

'I've thought about that,' said Denis Denitsev. 'I have the ideal messenger.'

'Yes?'

'Why don't we ask Annabella to deliver it?'

'Annabella? Annabella Markova-Casillias?'

'Yes, that Annabella.'

'But she's only a temporary! She will be out at the end of the year.'

'Yes,' said Denis, 'she will indeed be out at the end of the year. She is desperate now that Potts is no longer here to look after her. Even if she did pass the faculty review, which you Hattie, are in charge of, she will certainly be demoted back to assistant professor.'

'I thought Potts had promised her a job at Georgetown if she goes stateside?'

'Ah,' said Denis, 'promises, promises. He might forget her and she won't get that job after all. On the other hand, if we offer her a positive evaluation and she keeps her job here, then she may come in very useful in the future.'

'Good thinking. You're a very devious man, Denis.'

'*Moi*, devious?'

It was the last Monday before the election. The city was still stunned by the events of the weekend. The Saturday riots had been bad enough but the murder of Caradescu and the arrest for it of Simonov had had a strange effect on the city's population. There was a quiet seething, a foreboding of yet more violence to come. The trade unions were planning a big demonstration that afternoon in Revolution Square. They would, the Chief of Police knew, be joined by all sorts of anti-social riff-raff - anarchists, Leninists, Trotskyites, weird fringe groups and troublemakers of all kinds. His men would need to be well-armed and reinforced.

Galpin met Zonkov in a different place. This time it was on a park bench in the Winter Park, whose daytime character was entirely different from what went on at night. It was the haunt of mothers and children, of joggers and courting couples, of elderly pensioners and retired working men playing chess. Galpin blended in with the last group - he was in the same peasant disguise.

'Is it OK?' asked Zonkov. 'You like how we remove Caradescu?'

'You did very well. Have the police been to see you?'

'Don't worry. Police no problem. Some work for me. I pay good.'

'What about Caradescu's men?'

'Already, they ask, Konstantin, my brother, you have job for me? I take them. Big army soon. Maybe Konstantin become president, eh? Good idea. President, he make many, many money! Ha, ha! '

'No more before the election. This afternoon's demonstration, just let it go. Let the police break a few bones. It will be on TV all over the world. Everyone will be expecting a repeat of last time. The police will restore law and order and no one will be able to point a finger at us.'

'That is bad. My boys, they were looking forward to action. They like fighting.'

'No, the police will be there in force. Let them sort it out.'

'OK. You're the boss. Oh, and boss, I get shipment. Very good. No problem.'

Denis Denitsev took Annabella Markova-Casillias on one side. 'Annabella, we have a little job for you.'

'Yes, Denis?'

'Yes. Have you heard from President Potts? How is he?'

'I think he is good.'

'You don't think he will forget you, now that he is back in Washington?'

'No, that is not possible,' retorted Annabella. 'Men do not forget me!'

'So, what do you think of David Balfour?'

'He's all right, for an old man.'

'No, I mean, how has he treated you.'

'Well, he tells me that my contract may not be renewed at the end of the year if I don't pass the faculty evaluation. But that will not matter. I can always go to Georgetown.'

'But if Potts forgets you as well and you don't get a transfer to Georgetown, then you are going to be jobless.'

'I think I can rely on Alaric Potts to keep his promise.'

'But, if Balfour were not here and you got a good report from the faculty evaluation process, then the new chair would be able to keep you on. It would be a little insurance in case Georgetown falls through.'

'So I need to go through the evaluation process again?'

'Yes, but it would be a mere formality. Professor Reilly is in charge of it.'

'So,' said Associate Professor Markova-Casillias, suddenly realizing that she was being offered a deal, 'what do you want me to do?'

'Nothing too difficult,' said Denitsev suavely. 'We just want you to make sure Provost Galpin gets this petition.'

'Can I see that?'

Denitsev handed over the unsealed envelope.

'But it says here that the entire faculty is demanding that Balfour is dismissed. I don't remember being asked,' she said.

'No, we, the longest-serving senior members of the department feel that we need to take this serious step on behalf of everyone. Someone needs to do something before the situation gets out of control. We are sure that Provost Galpin will take more notice of it, coming from a friend of General Potts.'

'OK,' said Annabella, 'I'll do it. When? '

'We have already made an appointment for you at five thirty this evening. The university will be nice and quiet by then.'

Provost Darius Galpin got up from the park bench after his meeting with Konstantin Zonkov and made his way to the exit of the Winter Park still disguised as a workman. Suddenly he heard a shout from behind.

'Professor, what are you doing here in daytime? Don't you recognize me? It's Malik! Yes, Malik who drives the taxi! Why are you dressed like a peasant from the country? You are usually so smart.'

Darius Galpin made a mental note to change his disguise for next time. After three supposedly coincidental, 'accidental' meetings, he was now certain that Malik the taxi driver was also working a second job.

'Are you following me, Malik?' demanded Galpin.

'Following you, Professor? Why should I follow you? I am your friend. I take you Winter Park at night when not like day. I drive you tonight? You have two girls like last time?'

'No! I not have two girls like last time! I am not

interested in whatever goes on here at night. Now, if you are not following me, then leave me alone.'

'I tell you what,' said Malik. 'You take my card. I can be useful to a big man like you. I have many contacts. I know everybody.'

'Just tell me,' said an exasperated Darius Galpin, 'who the hell are you working for?'

'Me? I'm just a taxi driver. No boss. Oh, here is your car. BMW! Very nice! You will change your clothes in the car? An important man should not go to the university looking like a peasant.'

Denis Denitsev was giving Annabella Markova-Casillias her last minute instructions.

'Soften him up. Sweet talk him. He's bound to like you. He likes women. There are rumors that he goes to the Winter Park some evenings.'

'Is that so?' said Ms Markova-Casillias. 'I've never seen him there.'

She took especial trouble with her *toilette* in the university faculty ladies' room. She brushed and plucked, she changed her blouse and she reapplied her makeup with slow deliberate care. When she was satisfied with her image in the mirror, she applied one last squirt of Chanel perfume and prepared to go to meet the provost. Almost as an afterthought, just before she stepped out of the makeshift boudoir, she bent down and with one practiced deft movement removed her panties and stuffed them into her purse. Then she was ready for Provost Darius Galpin.

Thirteen

In the last few days before the election, there was a very high police profile. The civilian police and the SSP, the Special Security Police, were under strict orders to keep a lid on any possible trouble. Known trouble makers were rounded up and others, those whom the police merely suspected of being troublemakers, were watched around the clock.

One could not travel far in the capital without being stopped and questioned. There were road blocks on all the main streets and every car was searched for bombs and guns. The long delays and tailbacks added to the general tension.

Darius Galpin was stopped twice on his way back to AUSB and it was nearly two in the afternoon before he got back to his office. He slumped behind the desk and his mind turned to Malik the taxi driver. He was sure now that the man was stalking him. The fellow had recognized him under his disguise and had probably seen him talking to Zonkov.

Why was he always there and who was he working for? Galpin went through the possibilities. Could he be one of ours? A check by someone inside the embassy that Galpin would not be working some kind of double cross? No, he thought, why should they bother? The same applied to his second possibility, that Malik was a fellow worker for the Company, the CIA. That still left the local civilian police or the state security.

He was particularly worried that it might be the SSP. The SSP were, in fact, the old communist era secret police. President Balashirov had not seen any point in disbanding such a useful arm of the state and he had left it virtually unchanged except for removing those very few senior officers who had been serious about their communism. Which was only a very small handful - most of the SSP top brass had quickly accepted the new political realities after the fall of communism and had simply changed sides. Their job descriptions would be unchanged except that now there would be more opportunities to make money.

So, Galpin continued, if Malik is not working for the Americans or the police or the state security, then he is either working for some other country or he was working for some major criminal – Zonkov perhaps? Maybe he was an independent operator? Galpin looked at the card which Malik had given him and he had an idea. He composed a short message and sent it encrypted to CIA headquarters at Langley. Where, he asked, is this phone located and who owns it?

He got his answer back within an hour. It read *'Phone owned Taliban Office, 14 St Maria Street.'*

The Afghan war had ended some years earlier with a humiliating NATO defeat which had been described by the then American administration as a 'victory for peace and reconciliation'. Since then, the Taliban had become semi-legitimate and were operating what they described as 'consulates' in many of the world's capitals. These were not usually recognized by most countries as full consulates with diplomatic privileges and were thus described by the sore losers, the western powers, as mere 'offices'.

So Malik was working for the Taliban and was stalking him. But why the Taliban? They were a long way away down at the other end of the Silk Road, or, as it really should be known these days, the Black Gold Pipeline. It was a puzzle. He was slowly filling in some of the pieces but he was still struggling with the reasons. What was it all about?

Anastasia Makarovna, caretaker prime minister, had asked the United States Ambassador for a meeting. He was well aware of the protocol that he was not supposed to talk to her until after the election.

'This will be purely unofficial, Your Excellency, a meeting of friend to friend. And, if I am privileged to be called upon to lead my country's government after the election next Sunday, then we can resume our official relationship,' she purred.

'On those terms, Madame Makarovna,' the patrician, well-mannered ambassador replied, 'it would be churlish, not to say downright rude, not to say yes.'

'Wonderful,' replied Anastasia and put the phone down.

Normally, it would have been the ambassador who would have visited the prime minister at her city center office but since she was now, technically, just an ordinary citizen like any other, it was she who made the trip, that evening, to the ambassador's private residence, part of a wing of the embassy compound.

Strictly speaking, he should not have allowed the visit because it could be interpreted as American interference in a local election, an attempt to affect the outcome. But Feldstein figured that she must want something, and want it badly enough to risk losing some of the not insubstantial anti-American vote should her visit ever became public knowledge. She could, who knows, even be coaxed into giving away useful information, possibly in the form of a deliberate red herring, for which the converse could be inferred. It would be an interesting meeting, he decided.

'Madame Makarovna!' said Ambassador Feldstein, 'It is so very good to see you! You are looking even more beautiful than ever!'

'Your Excellency! You are so gallant! So kind of you!

145

'   'Tell me, how is good President Balashirov?'

'He suffers heavily at the way this quite uncharacteristic violence has harmed the peaceful democratic reputation which our country has always enjoyed.'

'And is he well?'

'Oh, yes, he is quite well. He and I are quite close, as I am sure you know, Ambassador.'

'I understand you were always in tune politically.'

'Let me tell you a little secret, Joseph. I can call you Joseph, can't I?'

'Call me Joe'

'Well, Joe, Leonid and I are more than just political allies.'

'Really? I am honored that you trust me with such a secret. It is quite safe with me.'

This was interesting, thought Joe Feldstein. She was offering a confidence. What was she expecting in return?

Actually, Ambassador Feldstein knew every detail of the personal relationship between Leonid Balashirov and Anastasia Makarovna, including full details of their every tryst, courtesy of American electronic ingenuity in the presidential bedroom. He knew also about Balashirov's vasectomy after Anastasia's hurried abortion a few years previously. Joseph Feldstein even had a copy of the poolside video.

She was direct because the direct approach sometimes works.

'I want something,' she said. 'What can you tell me about the proposed new United States air base in my country?'

'I can't say much because I don't know much. As I understand it, and all this is all in the public domain, we, that is, NATO, with the US bearing the lion's share of the cost, will be doubling our defensive capacity in your

146

country by building a second base. It will provide revenue in the form of annual rental payments plus much-needed jobs in both the construction and operation. That's all I know.'

'Yes,' said Anastasia Makarovna, 'that is what it said in the official communiqué. They are going to call it Operation Warm Blanket and NATO will be doubling up its airbases all the way from the Adriatic to the Great Wall of China.'

'That's about it. Why do you ask?'

'I don't know. Why now? We have peace in the Balkans and much of Asia. It just seems an odd move. Of course, for us it is good. It must be good for all the countries involved. It brings money. We are a poor country and the dollars from your base at Altameda means that we can provide a little better for our people. They don't want the old poverty. They want cellphones and Coca-Cola and new sneakers. If I can bring the base here, it will help them get a modern life. Not like under the communists!'

'Weren't you a good communist, yourself, in your younger days?'

'Of course, you had to be. We all pretended to be in love with communism and then we went home to watch Miami Vice on TV and wish to be Amerikanski! Then the end of the Iron Curtain came and all was good. Except that it is very difficult to get dollars. If this base is not built, then there will be big trouble! I know it.'

'Well, Anastasia, all I can tell you is that as far as I know, it is all going ahead.'

'There have been some rumors that the new base will be the home to unmanned flying machines called drones. Have you heard those rumors? Is there any truth in them? If there is, it would be very serious.'

'I have heard absolutely nothing. As you know,

President Bedford has made a number of statements against the use of drone warfare because of the risks drones pose to civilian life. I think you can rest easy on that one, Anastasia.'

'Thank you Joe, that's all I need to know.'

'Good luck on Sunday. I know I am supposed to be impartial, but just between you and me, strictly confidentially, you are our preferred winner.'

'Thank you again.'

Sitting in her car, Anastasia Makarovna's sharp political instincts were demanding attention. Feldstein's last remark had set her thinking. So she had been Washington's choice, had she? Why was Feldstein telling her - to make her feel grateful, perhaps? So that she would be available for use at some future date? It would not be the first time the US had swung a tight election in a poor but strategic country.

Or could Feldstein have just been making an empty reassuring compliment. No, no, she dismissed that idea as too naive. Anastasia had been a very good chess player as a schoolgirl and she knew full well that there is always a reason behind every move even if you don't see it at first. Feldstein had told her because he wanted her to know. And what were the implications of that? Had the Americans arranged the murder of Caradescu? And the violence in Revolution Square, were they responsible for that as well?

What if she were being set up as an American stooge? The logical deduction from that was too awful to contemplate. It meant that if she could no longer deliver what the Americans wanted, then she, herself, legally elected prime minister or not, could be removed the way they had removed Caradescu. Suddenly the presidency of the State Bank looked beguilingly appealing..

Across town, another meeting between an older man and a beautiful younger woman was taking place. Associate Professor Markova-Casillias had been admitted into Provost Galpin's inner sanctum. He motioned her to a chair where she pulled up her skirt and sat down, displaying her long brown legs. She was not wearing tights or stockings because it was still late summer and the temperatures were often as high as 30C. This was the time of year when the perversely named Winter Park saw the peak of its after-hours activity.

'What can I do for you, Annabella?' asked the provost.

'I have been asked to bring you this.'

The provost read the paper which she handed to him. 'Why do you want to get rid of Balfour?'

'Like they say, he is becoming difficult. He is making problems for the working faculty.'

'The entire faculty or just these four?'

'Certainly those four, I can't say for everyone. Most of us don't have votes. The rules are set up so that we don't really have much of a say. But Balfour is a disciplinarian and they don't like it.'

'Were you approached by these four senior professors?'

'Oh, yes, they discussed everything with me and explained the situation.'

'So,' asked Darius Galpin, 'what will it mean to you if Balfour stays or if he goes?'

'If he goes, then I have a chance of getting another year or more in this job.'

'But I thought you were going to Georgetown on the recommendation of President Potts?'

'That might not work out,' said Annabella.

'So you are going along with this little mutiny in order to back your horses both ways?'

149

'A girl must protect herself,' said Annabella. 'It's still a man's world.'

The provost laughed. He was starting to enjoy himself after a few stressful days. 'A woman like you could probably take care of herself without help from a man,' said Darius Galpin.

'Oh, I don't know,' she replied, 'it's more difficult than you think. A lot of men just see you as some kind of bimbo - until you get to be fat and middle-aged, when they ignore you completely.'

'Are you thinking of anyone in particular?' The provost pointed to the petition.

'Ha, ha! You don't mean Hattie Reilly, do you?' asked Annabella.

'Hattie Reilly 'P' 'H' 'D', as she always likes to be called,' replied the provost.

'She is a strong and confident woman,' said Annabella.

'As you say, she is indeed a bossy and self-important woman,' answered Darius Galpin.

'Does that mean you are going to reject the request?'

'Not at all, it's a good idea. I think David Balfour may be too disruptive. Mike Mulvaney should never have appointed him in the first place.'

'Shouldn't it be a matter for Dean Mulvaney then?'

'Not necessarily. I can overrule Mike if I have to.'

'Will you, if the Dean doesn't want to remove Balfour from the chair?'

'I may have to do it for him. Dean Mulvaney doesn't like problems.'

'I would have thought he'd be used to problems by now.'

'Mike Mulvaney just wants problems to go away. He isn't the strongest of men.'

'Sometimes, a kind and gentle streak can be very attractive in a man.'

'But,' said Provost Galpin, 'I am sure you prefer a man who shows a little more initiative?'

'Provost...'

'Call me Darius.'

'Oh, Darius, I think you are flirting with me.'

'You don't seem to mind.'

'No, Darius, it's very flattering to be flirted with by a strong man.'

Darius moved around the desk so that he was standing over her. Annabella looked up at him and he bent down to kiss her. Her arm went around his neck as she pulled him to her. Then his hand was inside her bra. They sank to the floor and Galpin pulled up her skirt. He realized with delight that she was not wearing underwear and she was already wet. He desperately tore off the rest of her clothes and then his own. It was quickly over.

'I hope you locked the door,' gasped Annabella.

'No, not locked,' Galpin panted. 'It's more exciting with the fear of discovery.'

'Just like the Winter Park.'

'Do you ever go there?'

'No. Do you?'

'No.'

Both were lying.

Dressed again, Annabella asked Darius Galpin about the petition.

'Leave it with me,' he told her. 'I will give you a decision later in the week.'

What he hadn't told her was that he had already decided, even before the gang of four had started their witch hunt, to dismiss David Balfour. The reason had absolutely nothing to do with anything academic. No, Balfour was being abandoned because of a confidential memo which had been circulated to the presidents of all American universities located in the NATO area, that all senior university officers, all departmental chairs, deans, provosts and presidents, in areas covered by Operation Warm Blanket, would need to be CIA members at some appropriate level of clearance. The removal of Alaric Potts from the presidency of AUSB had been just the first step. Since Balfour was not Company, he would be going anyway. But Galpin did not see any point in telling that to Associate Professor Annabella Markova-Casillias, that exotic creature who had come to his office without underwear. At least not until after he had got to know her a little better, maybe twice or even three times more.

Malik the taxi driver was waiting as Provost Galpin left the university that evening on his way to the United States Embassy for a meeting with John Sieghart.

'Hey, Professor, you want taxi? Not drive own car. Traffic very bad! I take you.'

'No thank you,' replied Galpin.

'No Professor, you come in my taxi. Very good. No fare.'

'I said no....', but Malik was holding him firmly by the elbow and was pushing him into the waiting cab. It took a moment before Galpin realized that he was being manhandled and abducted by a very strong man indeed. Malik then pushed Galpin down on to the back seat and locked the doors. He started the car and pulled away from the kerb.

'Where are you taking me?' asked Provost Galpin.

'Don't worry. You will come to no harm. I just want a little talk.' Malik's English had suddenly become more fluent. He was no longer the bumbling taxi driver. In fact, Galpin realized, he had taken on the appearance of a very nasty professional thug.

'What can I tell you? Do you want some student grades changed? I know, your girlfriend is one of our students and you want her to pass. Is that it?' Galpin had often been approached by people like this new version of Malik, people who were prepared to pay well for academic favors.

'No, Professor, I don't want anything for my girlfriend. Let's be serious, shall we? Let's talk about your proper job, not your pretend work at the University. Let's talk about your real work with the American Embassy.'

'Whatever are you talking about?'

Malik stopped the car suddenly. 'Do not, Mister Professor,' he said sharply, 'waste any more of my fucking time! Do you understand? We know all about your meetings with the gangster Zonkov and we know what he has been doing for you. How are you going to pay him? In drugs?'

Galpin said nothing.

'Look Mister Professor, I don't give a shit about what you get up to with Zonkov. It's not any of our concern. We do not care either if some stupid gangster rubs out some stupid politician. It's their country. Let them screw it up on their own.'

'So,' muttered Galpin, 'what do you want?'

'That's more like it. A little bit of friendly co-operation. Now, I am guessing you don't spend too much time on your academic duties. Your main job is keeping you busy enough. Am I right?'

Galpin nodded.

'And,' Malik continued, 'your job as CIA field operative is more important than being a professor, at least until after the election, yes?' Galpin nodded again.

'Now, what my bosses want to know is very simple. Why are the Americans going to all this trouble to fix an

153

election in a small country like this?'

'I don't know why,' said Galpin. 'You and I are professionals. We just obey orders. That's what I'm doing, just obeying orders.'

'Look,' Malik told the provost, 'those were damn' big orders. Kill Caradescu, get Simonov arrested, start riots. The Americans are going to a lot of trouble for a routine election.

'You know about all that?'

'Of course, we have our sources. And we've been following you for weeks. Ever since those two jerks got sent home and you were brought in. We knew you'd be the CIA main man. We also know about Sieghart. But he's just a desk man now. He's too old for dirty tricks.'

'You keep saying 'we'. Just who are you?'

'Guess. I am not from this country and my government needs some very important information.'

'Can you tell me where?'

'Oh, you know where already. I am sure the CIA has a file on me. But don't worry, American. I am not going to harm you. We are not looking to make enemies out of the United States, unless we have to, of course.'

'So what can I tell you that'll make you leave me alone?'

'What we want to know is why you are fixing this election for Balashirov's whore?'

'Why? I can't tell you. I don't know. My orders are just to do it. And keep the CIA out of it. That is why we are using Zonkov.'

'Oh yes, you are using our gangster friend so the Company's hands can be kept clean. Useful now but come Sunday, you will have new orders for Zonkov, eh?' Malik made the throat-slitting gesture.

'Maybe, who knows?'

'Maybe,' agreed Malik. 'Maybe, if you're too

frightened, we'll do it for you? No, I make a joke. Zonkov is too useful. He also works for us from time to time.'

'Look,' asked Galpin, 'what's all this about? I have a meeting. I'm late. They will be suspicious.'

'Blame the traffic! Not in a hurry to get to the Winter Park, are you? Anyway the girls will not be there so early. No, your meeting is with Sieghart at the US Embassy.'

'OK, I'm meeting the CIA desk man.'

'Maybe you can ask him what he can tell you about Operation Warm Blanket?'

'Operation Warm Blanket?'

'Before I take you to Colonel Sieghart, why don't you tell me what you do know? Exactly why is the United States so anxious to make sure that Makarovna wins on Sunday? Why are you prepared to take the risks of getting mixed up with the likes of Zonkov? What you usually do is wait until the new guy, the president or the prime minister is elected fairly, or at least as fairly as they do things around here. Then you carefully explain to him what you expect him to do for you Americans. Which is that he had better do as he is told or kaput! Isn't that the American way? '

'Yeah,' agreed Galpin, 'that's the way it's usually worked in the past.'

'But Anastasia Makarovna is just about the only person in this goddamned country who can be relied on to do exactly what Washington wants without even waiting to be asked, right?'

'Right.'

'So, just to make it absolutely sure, it would be better to fix things so only she can win? That means that it is big, yes?'

'Yes, it's big. But I don't know why. I'm just an operative.'

'So, Mister American Professor, tell me what you know about Operation Warm Blanket.'

'All I know is what I've read about and seen on TV. It's a new line of NATO airbases across from the east, all the way to central Europe. It doubles up defensive capacity along the line of the oil pipeline.'

'Yeah, yeah, yeah,' said Malik. 'That's the official line from O.B. and those assholes in Washington. And Milady Makarovna must win here because that will make it easy for them. Unlike Caradescu or Simonov who will make trouble, ask questions, maybe even demand more money.'

'That's probably about it,' said Galpin.

'Do you know what they are saying in my country?'

'No what? '

'They are saying that Operation Warm Blanket is not genuine. They are saying that there is some other plan which the Americans are not telling us about. We need to know all about it. You, Big American Professor, you will find out for me.'

'Oh, shit,' said Galpin. 'Is that true?'

'It could be. Why not ask your Colonel Sieghart?'

'So, do you think Caradescu and Simonov knew something even I haven't been told and that is why they had to be shut up?'

'Possibly' said Malik, starting the car. 'But we need to know exactly what the Americans are up to.'

'Why do you need to know? Your country's not a member of NATO. We're not planning bases on your soil.'

'Look, we only just got rid of the Americans and we don't want them back. Before that we got rid of the Russians and we don't want them back either. Before that we got rid of the British who came to our country to steal what they could. We have been fighting foreigners in our country for two hundred years and we always win in the end. You Americans don't like to be beaten and now we think you are up to something and we want to know what it is. We need to be ready.'

'I can't help you. Sorry.'

'I'll tell you what. Why not get me all the facts from Sieghart and in return, we will not execute your Ambassador in Uzbekistan. That's fair, is it not? I'll drop you at the embassy. Or maybe you'd prefer the Bar Whiskey? You look like you need a drink. Or I could stop at the Winter Park, if you like. The whores should be arriving by now. Get yourself two nice ones before they get too tired!'

Galpin groaned. Just a little oh-fuck-how-the-hell-did-I-get-into-all-this sort of groan. He was starting to regret the Faustian deal he had made with the CIA. How much easier it would have been, just to be a straightforward university teacher, with no second life.

He immediately dismissed the unworthy thought. Not only was he serving his country by this Jekyll and Hyde existence but he would be no more than an associate professor by this stage in his life.

'I'll tell you for sure on Friday,' Annabella Markova-Casillias reported back to Denis Denitsev.

'He wants to see you again? 'Denis asked.

'Of course,' replied Annabella. 'I have him hooked.'

'Did he say anything about Balfour? What about our petition?'

'All he said was that it might be a good idea if Balfour was removed from the chair. He also said that he would need to make things right with Mike Mulvaney.'

'Maybe you should try to work your charms on the Dean. It might speed things up.'

'I could, but he is such a cold fish. I can't see Mike Mulvaney showing a girl much affection. Maybe it won't

157

be necessary.'

'But for the good of the department, I am sure you could shut your eyes and think of Georgetown,' suggested Denitsev.

'By the way,' he asked her, 'does the provost have any idea about your, er..'

'My little problem? No, he is just like all you men. Well, not you, Denis, but most. Once the balls are full, the brain is empty.'

'But still, not a nice thing for him to take home to Madame Provost.'

'Especially since she is so important in the World Council of Churches! '

'How many more times will you see him?' asked Denitsev.

'Two, maybe three,' answered Annabella, 'these little flings burn out quickly.'

'Then you can go back to your second job at the Winter Park.'

'No not a job! I never take money! The Winter Park is for pleasure only! I am not a whore!' Annabella Markova-Casillias was quite indignant. Denis realized he had gone too far. His tone was placatory.

'I am so sorry,' he told her abjectly, 'of course you are a good girl. And you have to look after your career. You are doing a great job with Doctor Galpin. We will certainly remember it for your end-of-term faculty evaluation.'

'You'd better. I'm writing it all down' were Annabella's final words.

Denis Denitsev could not wait to report back to Reilly, Nyborg and Smalley. 'I think you can say that it's in the bag!' he told them triumphantly.

'How so?'

'Well, the provost hit it off brilliantly with our

seductive little friend. Romance is in the air. They may have to meet again a couple of times more. Galpin is fairly pissed off with Balfour already, according to Annabella. He will not mind if Balfour goes.'

'She will do all this for a good faculty evaluation from us?'

'Of course, if Potts has already decided that Miss Markova is out of sight and therefore out of mind, we are her only job opportunity. Without our recommendation she will be unemployed.'

'I can't imagine Professor Markova-Casillias ever being unemployed. Not with a talent like she has.' said Nyborg. 'And I don't mean academic,' he leered.

'Let's get back to the main point,' said Denitsev. 'We now have several ways we can get rid of Balfour even if our petition doesn't do the trick on its own.'

'And they are?' asked Hattie Reilly PhD.

'Well,' said Denis Denitsev slyly, 'there is also the threat of a sexual harassment charge against Galpin like he did to Potts. Not to say good old-fashioned, honest-to-goodness blackmail.'

'OK,' put in Nyborg. 'First, is Annabella willing to go along with the sexual harassment thing?'

'Oh, yes,' replied Denitsev. 'I think we have her loyalty. She could be out as well unless she co-operates with us.'

'You mentioned something else,' asked Smalley, 'blackmail?'

'Yes, indeed, blackmail,' said Denitsev. 'Did you know that Mrs Galpin is very important in religious circles? She's something like a Knight Imperial Dragon of the World Council of Churches.'

'So?'

'So, our young colleague could very well have made a very positive donation to the good lady, via husband

Darius, without him actually knowing, of course.'

'You can't be serious!'

'Oh, but I am,' said a gleeful Denis Denitsev. 'I have the medical records of our very sexually active associate professor!'

'How did you get those?' demanded Hattie Reilly PhD.

Denitsev just patted the side of his nose. 'Friends at the Ministry of Health,' he said, 'important friends.'

Fourteen

Malik dropped Galpin off at the American Embassy for his meeting with Sieghart.

'Did you know the Taliban are in town?' Galpin asked Sieghart.

'Yeah, of course, they have an office in Saint Maria Street.'

'And we are watching them?'

'Naturally, and they are watching us. It's all standard stuff. Why do you ask?'

'Well, one of their spooks had a long talk with me only an hour ago. He asked some interesting questions.'

'Go on.'

'Well, this guy, his cover is taxi driver, is very interested in Operation Warm Blanket. Seems to think O.B. was not being completely truthful when he announced it.'

'Yes?'

'The Taliban seem to think that Warm Blanket is a cover for a different plan. He thinks that is why we are going to all this trouble for Makarovna. This will be the first country to be told what the real plan is all about.'

'There has been some talk, yes,' said Sieghart, 'but the official word is that we are doubling up real live NATO stations to integrate our defenses and bring incidental economic benefits to the countries involved. There has been some talk about drone stations, but nothing official until after our girl is safely home.'

'And the unofficial word?' asked Galpin.

'Unofficially, I don't know. It's a maybe. I can't tell you.'

'Well then,' replied Galpin, 'how about this? This Malik I was speaking to is deadly serious. He knows all about Caradescu and our connection with Zonkov. Zonkov works for them as well. Did I mention that? '

'Zonkov works for them as well? Jesus, is there no one we can trust?'

'It seems not. Malik the Taliban sounded pretty certain. It was almost like he had inside information.'

'He don't have squat!' answered Sieghart. 'As far as we are concerned, the plan as announced by Bedford is the only game in town. Tell the little fucker that!'

'So, the boys back home haven't told you everything, is that it?' asked Galpin, 'and they can't tell you because it's 'need to know' and if it got out it would screw things for Lady Mak and her boyfriend in the presidential palace? Am I right?'

'Darius, you know my hands are tied. I can't give out that kind of information, even to you.'

'Do you think NATO is going to pull all its air forces out of Eastern Europe and Asia? Go over to that – what did you call it? – geeky stuff. All unmanned? '

'OK, yeah, it's something like that. I don't have details and it's not yet finalized. Drones are cheaper and they don't cost American lives. I hear whispers. There are rumors that the entire USAF will soon be drones and Warm Blanket is just the first step. There's been a lot of talk lately at a high level. But that's all I know, mainly rumors and gossip. But it all makes sense.'

'Including delivery of nuclear weapons?'

'I guess so. The geeks are very proud of the plan. Thinking is that this is the future.'

'So the Taliban taxi driver is right. There's a lot more to Warm Blanket than we've been told.'

'That little piece of information is classified at the highest level. Even you shouldn't have it.'

'The Taliban may already have it! Where did they get it from?'

'Christ knows! They probably tortured one of our guys or bought it from someone like Zonkov.'

'There's one thing I haven't mentioned,' said Galpin, 'and that is that the Taliban taxi driver needs details from us right now or...'

'Or what?'

'Or he will murder our Ambassador in Tashkent.'

'Oh shit!'

'So,' asked Galpin, 'what do I tell him?'

'When do you meet him next?'

'Probably tonight, certainly no later than tomorrow morning. The bastard's stalking me. He's probably waiting outside right now.'

'Can't you stall him? The real deal on Warm Blanket mustn't get out before Sunday's election. If our girl loses then the first thing the new government will do is tear up the treaty and if they do that then every other pissy-assed little country from here to China will do the same.' said Sieghart.

'And if Madame Mak wins, then we spring the good news to her about Warm Blanket when she is safely in power for the next four years. And she can only stay in power if she follows our instructions? '

'To the letter, except that we will help her stay in office even longer than that. Our boys will help her see the benefits of not having any sort of opposition to worry about. A pro-US one-party democracy is just what we need. And what we need, we'll make sure she gets.'

'So, what do I tell the Taliban cab man?' asked Galpin.

'Tell him he's talking complete shit and tell him that if he lays one finger on any of our people, we will bomb his crappy little country back to the Stone Age. Meanwhile, I'll alert State about an assassination threat. Tell them to double the guard, put everyone on high alert.

I'll phone Bland and get him to pass the word along. Remember, Darius, keep a lid on this thing, at least until next Sunday.'

David Balfour was in a tense meeting with Hattie Reilly PhD. 'Next semester I want you to take on a new course. I am thinking that we can probably get the faculty committee and the university executive council to agree to widen the curriculum. So I am going to ask you to develop a new course in organizational behavior. Here is the standard syllabus from the US National Business Education Council. You can adapt it as you see fit.'

'What!' shouted Hattie Reilly PhD. 'You expect me to develop a completely new course, just like that! With my work load! On top of all I have to do!!'

'We do need to expand the range of courses,' explained Balfour, patiently.

'Why me?' she screeched.

'Well,' Balfour continued in emollient vein, 'the course is essential. It's a core course in most business programs and you are an expert on organizations.'

'Yes, I am an expert and that is why my courses in hotel management are so successful. Because I've made them perfect over the years! Why not ask one of the younger people? Or do it yourself? Or get someone in?'

'All, I am asking, Hattie, is that you, as our leading expert, should spearhead this new advance.'

'I refuse. I am not going to do it! I have far too much to do already. You are trying to exploit me!' With that, she stormed out of Balfour's office, flinging the door wide open. As Balfour went to the door to close it, he noticed her down the corridor in animated conversation with Nyborg. He could only hear bits of what she was saying but her grim expression told him what the gist would be.

'... told me... new course... after all I've given....who does he think he is...see the dean...'

Next Balfour called Nyborg.

'Morten, please, could you spare a minute?' Nyborg, with set face, slouched over to Balfour's office. When the door was closed, Balfour asked Nyborg if he, too, would be willing to develop a new course. He tried a tack less confrontational than the one which had failed with Hattie Reilly PhD.

'Morten, we need to bring our whole program into line with national business program guidelines, which means some new courses. One of them is financial modeling. Here is a specimen syllabus which I copied from the University of Wisconsin website. What do you think?'

'Well,' said Nyborg, 'it looks very interesting. Are you going to offer it here?'

'Yes, we are,' said Balfour. 'In fact, I thought you might like to write the syllabus and take it over.'

'What? Me? You must be joking. With all I've got to do already? When am I going to find time to do it?'

'Well, Morten, I happen to know that you also moonlight for two online distance education colleges. That must take a lot of time. Remember, we pay your salary. You could drop one of those and work for us instead.'

'I don't do any moonlighting. What I do outside is part of my - what do you call it? – my 'self-managed scholarly activity'. I am staying abreast of my subject as my contract requires me to. And what's more, I'm doing a great job full-time here without taking on new courses.'

'No you're not. You are working for these two online colleges, namely, Isaacstown Community College and the University of Rochdale, just for the extra money, not for any academic prestige. And that is affecting your job here.

165

I understand that you will shortly be evaluated. Papers published? Conferences attended?'

'Anyway,' said Morten Nyborg, 'I don't know anything about financial modeling.'

'That is strange,' said Balfour, 'since financial modeling is what you are teaching online for Isaacstown College. I even downloaded your syllabus from their website. A lot like the standard syllabus you are holding in your hand right there. Now if you can teach it for them, I don't see why you can't teach it for us.'

'Screw you!' said Nyborg, got up and walked out, slamming the door loudly behind him.

Sure enough, as Darius Galpin had predicted, Malik was waiting for him next morning outside the entrance to AUSB.

'Hey, Mister Big American Professor,' he shouted at Galpin from his cab, as Galpin was pulling into his designated parking space, 'you have something for me?'

Provost Darius Galpin walked over to Malik's car. 'No, I haven't anything. You are all wrong. There is no plan for drones. We don't know who planted the idea. Have you been talking to Zonkov? He's full of shit. Just like you if you believe him.'

'Maybe you are right, Big American Professor. Maybe we'll kill the ambassador anyway. Then you'll know we are serious.'

'That would be murder - for no reason. There would be big problems for you if you did.'

'You don't understand, American. We are not in your country. You are foreigners who come to my country to kill our children and take our oil. Uzbekistan is not your country either. Now, I give you one more chance, Big American Professor. You tell me the real details of

Operation Warm Blanket and your Ambassador in Uzbekistan, who is called Suzanne Fernandez, she will not be harmed. You have until this time tomorrow.'

'I don't have any information to give you. All I know is that NATO is going to build a second airbase here and it will be like all the others. It will be manned by NATO personnel from this country and other friendly countries.'

'I think you lie to me, American. Twenty four hours.'

Darius Galpin slumped in his office chair, wondering what sort of a mess he could have gotten himself into. He tried to put the best gloss on it by telling himself that Suzanne Fernandez would be well-guarded around the clock. She would probably be spirited safely out of Uzbekistan. But he knew just how efficient professional hit squads could be. There is no doubt that the Taliban hitmen would not be too careful when it came to taking out the Ambassador's guard detail as well. He could tell Malik that he had been right that Operation Warm Blanket was just a cover for a different plan, one to build a wall of unmanned drone stations.

If he told Malik what he knew, it would save the life of Suzanne Fernandez. But if he did, his career would be over or worse, knowing the CIA way of doing things. Who knows who Malik was in cahoots with? Maybe Malik was working with Simonov or what remained of Caradescu's party? There was still time to disrupt the election - there were three days left. If, as Sieghart had told him, he could keep a lid on things then all would be well. Maybe the Taliban wouldn't be able to get to Ambassador Fernandez? Maybe Anastasia Makarovna would win Sunday's election easily. Maybe, maybe.

Annabella Markova-Casillias still had to earn her prize, a smooth ride through Hattie Reilly's faculty evaluation procedure in return for delivering the head of David Balfour. She still had some work to do on Provost Darius Galpin.

She phoned him. 'Darius, my dear,' she purred, 'I can't forget our wonderful experience in your office. You won't keep a girl waiting any longer for more, would you? That would be teasing me.'

'Annabella, my sweet, you are never out of my thoughts. Look, why don't you come to my apartment at the embassy compound after your class this afternoon?'

'That would be wonderful darling, but what about your wife?'

'Don't worry, my dear, my wife is attending the International Ecumenical Conference in Kuala Lumpur. She won't be back until next week.'

'So, I could stay the night?'

'Yes, darling, stay the night.'

In and out of bed, that evening and through the night, Darius Galpin and Annabella Markova-Casillias, between bouts of enthusiastic unprotected love-making, discussed many things, including the future career path of Professor and Chair of Business David Balfour.

'OK, darling! Yes..ah..ah. I promise. He will be fired....oh...oh. You do that so well.'

'A girl must be sure. You promise me that Balfour will be out, and Darius, darling, I will do that to you again.'

'Oh, yes, yes please. You must do it again.'

But no pleasure lasts forever, and Darius Galpin, physically exhausted by the expert erotic skills of Associate Professor Markova-Casillias and emotionally exhausted by the stresses of corrupting a national election, arranging the murder of a leading national politician and keeping a state secret at the possible cost of the life of one of his country's most distinguished diplomats, fell into a deep and troubled sleep. Images of deaths, of diplomatic shootings, of ballot forgeries, of unmanned airplanes and hydrogen bombs, of street riots, of the luscious charms of his bedfellow, of the removal of the chair of business, of the sinister Malik and of the drug baron cum executioner Zonkov - all these merged together into one long obscene nightmare.

He woke up suddenly in a cold sweat. Annabella was sitting on the chair at the side of the bed.

'You woke me up,' she said. 'You were talking in your sleep.'

'A lot on my mind,' he told her.

'I know,' she answered, 'what was that about drones and airbases?'

'Nothing,' he said, sleepily.

'You talked a lot about Zonkov and Caradescu? You know these people? Zonkov is a very bad man. They say he killed Caradescu.'

'Only what I've read.'

'In your sleep, you said that you killed Caradescu. And you will kill Fernandez. I don't know that name.'

'No, I don't know it either.'

'Then why were you shouting it out loud?'

'I don't know. You know what nightmares are like. Just fantasies. Nothing real. Let's go back to sleep.'

Darius Galpin found it difficult to get back to sleep. What, he wondered, had his subconscious been doing to him? What had he revealed to Ms Markova-Casillias? Would she stay silent in return for his getting rid of Balfour?

He knew what he had to do first thing in the morning and that was to remove Balfour from AUSB immediately. Annabella Markova-Casillias had only asked for Balfour to be removed from being chair of the department. Better to fire him altogether and just hope that Annabella keeps her mouth shut. She might even be grateful enough to forget his nocturnal ramblings. He would need to warn her to forget everything she had heard. With Balfour gone, the gang of four would get off his back and they could occupy themselves over the election weekend with the vital task of finding themselves a new chair.

He would also need to make a few phone calls - to ex-President Potts to remind him of his promise to his former mistress, to Georgetown University and to the CIA Headquarters in Langley, VA. It would be better all round, he decided, if the exotic seductress were safely on the other side of the Atlantic as soon as possible. Maybe he could even get her an interview straight away so that she would be away during the final run-up to the election?

Fifteen

The next morning, Darius Galpin drove Annabella Markova-Casillias to the AUSB car park. They had had a long talk over breakfast and it was agreed that it would be today that the university would be firing David Balfour.

'I don't know what I was talking about in my sleep, last night,' Galpin had told her, 'but you must never mention it to anyone, ever. That is very important.'

'Of course not, darling,' Annabella had told him.

'You want me to fire David Balfour. Well, I will do that today. But, in return, you must promise me absolute silence. Understood?'

Once in his office, the provost called Mike Mulvaney, who was, as every day, in his place early.

'Mike,' said Galpin, 'can you spare a minute?'

'Mike,' began Galpin when Mulvaney had arrived, 'what is your opinion of David Balfour's work?'

'He seems to be doing a good job, from what I hear.'

'But, Mike, don't you feel that his management style is a little too, er, confrontational? Too abrasive? '

'Well, he doesn't beat about the bush. He is trying to move things along. He's bound to ruffle a few feathers. You can't make an omelet without breaking a few eggs.'

'Quite. But I've had a faculty petition requesting his dismissal.'

'What are you going to do about it? It could be some faculty troublemakers with a personal grudge.'

'Yes, it could. But I think it is best to be on the safe side.'

'So you are going to dismiss him without hearing his side of things on the say so of some malcontents? And I know malcontents. The whole department should be called the Malcontent Department. Can I just say that I disagree? He has done nothing wrong. We even gave him a new contract for three years only last month.'

'Yes, I think it would be better if we persuaded him not to try to make case out of it.'

'So, said Mulvaney, as the penny dropped, 'it's wheels within wheels, OK?'

'Precisely,' said Galpin. 'It's wheels within wheels, Company wheels. Just do it. And fast, please.'

'This unseemly haste wouldn't be anything to do with Sunday's election, would it?'

'In a way,' said Galpin, 'but not directly. By lunchtime, if you can?'

Mulvaney left Galpin's office with a bad taste in his mouth. He actually liked Balfour, even if the man came often to his office to make his unreasonable and strident demands. He was not going to enjoy terminating Balfour's career. Dave Balfour would find it difficult to get another job at his age.

Galpin then got down to the sensitive business of phoning Bland at the CIA. Bland wasn't available because it was the middle of the night on the American East Coast. He spoke instead to the duty officer on the East European desk and used that day's code word. He followed this up with an encrypted email requesting full support for getting Associate Professor Markova-Casillias out of the country for a while, maybe even permanently. He then left a message on the cellphone of Eastman Stahl, the President of Georgetown University, and sent an email to General Alaric Potts.

Annabella Markova-Casillias, sworn to secrecy, had reported back to Denis Denitsev as soon as she got into the university. Denitsev could not contain his delight.

'Are you sure? Are you sure he told you that Balfour would be leaving? Did he really tell you that Balfour was being fired from AUSB completely and not just as chair of the department?

'Yes, Denis, I am completely sure. He will be going right away, maybe even today.'

'That's wonderful, Annabella! You have done great work. You will certainly have no trouble with the faculty evaluation now. Tell me, because I am curious. How did you do it? Did you sit down and discuss it over a glass of wine, or was it, maybe, er, pillow talk?'

'Oh, Denis, you can't expect a girl to go into details. You make me blush.'

'Oh, sorry,' said Denis.

'In fact he made me swear never to breathe a word to anyone. Twice.'

'What do you mean? The moment Balfour is out, news will be all around the university in minutes.'

'No, not about Balfour, I mean the other thing.'

'What other thing?'

'The other thing. He talks in his sleep.'

'He talks in his sleep?'

'Yes,' said Annabella. 'He was saying all sorts of strange things.'

'What kind of things?'

'I can't tell you. I promised. Anyway, it is nothing to do with this place.'

'So, what is it all about then, Annabella? Tell me what he said in his sleep. It might be important.'

'OK then. What he was saying. It was very difficult to be clear. I heard the words 'wet blanket' and then 'drones' and then 'no more airbases'. Then he said a lot of stuff I couldn't make out but I distinctly heard him say out loud 'kill Caradescu'. He said that quite loud. I am sure about that.'

Denis Denitsev was making notes. '..'wet blanket, 'drones', 'no more bases', 'kill Caradescu'. Are you sure that is all you heard? What do you think he meant?'

'I don't know. You don't think he killed Caradescu, do you?'

'I don't think so,' replied Denitsev. 'They put Simonov in jail for that.'

'Could he be involved in some way?'

'I don't know. I don't think he has any connection with criminals here, or politics for that matter. The university is always telling us that we must never get involved with local matters. Look, when are you due to see him again? Tonight?'

'I guess so. His wife isn't back until Tuesday, so he will probably invite me back again.'

'Just keep your ears open. It could be nothing or it could be important.'

David Balfour was sitting across the desk from Mike Mulvaney.

'I don't like to do this, Dave,' said Mulvaney. 'I'm sorry. I am removing you from the chair of business. It's not you, Dave, in my book you are one of the best. But you know what it's like in a place like this. There are always lots of petty politics.'

'So,' replied Balfour,' you are going to just give in. Just like that? You just said I am one of the best in your book. So why not stick with the best?'

'I really wish I could,' said Mulvaney, 'but I can't overrule the faculty decisions. There has been a complaint about you from the whole faculty. Do you know they sent a petition to the provost? You have upset some people, so I am afraid you are going to have to go.'

'But you told me I had your complete support!!'

Balfour was now getting angry. 'Why don't you give me that support now, instead of just rolling over? Anyway, what petition? There was no petition or I would have heard about it! You can't keep that sort of thing quiet in small place like this!!'

'My hands are tied, Dave,' said Dean Mulvaney, shamefacedly, 'I wish I could keep you on. You've been a great chair. But some of the senior members of the department are complaining and I just can't afford to ignore faculty complaints.'

'Have you seen this petition? Can I see it? So I know what I am being charged with!'

'Dave,' whinged the Dean,' it's not like that. You are not being charged with anything. And yes, I have seen the petition. The provost showed it to me.'

'So, can I see it?'

'Sorry, Dave, it's confidential. The provost has the only copy.'

'So,' expostulated David Balfour, 'I am being fired for no reason and I am not even being allowed to see the charges against me. Whatever happened to due process, or American justice?'

'But I keep telling you, Dave, there are no charges against you. We are just asking you to step down from the position of chair in response to your colleagues' democratic request.'

'And if I refuse?'

'Then you will create a great deal of departmental disharmony. You wouldn't want that, would you?'

'Look, Mike, there is already departmental disharmony. I am the sixth chair in five years! Don't you think that is departmental disharmony enough? Have you ever wondered what, or rather who, is the source of the departmental disharmony?'

'Oh, come on, Dave, surely you are not suggesting

175

that our colleagues are conspiring against you?'

'Mike, use your eyes! There are some people in the Business Department who will conspire against anyone who takes on this job. You could give the job to the Archangel Gabriel and they would conspire against him!'

'Oh, I don't think that's the case. The entire faculty is completely loyal.'

'So you want me to step down from chair to satisfy some troublemakers, names unknown, who are hiding behind a secret petition? Which you won't let me see! '

'That's putting it a bit strong, Dave.'

'No, it's not! That's exactly what it is! How would you put it, Mike? '

'Never say never, Dave. Maybe you'll be back one day. Look at Pavlovski. He said never again and he came back for a term. He was even technically disqualified because he refused to take the faculty evaluation, but he still came back. So never say never, eh?'

'You say 'came back'. Where am I supposed to be coming back from?'

'Sorry, Dave,' said Mike Mulvaney, 'but it's not just the chair's job we are asking you to step down from. The provost is asking for your complete separation from AUSB.'

'What!!'

'Yes, Dave. You've done a great job here, but the provost feels that the harmony of the university would be better served by a complete break.'

'But I've just got a new contract!'

'And I am sure the university will honor the contract as regards early resignation.'

'But I am not resigning, I am being fired!'

'I'm sorry, Dave. I would like you to stay, myself, but, as I told you, my hands are tied.'

Meanwhile, Darius Galpin was getting impatient with the seven-hour time difference between AUSB and Georgetown. He had spoken to the CIA liaison already and they would talk to the president of Georgetown University as soon as it was a civilized hour. There would be no communication before 3pm local time. The call came through late Friday afternoon as the university was winding down for the weekend.

'This is a helluva favor you Company boys are asking from me at short notice,' said Eastman Stahl, a long-time senior diplomat and Company man who had effortlessly transferred to academia where he could oversee recruitment into both of his previous careers, as well as stay on the DC scene.

'Can you do it, sir?' asked Galpin.

'Yep, we'll do it. Get her in my office no later than noon tomorrow and I'll wire the invitation to President Spring. Goodbye, Galpin.'

'Goodbye, sir.'

The email invitation to Associate Professor Annabella Markova-Casillias to attend the President of Georgetown University to be interviewed for a tenured position as a professor of business appeared almost immediately, with copies to President Spring and Provost Galpin. Annabella went to the AUSB Human Resources Department and asked them how she could get there.

'There's only one flight,' she was told. 'It leaves here at ten fifteen this evening. Change at Frankfurt and Atlanta, arriving at Dulles at nine thirty eight in the morning, Eastern Standard Time. You should just about make the midday interview. If you pay us now, you can get a reimbursement from Georgetown.' Annabella handed over her credit card and the HR Department clerk made the booking.

She met up with Galpin. 'Oh, my darling,' she told

him. 'We cannot be together tonight. I have to be in Washington by lunchtime tomorrow. I am so sorry. But be happy for me. I have a very important interview at Georgetown University!'

'Darling, I will miss you. But I am so glad that you are going to such a great university. Your friend President Potts has kept his promise, then?'

'Yes, he has been very kind, just as you have been, my dear.'

'What time is your flight?'

'Ten fifteen. I will sleep on the plane.'

'Would you like me to drive you to the airport?'

'Oh, there is no need, my darling. Denis Denitsev has already offered to take me. You must rest!'

'Have a good flight!' said Galpin. 'We'll see you next week!'

So, thought Provost Darius Galpin, that was one problem temporarily solved. At least Annabella Markova-Casillias would not be telling the world what he had been talking about in his sleep.

She went home and hurriedly packed a bag. As she did so, she wondered why Denis Denitsev was so anxious to drive her to the airport with still four hours before take-off. He picked her up from her apartment on the dot of 6pm.

After a few minutes she could see that they were going the wrong way. 'The airport is in the other direction,' she told Denitsev.

'That is why we are so early. There is a good friend I want you to meet. Don't worry, we have plenty of time.'

They sat in silence until Denitsev drew up outside a grotesque vulgar Balkan pastiche of *Le Petit Trianon*. It was the sort of house that only piratical businessmen or corrupt government ministers could ever afford. The two armed guards obviously recognized Denitsev because they immediately opened the iron gates to let the car in. There was no-one to greet the two AUSB professors in the garden but the door was unlocked. Denitsev was obviously familiar with the place because he quickly took Annabella inside without ringing the bell. Waiting in the hall was General Alexei Alexandrov who greeted Denitsev like a favorite son.

'Denis! What a pleasure it is to see you! You know, you don't come to see me often enough! And who's your little friend?'

'Alexei, this is Professor Annabella Markova-Casillias. She is from the American University.'

With old-fashioned gallantry, Alexandrov kissed her hand. 'My dear, I think you are far too beautiful to be a professor. Professors are old men with long grey beards. You should be a model or an actress!'

'That is very kind of you!'

'Not kind, my dear, I am just being truthful.'

'Thank you!'

Denis Denitsev cut in. 'Sorry to hurry you, General, but the professor has a plane to catch. She has not much time but she has something to tell you.'

'Go on, my dear,' said Alexandrov and Annabella told him what she had told Denitsev that morning about Darius Galpin's nocturnal ramblings, She told Alexandrov about the words Galpin had used - 'wet blanket', 'drones', 'kill Caradescu' , 'no more airbases'.

Although they had meant nothing to a simple nymphomaniac, Alexandrov instantly understood their importance. He had been with Prime Minister Anastasia Makarovna when she had signed the treaty for Operation Warm Blanket. He was also aware that there was a lot of unofficial speculation that Warm Blanket might just be a cover for replacing all NATO airbases with drone stations and he also knew, which Annabella did not, that AUSB, the

American University of the Southern Balkans, was kept going financially by the CIA as a low-level intelligence-gathering operation. Alexandrov also knew that Provost Darius Galpin was, at that moment, the CIA's top field operative in the region.

Alexandrov affected a lack of interest. 'Yes,' he said, 'it could mean something, or maybe nothing. Have you told anyone else apart from Denis and me?'

'No one, General.'

That was literally true because although she did not realize what the game was, she was absolutely sure that she was in the middle of some game or other. So she had told no one apart from Denis, and now, General Alexandrov. Instead, she had written it all down in a well-hidden notebook. A girl must always have a little insurance.

'Denis,' said Alexandrov to Denitsev, 'thank you so much for bringing Miss Markova to me. You do not need to take her to the airport. I will have my limousine take her instead, with a couple of motorcycles. She will arrive like a film star! That will be much faster than your old car. And it will give me a little more time to talk to the good professor.'

Denis Denitsev knew when three's a crowd and when he was being dismissed. So he turned and went back to his car. As he closed the door, he saw the look in the General's eye which left no doubt what Annabella was expected to do next. She knelt down in front of the General and slowly unzipped his pants.

What a perfectly wonderful evening this has turned out to be, thought General Alexei Alexandrov. Not only was he being attended to by this exquisite and delightful creature, but he had also been delivered of the sort of information which he knew would be sufficient to sink Makarovna's government should he ever need to. He could not quite decide which of the two gave him the greater pleasure.

Darius Galpin was just starting to congratulate himself on the way he had managed to get rid of the problem of Associate Professor Markova-Casillias. She would be well on the way to the airport by now, he told himself. He was rudely woken from his reverie by a phone call.

'Your twenty four hours is up, Big American Professor. You still haven't given me details of Operation Warm Blanket.'

'But I told you all I know. I don't know anything else.'

'Yes, but you are lying, Big American Professor!'

'I'm sorry but that's all there is.'

'You got TV, Big American Professor? You switch on your famous CNN right now. I told you we are serious.'

Galpin switched on the TV.

'..we are getting reports from Tashkent in Uzbekistan of an explosion at the American Embassy there. We understand that the car of the American ambassador was attacked and there have been some fatalities. Quintin Allibone is our central Asia correspondent and he is in Tashkent right now. Quintin, what do we know?'

'Well, Monita, there was a large explosion at about seven pm local time. It completely destroyed the ambassador's car and did some damage to the surrounding buildings. It is believed that the ambassador, Suzanne Fernandez, may have been inside the vehicle at the time. So far, no one group has claimed responsibility for

181

the attack, which is being described as a 'terrorist action'. Monita.'

'Thank you, Quintin. We'll bring you updates on that breaking story just as soon as we have them. Next..'

The phone rang again in Galpin's study. It was Malik again.

'So, Big American Professor, you still think we are not serious? You know what we want. Tomorrow morning, ten am, Winter Park.'

'I'll be there.'

'I'll be parked outside the main gate.' The phone went dead. Then it immediately rang again.

'Provost, I am glad I caught you in at this time. Can I drop by your office right now?'

'Professor Balfour. Yes, of course. Please come right around.' David Balfour was not a man to hide his feelings and he was bloody mad. He did not like Darius Galpin one little bit.

'Is it true that you are firing me?' began Balfour.

'Yes,' answered Galpin bluntly, 'you are detrimental to departmental and university harmony.'

'Who says I am detrimental to university harmony?'

'I had a petition. It would have been irresponsible for me not to act on it.'

'Can I see it?'

'I'm afraid not.'

'Why not? It would be fair, would it not, for me to see the evidence against me so that I could challenge it? Even murderers get a fair trial,'

'I'm sorry you feel so strongly, but it would not be in the best interests of the university to show it to you. For two reasons, one, it was not addressed to you, it was addressed to me – confidentially. And I cannot break a confidence. Secondly, if you see the names on the list, it might damage their future careers if you ever move on to a senior position. Sorry.'

'Don't worry. I already know their names. It's the old guard isn't it - Nyborg, Denitsev, Reilly and Smalley? They are the departmental troublemakers.'

'Troublemakers? I prefer to call them distinguished colleagues. All of them have given years of service to AUSB.'

'No, they are troublemakers and you know they are. They will screw the next guy, just like they screwed me and all the others.'

'I'm sorry, I can't comment on your wild accusations, except to say that you still have the option of resignation. It will look better on your résumé than being fired. I have been looking at your contract. If you resign, you will get severance pay.'

'Severance pay?'

'Yes, in return for a resignation letter you will get, let me see – your contract is for three years at one week per year - you will get three weeks salary as severance pay. But if we fire you, then nothing.'

'Screw you! I'll see you in court!'

'That would be a waste of time and money. You couldn't possibly win. The university will have better lawyers and we will make sure there is a rock-solid case against you. If you are stupid enough to take us on, we will destroy you. You're not a young man, Balfour. Do you really want to spend your retirement on welfare in some trailer park?'

'You bastard!'

'There's another thing. Before you leave here, for the last time, you must never, ever, speak about what has happened to anyone, either here in the university or back

183

home in the states. Read your contract. There is a non-disclosure clause which you signed up to. We advise you to leave right away, maybe before tomorrow. All staff and faculty here will be told not to talk to you or they will risk instant dismissal.'

'You can't do that! Where the hell do you think you are, North Korea?'

'Oh, yes we can,' said Galpin. 'You will find it healthier to do exactly as we tell you.'

'Healthier?'

'Yes, definitely healthier. It's wheels within wheels, you might say. Go clear your desk. You have one hour.'

Sixteen

Galpin had slept badly for a second night and was not pleased at having to be at the Winter Park gates at 10 am. He drove there in his car, wearing his usual workman's disguise. The city was quiet on the eve of the election. It was a sullen, heavy silence as if the city were waiting for a summer storm although the storm season had already passed and the unmistakable smell of autumn was in the air.

There was to be a rally in Revolution Square by Simonov's liberal party that afternoon. Simonov was still in jail awaiting a formal arraignment but his supporters were predictably angry and some level of violence was not only expected, but almost inevitable.

The Chief of Police was planning a major show of pre-emptive force. All police leave had been cancelled and riot control officers were being equipped with all the latest up-to-date weaponry necessary to contain a major disturbance. Just to be on the safe side,

President Balashirov had ordered all the streets around the square to be closed off and to have tanks and armored cars parked under the trees. Many residents had fled the city for the beaches to take advantage of the last of the warm weather as well as to avoid the promised Saturday afternoon violence.

Galpin immediately spotted Malik waiting for him. Malik motioned Galpin to get into the taxi.

'So, big American Professor, you see the pictures from Tashkent? Your Ambassador is dead and two of your marines also. It's a dirty business. Now you talk, yes? We like your Mister Ambassador Feldstein. We wouldn't like anything like that to happen to him.'

Darius Galpin considered the threat to Ambassador

Feldstein, which Malik was obviously capable of carrying out and quickly made the calculation that the election would be the next day and Makarovna was sure to win, so it didn't matter anymore if he told Malik all he knew. Keep a lid on things until Sunday, Sieghart had told him. Well, with just one day to go, and the election in the bag for Makarovna, Galpin considered that he had done his patriotic duty. At least Joseph Feldstein would not be harmed.

There were many more countries where unmanned airstrips would be replacing regular airbases. If Operation Warm Blanket were to succeed, it would need all of them to go along with the plan. Once word got out, the whole plan would fall through. But Galpin no longer cared about his country's long term interest. He just wanted the whole nightmare to stop. So he told Malik what he knew.

'OK Malik, if that's your real name, I'll tell you. The eventual plan is to remove all NATO air force personnel from Europe and Asia and replace them with an air force of drones, completely unmanned, some with nuclear weapons. That's all I know. I don't have any details.'

'Tell me about why you fixed the election tomorrow? Why do you get mixed up with that stupid criminal, Zonkov?'

'That was insurance. We want Makarovna to win. Caradsecu and Simonov would have been more difficult to deal with. O.B. wants Warm Blanket to go through as easily as possible.'

'And you've paid her well?'

'No need. She knows her duty. She knows that she is safer working with NATO than with some of the crazy countries further east. You can tell your bosses that Operation Warm Blanket is just a cover for the real plan.'

'So, if Makarovna accepts this drone plan, it will be easier to get all the other countries to accept it as well?'

'Certainly.'

'Thank you, Big American Professor! Drones, eh? It makes sense now that you Americans can't afford real soldiers anymore. So now you can kill our children and our old people from a safe rat hole in California.'

He nodded at the iron gates of the Winter Park. 'It's too early for your girls, eh, Big American Professor? Ha, ha, ha!'

Hattie Reilly PhD called a meeting of her little group at a coffee shop near the university building for midday Saturday. 'He's gone, I hear,' she began.

'Yes, kicked out without a hope, was what I heard,' said Denitsev.

'I think we can consider that a job well done,' put in Smalley. 'I never liked the little so-and-so. He just wasn't right for this department. However did he get appointed in the first place?'

'Beats me,' said Morten Nyborg. 'He was Mulvaney's choice after Oliviera left but he wouldn't take it at first, so Mulvaney did it until Balfour's arm could be twisted hard enough.'

'As I recall,' said Reilly, 'Mulvaney was fed up of doing the job himself. So any warm body who could walk upright would have been OK for Mike.'

'It is definitely something which needs changing,' said Nyborg. 'I mean, all the regular professors have to go through our evaluation process before they can be appointed and that is as it should be, an open democratic process.'

'You are right there,' put in Hattie Reilly PhD. 'I designed it myself. It has worked well. All you three have been through it. Although your five year review is due, isn't it, Morten?'

187

'Next year,' replied Nyborg.

'Don't worry, you will be fine,' Reilly assured him.

'I think we need the same sort of democratic process for choosing the chair,' said Denitsev.

'That's right,' said Smalley, 'a vote of all faculty members. Or at least those with voting rights.'

'Which is just as four,' said Reilly. 'We are the only faculty in the Business Department with tenure.'

'It will take too long to change the rules in a faculty meeting, so this time we will have to leave it to Dean Mulvaney to appoint someone. And change the rules as soon as possible so that Mike doesn't have to make the choice next time,' said Smalley.

'Which means that we need to find a new chair pretty quick and present the choice to Mike Mulvaney. If we do it right, he can be made to think it was his own idea,' said Morten Nyborg.

'It has to be someone we can trust - someone like us. Maybe even one of us?'

'Well,' said Reilly, 'it doesn't have to be someone who's tenured. Anyone could do it. They would need to be here for a while, so they would need to be through with the faculty evaluation process for a year or two.'

'Speaking of going through the evaluation process,' said Smalley to Denitsev. 'What about your little *protégée*, Annabella Markova-Casillias?'

'Oh, I forgot to mention,' said Denitsev, 'Annabella is not here.'

'Not here, what do you mean?'

'Well, late last night, she suddenly got an invitation to go for an interview at Georgetown University today. Apparently she is seeing the president there, Eastman Stahl, about a job. She should be there just about now.'

'When did she leave?'

'Last night, on the Frankfurt plane.'

'The same plane as Balfour?'

'Could be.'

'Wowee!!' said Nyborg. 'That is big time! Wow! Georgetown!'

'Don't wet yourself,' said Reilly. 'It must all be courtesy of our ex-president and sexual harasser, Alaric Potts, who has connections.'

'Do you mean,' asked Smalley, incredulously, 'that Potts fixed it for her?'

'How else? Potts lives in DC. He wants her nearby.'

'I'm amazed,' said Smalley, 'I never thought that sort of thing went on. She still has to pass the interview, though. She might not get it.'

Hattie Reilly PhD was sarcastic in reply. 'Get real. Potts is a three-star general who knows everybody who matters. Eastman Stahl is President of Georgetown and long-time DC wheeler-dealer, Christ knows how many favors he owes Potts. Can't you just put two and two together? Of course she's going to get it.'

'So Annabella is off the candidates list for chair here,' said Smalley, chastened by Hattie Reilly's rebuke.

'Well off,' answered Denis Denitsev. 'I don't even expect to see her back here on Monday.'

'So,' concluded Hattie Reilly PhD, 'it's one of us four.'

'Not me,' said Nyborg. 'I have far too much to do. I have to prepare for my re-evaluation.'

'Nor me,' said Denis Denitsev. 'I need to spend a lot of time with the Ministry. I do a lot of liaison work for AUSB. I couldn't do that if I were chair. What about you Hattie?'

'Oh, I don't think I could do it. I just have so much to do. Articles, meetings, it never ends.'

'So that just leaves you, Richard,' said Nyborg. 'Would you like to be chair?'

'Not me, thank you. I've seen the workload,' replied

189

Richard Smalley. 'Anyway, it should be an American. Besides, I have my research to consider.'

'Research, you actually do research?' asked Morten Nyborg, incredulously.

'Yes, research. This is supposed to be a seat of learning.'

'And what are you researching right now,' asked Nyborg with a sneer.

'If you must know, I am writing a paper on the development of ethical standards in the negotiation procedures for administering the European Common Agricultural Policy.'

'Tell me, Richard, will you be getting George Clooney and Julia Roberts to play the leads when they make it into a film?'

'Will it be R-rated - with lots of sex and violence?'

'Very funny! You can laugh, but I happen to think that research is important.'

'Look,' said Hattie Reilly PhD, 'research is all very well if you want to spend forty years in one place and get promoted slowly. But the quick way to get on is to become departmental chair. You do a good job here, Richard, and it will look great on your résumé, a fast track promotion. You will still have time to do your research.'

'I don't know,' said Smalley.

'You can do it, Richard, certainly better than that jerk, Balfour. Better than Oliviera. Even better than Mulvaney,' Reilly tried to persuade him. She actually thought that Smalley would be a good pliable choice. Not that he possessed the gravitas for the job, or the human qualities essential for someone who would need to spend a lot of time in face-to-face contact with his colleagues. He was definitely not the cleverest member of the department, although he thought he was. No, Hattie Reilly PhD wanted Smalley as chair because she could manipulate him and browbeat him easily.

'I'll think about it,' said Smalley.

Annabella Markova-Casillias had had a long flight and she had made it to the office of President Eastman Stahl of Georgetown University with only minutes to spare before the noon appointment. She was a little disheveled and tired. Trying to sleep on a plane is always difficult for anyone over the age of five. Annabella's night had further been interrupted by the attempts at conversation by a surprise fellow-traveler, her departmental chair, Doctor David Balfour himself.

'Whatever are you doing here?' asked Balfour.

'I might ask the same. I am going to Georgetown University for an interview at noon tomorrow. And you?'

'Oh, something has come up suddenly. I have to get back to Oklahoma.'

'Must be serious?'

'Yes, it is. Isn't this a coincidence? You and I on the same plane.'

'Yes, a real coincidence. Change at Atlanta?'

'Yip, change at Atlanta.'

Both were thinking the same thoughts - why is he/she on his/her way across the wide Atlantic at this very time and would he/she be coming back to AUSB? Once again Annabella got the powerful feeling that she was in someone else's game as a pawn, not a player. Balfour felt exactly the same. The brutality and urgency of his dismissal were of a degree he had never experienced before, even in the squalid, peevish world of university politics. Something was definitely going on and they had been removed, both realized, because they were, somehow, in the way.

As Hattie Reilly had predicted, Annabella passed the

cursory interview and was quickly offered a tenured, five-year position as an associate professor.

'We'd like you to start as soon as possible, Miss Markova,' said President Eastman Stahl. 'Do you have much to do back home? Packing and stuff?'

'Nothing much, I can get shippers to pack up my apartment and have it sent on. But, isn't it a bit unusual for me not to give notice and to start immediately.'

'Don't worry about that,' said Stahl. 'I have cleared it with Curtley Spring. We go back a long way. We've got you a room in the University Lodge for the next week or so. Welcome to Georgetown.' Stahl held out his hand.

'Thank you,' said a bemused Annabella.

From the Georgetown University Lodge she sent news of her success back to all her contacts via *Facebook*. She also sent private emails to Galpin, Denitsev, Spring and Alexandrov. All four were fulsome in their congratulations. For Galpin, Denitsev and Spring, her appointment was just what they had expected. Only General Alexandrov was surprised. If the Americans will remove such a minor embarrassment so efficiently, he reasoned, then his deductions about what Annabella had told him concerning Galpin's sleep-talking must be true.

The Saturday afternoon eve-of-election rally by the Simonovistas, as the leaderless liberal group now called themselves, had passed off with only the normal amount of bloodletting and the Chief of Police had not had to call upon his armored riot police, nor had Balashirov had to authorize the use of his heavy artillery. Zonkov, having been told not to interfere any more, had gone back to his non-political business activities.

The rally had taken the form of a protest march from Revolution Square through the main shopping street, King Cyril Street, to gather outside the American Embassy and chant 'Free Simonov!' Then there was the traditional burning of the Stars and Stripes and a little token stone throwing.

Joe Feldstein observed, as he watched the demonstration from a high window, 'it's almost as if they've given up.'

'Well with one leader dead and the other in the chokey, there's not much organized opposition to our girl. She probably has it in the bag already,' replied his deputy, Assistant Ambassador James Groznow.

'All without dirty tricks, eh, Jim?'

'Not from our side, Ambassador, you can be sure of that.'

'I'm glad to hear that, Jim. If this thing comes apart, some important heads are going to roll.'

By Sunday evening, the re-election of the Conservatives was confirmed. Anastasia Makarovna would be prime minister for at least four more years. Her win had turned out to be quite decisive. It had been predicted that the vote would be a three-way split with Makarovna getting about 40% of the poll. But, in the event, Makarovna's count was well over 50% and she had scored an outright victory.

There was a small gathering of embassy officials in the embassy compound clubhouse bar late on Sunday night. The Ambassador made a toast to continuing co-operation and good will between the host country and the United States and announced that he had already spoken to Prime Minister Makarovna and congratulated her on her success.

'You know,' he said to Sieghart and Galpin, as he circulated, 'this is the best result we could have hoped for. Do you realize that she got about half a million more votes than anyone expected? Thanks to our honest, democratic way of doing things.'

'Thanks,' said Sieghart to Galpin, quietly, after the ambassador had moved away, 'to Konstantin Zonkov for photocopying all those ballot papers. That's what he should have said.'

In the splendid bedroom of the presidential palace, newly re-elected Prime Minister Anastasia Makarovna and long-time President Leonid Balashirov were drinking champagne and watching the late election results come in. It was already midnight.

'You'll need to go down to the Square for your victory speech,' said the president.

'I have it written. Since yesterday.'

'You were that confident?'

'Of course, that demonstration yesterday was a washout. There is no real opposition anymore. You didn't need to bring up those tanks.'

'Oh the tanks were a very good idea,' said Balashirov. 'It helps keep the peace if the people are reminded now and then just where the power lies. It's like showing a dog the whip. You don't have to use it, just let them see it.'

'I like that. I like a strong government with a strong leader. Now that the government has an overall majority at last, we will be able to drag this country to its feet.'

'Had you thought who is going to be in your new cabinet?'

'The same faces, mostly. Rumescu, Nikolaides, Deltov, Alexandrov...'

'Alexandrov, are you keeping him?'

'I think I have to. Better to have him inside the tent pissing out, than outside the tent pissing in, as Lyndon Johnson once said.'

194

'Think twice about Alexandrov, my dear. He's a crook and a traitor. My advice would be to kick him out now and then have him charged with tax evasion, or stealing state assets. Something like that. He could be on trial for years and while he's in jail, you'll be safe.'

'I'll think about it. You've always given me good advice.'

'If you are going to fire Alexandrov then now is the time to do it. Now get dressed and go make your speech.'

As soon as the university opened on Monday morning, Hattie Reilly PhD began her enthusiastic lobbying to have Richard Smalley made Chair of Business She went to see Dean Mulvaney first.

'Mike,' she told him, 'I must say, it was damned rude of Balfour just to leave like that, without even a word.'

'He had sudden family matters to attend to in Oklahoma.'

'We will miss him. He was a good professor.'

'So you didn't sign a petition to have him removed, then, did you Hattie?'

'That was just a request to get him to step down as Chair. We didn't expect him to storm off in a sulk. Still, we need a new chair.'

'Yes,' said Mulvaney wearily, 'I suppose we do. Are you putting yourself forward for the job?'

'No, Mike, not me. I think you should offer the job to Richard Smalley.'

'Does he want it? I thought he was all tied up with his research into - what? – the business practices in the automobile industry or some such.'

'Oh, I think he can be persuaded to take it, if the offer is right.'

'You know what I think, Hattie? I think the guy

195

would be a disaster in the job. Balfour was good at the job because he knew how to handle people and he stood no bullshit. Smalley is lousy with people. He hasn't got any friends anyone's ever seen him with. He's about as cold as a human being can be, without actually being dead.'

'Think about it, Mike. There's nobody else, unless you want to take it over again yourself?'

'OK, I'll think about it. I'll check his file. Before he was appointed, we would have to see if we can get him Company clearance with Sieghart.'

'Good point, Mike. We can both vouch for him.'

'True, Hattie, but Richard being Australian, might be a problem with Sieghart. We can only try.'

During the next few days, Hattie Reilly PhD was busy talking to all and sundry, boosting the case for making Smalley the new chair. Even the non-voters were lobbied, just in case the dean would ask them their opinions, which, of course, he wouldn't.

She decided it was better to build a groundswell of support so that when Smalley took the job, as Reilly was now certain she could persuade him to, there would be no possible dissent from any quarter. When she approached Smalley a second time, a couple of days later, Smalley accepted with his natural ill-grace.

'All right,' he said. 'I'll do it - for the time being.'

Although Mike Mulvaney was a long-time CIA man, his clearance, and now his age, meant that he had never had to get involved with anything more than a little informal reporting of everyday gossip – who was in and who was out, who had been heard making anti-American noises etc. He regularly reported this tittle-tattle back to Colonel Sieghart at the embassy when they met every few weeks at some embassy function or other. So low was the level of his clearance that he had met the Ambassador only once. Today he went to see John Sieghart who welcomed him warmly.

'Mike, it's good to see you! What's new?'

Mike Mulvaney told him the details of the sudden departures of Annabella Markova-Casillias and David Balfour while Sieghart made notes. When Mulvaney had finished his report, Sieghart asked him who would be taking over from Balfour.

'This man,' said Mulvaney. 'He's called Richard Smalley,' and handed over Smalley's personal file.

'Yes,' said Sieghart. 'We know about Smalley. He's Canadian, isn't he?'

'Australian,' corrected Mulvaney.

'I don't know if your provost, Doctor Galpin, has told you, but there has been a new ruling. From now on, everybody in our universities at chair level and above has to have CIA clearance.'

'Yes, that's what I came about. Can we bring Smalley in, as a temporary at the basic level?'

'Could be possible,' replied Sieghart. 'I'll need to speak to him myself. Can you arrange a meeting? I could come over to the university.'

As a new chair, Smalley was interviewed by Darius Galpin and Mike Mulvaney. Richard Smalley could not quite understand why this sixty-something ex-soldier was sitting in on the meeting. The man asked no questions but seemed to be writing copious notes. For some reason, there was also a tape recorder running. Finally, the interview ended with Smalley none the wiser as to what it had all been about.

Darius Galpin shook Smalley's hand and thanked him for attending.

'Good talking to you, Richard. Remember, anything you hear which may be of interest to the security authorities, just let me know and I will pass it on to the Colonel here. And congratulations on your new job!'

After Smalley had left, Sieghart told Galpin, 'Yeah, he'll do. We'll grade him F-3, so he doesn't get near anything classified.'

'Thanks, John. Appreciate it.'

'What was all that about?' said Smalley to himself once out of Galpin's office. He did not even realize that he was now an unpaid CIA informant, grade F-3.

Seventeen

Prime Minister Makarovna began work early on the Monday morning after the election. Even though she had not got to sleep until nearly three am after the round of victory parties, she was at her desk by nine. Her first job was the appointment of her ministers. She had taken Balashirov's advice. Alexandrov was not called. Instead, she made Fatih Nikolaides her Minister of Defense.

Alexandrov had been waiting by the phone for his summons. When it had not come, he phoned the prime minister on her direct line and she agreed to meet him at her office. His driver took him to the front entrance and he marched right in. 'Am I not to be in your government, Tasha?' he asked.

'I am very sorry, Alexei, but no. Fatih Nikolaides is Defense Minister.'

'Nikolaides! Nikolaides! The little corporal? What the hell does Corporal Nikolaides know about defense? I am a trained military officer! A general! When Nikolaides did his military service, he was a driver for officers! You are making that man Minister of Defense instead of me? Me, a full general! Why? Why, Tasha? Haven't I been like a father to you all these years? Why are you deserting me now?'

'I think you know why, Alexei. You've been too much involved with buying weapons and planes for our armed services. You are in collusion with some people in the Finance Ministry and between you, you've all become very rich. People are noticing, Alexei. They see your big house and your country estate and your expensive mistresses and your regular trips to Geneva to visit your money. I want this government to be honest and to look honest as well!'

'So, you are casting your good friend aside, just because you don't need him anymore. Because you couldn't fire me before when you needed me and you needed the army because were clinging on to power by your fingertips. But now it's OK, yes? Now you are safe and you don't need your old friend anymore!'

'That's politics, Alexei.'

'Well, let me tell you, Madame Prime Minister, that you are doing a very stupid foolish thing if you try to get rid of Alexei Alexandrov like an old boot! Madame Prime Minister, you and I are now enemies and I have some big, important friends! You'd better believe me!' And with that, he turned, flung open the door of the prime ministerial office and stamped down the stairs shouting curses about 'that woman' and her treachery and ingratitude.

Makarovna's next meeting after Alexandrov had left, was with Joseph Feldstein, the US Ambassador. She greeted him warmly.

'Mister Ambassador, what a pleasant surprise. How good to see you! '

'The pleasure is all mine, Prime Minister.'

'May I personally offer my government's deepest sympathy and condolences to the families of the victims of the appalling events in Tashkent. I have already sent a message to President Bedford.'

'Thank you, Prime Minister. I knew Suzanne Fernandez and her family very well. She and I were at Harvard together. This modern world, with its terrorism! Sometimes I despair. Anyway, I am here now to congratulate you personally on your outright victory. It must feel good to be safe for a few years.'

'Yes, indeed. I think my party can stay in office safely and make some important improvements. This is why Operation Warm Blanket matters so much to my country. It will bring jobs and much needed foreign exchange. I was so happy to receive your assurance last week that NATO still intends to implement it according to the treaty.'

'Yes Anastasia. It remains in place. Only the final details and project schedule still have to be finalized.

'That is good, Joe. I know I can trust the United States.'

'I have one other thing to talk to you about, Anastasia.'

'Oh yes? And what is that?'

'Well, this is a little delicate. The Secretary of State, Alison Treadwell, whom I believe you have already met, will be going into it in more detail when she visits next month.'

Prime Minister Makarovna looked puzzled as the Ambassador continued.

'We in the United States foreign service are very conscious of the importance of stability and democracy in our sister nations,' he began. 'We are very keen to make sure that only sensible, pro-western governments are supported in this region. We also see the need for continuity and steady development.'

'As do we all, Joe, as do we all.'

'Yes Ma'am. What we are concerned about is not having any avoidable disruption by constant changes of administration. Ideally, we would prefer to see a government like yours in place for a long enough time that you can achieve the goals you have set yourself for your country. We see your government, Anastasia, with its outright mandate, as being in a position to consolidate, maybe even permanently, your control of the country. It would be in the joint interests of both our nations, of course.'

'Of course, Joe, but we, like the United States, have a

constitution which guarantees four-yearly elections. We can't change that.'

'No, no, of course not. Nothing must subvert the democratic rights of the people. I think Alison has some more ideas. I am sure she will be able to explain what we have in mind when you meet her.'

'I am looking forward to it, Mister Ambassador.'

When he had gone, Anastasia went over the conversation again in her mind. Was the United States, upholder of all that was fair and democratic, really asking her to fix things so that the country was turned into a one-party state with her as prime minister for life? It certainly sounded like it.

Richard Smalley began his reign as chair of business with a triumph of self-importance. Believing that his minute-by-minute schedule would be of vital interest to every one of his colleagues, he was not slow in advertising his indispensability as a man who would be on call every minute of the day. A list of times when he would be able to receive his colleagues in audience was pinned up outside his office and emailed to the entire university.

Then he took to emailing everyone in the department with his casual thoughts about the university and his role in it. These ideas, invariably commonplace and banal, were transmitted at intervals of an hour or less as if they were magisterial pronouncements of historic importance. The professors were assailed with a torrent of email messages about his quotidian trivia.

For example, he might write

'..from 08.00 am until 08.25 am, I will be in conference with Assistant Professor Ivan Petrov-Smith. As you will know, Professor Petrov-Smith is the Business Department representative on the inter-departmental library advisory sub-committee. We will be discussing the very important matter of the mechanism for reporting faculty concerns over library opening hours back to the main University Executive Council.'

or,

'..from 12.15pm to 12.45pm I will be at lunch. (If nothing turns up before then!)'

The parenthetic clause was Smalley's feeble attempt at self-deprecating humor. Unfortunately, he was not possessed of a real sense of humor and so all such attempts merely came across as inverted arrogance.

The snowstorm of electronic vanity was ignored by the majority of the faculty and after a week or two, most of its recipients would automatically delete it unread.

Like many newcomers to authority, Smalley had ideas about developing the social activities of his new little realm. Attempts to develop an *ésprit de corps* through shared socializing are a standard ploy of the novice manager.

If, the simple-minded thinking goes, ordinary rank-and-file workers can have regular get-togethers, maybe dinner, if the work-force is of mixed sexes, or a drinking session if it is all-male, then there will be some synergistic bonding which will be of benefit to all.

So the new manager, filled with optimism about the beneficial effects of such an initiative, institutes some social event - or possibly several of them - with the naive expectation that that is what his underlings actually want.

A moment's thought would have told him that his expectations are definitely ill-founded. There are, indeed, many excellent reasons why off-duty semi-compulsory socializing is a very stupid idea.

The first and most obvious reason is that it does not need a manager to organize a dinner. The ordinary toilers can quite easily do it for themselves. That they haven't done so would lead the average logical person to the obvious conclusion that the reason why there haven't hitherto been any social events for the departmental rank and file is because the departmental rank and file don't want them.

People prefer to choose their own off-duty companions. Being forced to spend valuable leisure time with people one does not particularly like, is not a relaxing pleasurable experience. It is a continuation of work by other means. In fact, the departmental dinner, after-hours midweek, is harder than regular work. For those many who are intimidated by social gatherings, such unasked-for overtime can be a real ordeal.

Tongues loosened by a few glasses of wine can expose animosities and resentments which sober prudence would keep hidden. A wise man will need not to drink alcohol at all at such gatherings if he is to avoid accidental career-damaging indiscretions. At the same time, of course, he will be carefully noting the lapses of others for future use.

A third problem with an off-duty social gathering is that many members of the group will not be able to attend, for very good reasons, such as domestic or family responsibilities. The event will certainly disadvantage such people, not because they are missing out on good fellowship or hospitality, which will be on limited display anyway. Any absentee can be certain that they will be talked about, especially if the gossipers are a bunch of well-lubricated off-duty university professors.

But, ignoring the received wisdom of ages that out-of-hours socializing is, at best, an unpleasant duty for all concerned, Richard Smalley embarked on a regular series of Wednesday dinners and duly sent out invitations. Older hands in the department gave the program a month before it would be quietly dropped.

For the first dinner there was a fair turnout, consisting mostly of the single, older, expatriate men, the 'old sweats' of the department, who were aware of the hidden dangers of combining duty with so-called pleasure. They gathered in the 'Tender Vines' restaurant at the appointed hour.

As is normal in the country, the food did not appear simultaneously for all the diners - each separate dish arrived at an interval of ten minutes or so with the result that only one person would be eating at any one time. The effect of phased eating, which may have been deliberate on the part of a restaurateur selling wine, was that the diners without food tended to drink more while waiting for their solid food to appear and absorb the alcohol. Consequently their tongues became looser quicker.

It might be expected by non-academic folk that discourse among a gathering of sixteen or so highly-educated full-, associate- and assistant professors, all with PhD degrees, might tend towards the sophisticated. Obviously there would be talk of university politics, of scholastic developments, of news in the world of higher education.

All this serious talk would be leavened with wit, with sharp insights and clever anecdotes recounted with incisive humor. As befits intellectuals in relaxation mode, the scholarly epigrams and the learned aphorisms, the sharp original observations and the well-rounded phrases would be presented in fully formed sentences structured with careful attention to the accurate use of subordinate clauses, subjunctive moods, precisely used prepositions and compound tenses.

The speakers would, naturally enough, also employ a vocabulary sufficiently wide such that every complex thought, no matter how subtle, would be precisely defined by the most perfect fitting *mot juste.*

There was a little desultory chitchat while the first drink was consumed. Soon, though, the wine began to work its usual magic.

'Here's a question!' said Morten Nyborg. 'Why can't eunuchs play football?'

'Because they've got no balls!' He completed the clever joke.

There was a roar of laughter.

'I've got one,' said Mark Kostik. 'What do you call a cross between a prostitute and a computer?'

'No, what?'

'A fucking know-it-all!!' screamed Mark.

All the table chortled.

Taking up the theme, someone else immediately offered

'How do you make a hormone?'

'Don't pay her!!'

By now the entire company was rolling in fits of laughter.

'Here's one,' said someone else. 'Why did a couple stop having children after their third kid?'

'Because someone told them that every fourth child born is Chinese!!!'

This happy banter went on for the next half hour or so as this bunch of senior university teachers vied with each other to tell the dirtiest and most puerile one-liners.

After the rich seam of the sexual and the scatological had been fully worked out, these beacons of higher learning moved on to more serious topics - in particular, the hilarious deficiencies of those of God's children who had been unfortunate enough not to have been blessed by being residents of God's promised land, the United States.

They began with a traditional target for the well-educated American.

'Did you hear the one about the Polish airliner that crashed? It ran out of coal!!!'

'What did the Polaks use to light their houses before they had candles?'

'Electricity!!'

A couple of the leading academics were now wiping their eyes with their handkerchiefs.

'Oh, yes, I've got another,' said one senior PhD. 'What is two hundred yards long and eats cabbage?'

'A Polish meat queue!!!' several shouted in unison.

Oh, how they laughed at that. But then there are always the French and their famous national shortcomings.

'What's the difference between a Frenchman and a sack of fertilizer?'

'The sack!!!'

Three or four of this band of fine scholars were now rolling about, so great was their mirth. But the Polish and the French were not the only nationalities to feel the cutting edge of the departmental razor-sharp wit.

'What's the difference between yoghurt and New Zealand? ' asked one full professor.

'Yoghurt has live culture!!'

For this brilliant witticism, he was even cheered.

And how could a festive evening possibly be conducted or be complete without a quota of amusing stories about the Irish and their stupidity? Or the British with their sexual inhibitions? Not to mention the Italians and their Mafia. Plus, of course, there had to be one or two hilarious jokes about slit-eyed orientals.

Even the Eskimos were not spared the coruscating rapier-like wit of Morten Nyborg and his fellow senior professors when he told a story which was something to do with a seal on the engine of a snowmobile and the Eskimo replying that he had frost on his moustache. That was very, very well received by most of the sixteen doctorates around the table, now half-drunk and well into jocular festive mood.

There being several Jews present, as is usual in American academia, the assorted party was careful not to be politically incorrect by any taint of prejudice or anti-Semitism, so no anti-Jewish jokes were offered. But good-humored joshing at the expense of the Catholics was quite acceptable in this glittering display of scholarly wit. The university's leading economist offered an original slant on the Roman faith.

'What happened when the Pope went to Mount Olive?'

'Popeye beat the shit out of him!!!!!'

'I've another,' he screamed. 'Why doesn't Jesus eat M&M's?'

'They fall through his hands!!'

By now the most brilliant intellects of the university were wiping the tears from their eyes, slapping their thighs and choking on their vino. How long could this clever Wildean repartee be kept up, they must have wondered?

'I've got one,' said a senior professor of economics. 'Two nuns in a bath. One says 'where's the soap'. The other says, 'yes it does!!' Ha, ha, ha!! '

Actually, this subtle joke had to be explained to one or two of the less sophisticated professors, which rather broke the mood. But soon it was restored, courtesy of Morten Nyborg.

Having done the Poles, the New Zealanders, the British, the French, the Italians and the Inuit, not to say the Roman Catholics, but not, of course, the Jews, because that would have been racist, Morten Nyborg was now ready to move on to the Canadians, there being no Canadians present.

'Why don't the Canadians water-ski?' Morten asked loudly.

'Because they can't find a lake with a slope!!'

This brilliant riposte restored the previous joyous mood which had been slightly spoilt by the over-cerebral 'nun' joke and the guffaws returned to the table.

Once the meeting had turned to Canada and its national characteristics, one diner, not possessing the wealth of humorous material which his colleagues were able to reel off so fluently, decided that his time had come to make his own small contribution.

'They do say that Canada has four seasons - May, June, July and winter,' he volunteered.

He was met with polite smiles.

'Yes, very funny.' His fellow diners were patronizing at this clumsy attempt at humor. But still the misguided fellow persisted with his Canadian theme.

'They also say that the Canadians could have had American efficiency, British government and French culture. But instead they finished up with British efficiency, French government and American culture.'

There was a deafening silence at this deplorable lapse of good fellowship by this man's ill-mannered departure from the jolly mood of the evening.

The silence was broken by Hattie Reilly PhD.

'I really don't think that's very fair,' she bellowed. 'What have the Canadians ever done to you? You shouldn't insult them like that. Whatever would they say? Have you no principles? Have you no conscience?

'I'm sorry,' said the miscreant. 'It's only a joke. You've been telling jokes all night.'

'But you are being insulting to our Canadian colleagues.'

'We don't have any Canadian colleagues. What about that joke about the Canadians waterskiing uphill? That was a joke about the Canadians.'

'That was a real joke,' said Hattie Reilly PhD. 'Not like your insults.'

'Mark used to be married to a Canadian lady,' she then added, irrelevantly.

All good things must come to an end and after three hours of this exciting revelry, the party broke up. Everybody had been fed, although all at different times, given the difficulty the kitchen restaurant had when it came to cooking more than one dish at a time. All the learned scholars were agreed, although most were not being entirely honest when they said so, that the evening had been a glittering success. Such a success, in fact, that it was repeated only twice more, with a smaller turnout each time, before off-duty quasi-obligatory socializing was abandoned awaiting whichever chairman would come next and who would, no doubt, come to the idea as if gifted by a revelation. For all of those who were not the chairman, i.e. the rest of the department, the ending of the experiment was, in reality, a blessed relief.

Alexei Alexandrov spent the next few days sulking in his mansion situated beside the river in the posh outer suburb where his neighbors, each in his own private walled estate, constituted the very summit of local social and financial success. They included financial wizards, banking geniuses, pharmaceutical distributors, owners of privatized national assets and other *glitterati* who, these days, constitute the very *crème de la crème* of a modern nation state and are therefore, by extension, the real owners of the country.

The average monthly income of the salariat was still $500, little changed in twenty years. The ordinary workers with their $8 a day were no better off than they had been before they had been liberated by the revolution. But it was still a matter of national pride that the country could now afford a small, immensely wealthy, plutocracy. It is a belief, held by many, that a country's status in the commonwealth of nations is a simple measure of how many billionaires it can produce.

Alexandrov was one of those billionaires. As a consequence of his importance as a self-styled national 'wealth creator', he felt, not unreasonably, since those have been the instincts of very rich men throughout the ages, that he was entitled to a say, and a big say at that, in exactly how the country ought to be run. Was he not a towering genius at having amassed such a huge fortune and did that not give him the right to an automatic seat in government?

After a few days of sulking and plotting, he picked up the phone to arrange a meeting with another billionaire wealth creator.

'Konstantin! How are you, my old friend? I haven't seen you for far too long! When was it? Oh yes, when we liberated the Bezaki Steel Corporation. We both did nicely out of that one! Ha, ha, ha!! Look, can you come round for a meeting? Today? Good. Something has come up. I think we can do some business together.'

Konstantin Zonkov was not surprised to find his talents in demand. He had done some good work for Alexandrov in the past but he hadn't heard from the

General now for three years, not since Zonkov's agitators and Alexandrov's soldiers, plus a little informal CIA assistance, had broken the strike at the Bezaki steel factory. Alexandrov had then bought the whole national steel industry at a fire sale price.

What did the General want now, Zonkov wondered? He knew that the General had been fired from his government job, so it must be something to do with that.

'Sure, Alexei, I will be round at your place in one hour.'

When Zonkov arrived at Chateau Alexandrov, he was taken straight to the General's office where Alexandrov locked the door and poured large glasses of iced vodka.

'Konstantin, we have a problem. It affects us both. That bitch Makarovna thinks she can run this country without Alexei. Alexei thinks she needs to be taught a lesson.'

'What kind of lesson?'

'A permanent lesson.'

'You want me and my boys to take her out?'

'No, no, Konstantin. You obviously don't understand politics. We can't take her out. Suspicion would fall on me because I have a reason. I also have association and the means. She is in the pocket of the Americans and she will do whatever they tell her to. If we delete her now, just after she has won an election, then the Americans will poke their noses in. And that could be uncomfortable. No, no, not erasure, not yet. Something more subtle.'

'What do you have in mind?'

'What we need to do,' explained the corrupt general to the criminal overlord, 'is to break her American connection. Then you can rub her out.'

'You have a plan? How can I help?'

'Well,' explained General Alexandrov, 'it just so

happens that a piece of very useful information just came to me recently from the American University. When it gets out, Makarovna will lose her American support and she can be removed. And if she goes, then that fat old bastard Balashirov will go as well. I am going to be interviewed on TV this evening on their big politics show and I am going to make some important disclosures. The journalist who will be interviewing me has already been told what to ask me. She has been well paid.'

'So, how do I come in?' asked Zonkov.

'After the broadcast, I want your people to start some protests. I am assuming you have enough people? How many can you raise?'

'Yes, General, I have enough.   I now have Caradescu's boys working for me. About seven, maybe eight, hundred.'

'That should be plenty. We need to stir up the entire population against Makarovna. So we need a big demonstration in Revolution Square. You know how to do that?'

Zonkov nodded. 'But why? What reason will we have?'

'Just be ready after the broadcast.'

'It'll cost money, getting all those people out on the street.'

'For something this important, my old friend, doll we can certainly find the money.'

The weekly politics TV show, called, as it is called in many countries, 'Politics Today', went out at 7pm that evening. The music faded out and the headshot of the presenter, Valentina Siumanova, came into view.

'Our guest this evening is General Alexei Alexandrov, former Minister of Defense, who was surprisingly dropped from Prime Minister Makarovna's new government this week. General Alexandrov, can you tell us why, after so many years in government, Madame Makarovna decided that she did not need you anymore?' asked the well-bribed Ms. Siumanova.

'Ha, ha! You would need to ask the prime minister that question. For myself, I am only happy to be able to serve my country in any way I can.'

'Could it be anything to do with the much-talked about Operation Warm Blanket, which Anastasia Makarovna and you signed up for in Brussels only a few months ago?'

'I don't know. It could be,' said Alexandrov, choosing his words carefully. 'Operation Warm Blanket is supposed to bring economic and security benefits to our country. There is to be a new base to be built at Nyo Brutske. It is supposed to bring new jobs and annual payments from NATO funds.'

'You say 'supposed', General. Do you think it might not happen?'

'If you want my honest opinion, no, I don't. There is a lot of talk that the official version of Operation Warm Blanket is just a smokescreen for a different plan.'

'A different plan, General?' asked Valentina Siumanova. 'What do you mean?'

'Military technology is advancing at a fast rate and the need for old-fashioned air defenses is less than it used to be. Many of our allies are saying that in the future NATO will not need new bases for planes with human pilots. The war of the future will be fought entirely with unmanned robotic vehicles, called drones, controlled from a safe distance.'

'So, General,' asked Ms Siumanova, 'are you saying that the planned new base will not be built?'

'Yes, I think that could be right. It makes sense. The

governments of the US and most of the NATO countries have all had serious financial problems since the banking crisis of two thousand and eight. This is not the time to be making large new investments when cheaper, more modern technological solutions for our defense requirements are available.'

'So,' Valentina Siumanova put the fatal loaded question, 'are you saying that not only will we not be getting a new base but the present base is going to be decommissioned as a regular base and converted to robotic control only?'

'That would be the natural conclusion, yes,' said the General.

'Does that mean that there will be no new jobs and unemployment for the workers at the present base at Altameda?'

'It would be even worse than that. We would have no control at all over how and when and why these drones would be deployed, or against whom. They will be completely in the hands of the Americans.'

'Will these so-called 'drones' also be armed with nuclear weapons?'

'That may be part of the American plan, yes. They haven't told us.'

'So, it looks like Prime Minister Makarovna was completely hoodwinked by the Americans at the Brussels negotiations?'

'It looks like it.'

'Thank you, General.'

'You're welcome.'

'And now we go over to Tashkent, where the authorities are still trying to piece together the reasons for the murder of the American Ambassador last Friday night. We hear that all the main terrorist groups have denied responsibility. Our reporter in Tashkent is Petros

Michaelis. Petros, do we have any more information about who caused this? '

'Nothing yet, Valentina.'

The TV in the presidential bedroom was abruptly switched off.

'What a bastard!' screamed Anastasia Makarovna. 'How dare he?'

'Is it true about the drones?' asked Balashirov. 'Can the Americans be trusted?'

'Feldstein gave me his word the deal was genuine.'

'You need to move, and move fast. You may have just won the election but this broadcast from Alexandrov is serious. Your enemies will already be plotting. I suggest you make a broadcast immediately and discredit Alexandrov. Say he was being unpatriotic. Charge him with treason. We could even have him killed, if you like.'

Eighteen

The prime minister's office immediately booked space for an announcement at 8 am the next morning. Anastasia spent half the night writing what she was going to say. She would tell the people that Alexandrov's treachery was because he had not been given a job in her administration, that what he had said about Operation Warm Blanket was a complete fabrication and that she had the assurance of the United States government, our loyal friends, that no such plan to replace the existing airbase with an unmanned base existed.

Alexandrov, she would tell the TV audience, was putting the whole future security of the country at risk for purely personal reasons. She wrote out her speech many times until she had got every word, every nuance, absolutely perfect. Then she read the speech in front of her mirror so that she could properly rehearse the body gestures and the facial expressions for shock, incredulity, disappointment and finally maternal reassurance.

She played the ten-minute speech back on her computer over and over again until she was as sure as she could be that her performance would be nothing less than perfect. When she was satisfied with it, the recording was sent to the TV station for broadcast after the main news at 8am that morning.

But it was all to no avail. By the time of the broadcast, the crowds had already begun to gather in Revolution Square. Konstantin Zonkov had been active through the night and he had bussed in many active supporters of Caradescu and Simonov. He had also packed the crowd with many of his own men, ready to light the fuse of the explosive situation which was developing.

As on the previous Saturday, President Balashirov had ordered his tanks to the perimeter of the square and the police riot squads were taking their places. But the crowd, growing larger and angrier by the minute, was now approaching twenty thousand in number and was pushing, pushing towards the row of tanks and the line of armored police who were blocking off the exits from the square. The push was in the direction of the road down to the presidential palace.

The shouts were 'SIM-ON-OV!' and 'CA-RA-DES-CU!' and 'DEATH TO MAKAROVNA!' Vainly, the police tried to push the protesters back while the tank commanders waited for orders to fire on their countrymen.

When the orders from Balashirov finally came, they were ignored. This was not just any routine demonstration, the commanders could see. This was a new revolution, just like the one that had first brought Balashirov to power sixteen years previously. They recognized a turning point in history, when the will of the mob is suddenly stronger than the established power of the state. It is the defining revolutionary moment - that moment when the defenders of the *ancien régime* change sides and join the protesting crowds.

The exact point which measured the end of the Makarovna government could be defined to the second. It was when the tank commanders ordered their guns to be turned away from the protesters and pointed towards the Presidential Palace. The police, against the orders being screamed by the Chief of Police, stood aside so that the avenue leading to the Palace was now open for the vast crowd to surge up to the railings around the building.

There they halted and waited for a tank to make its way through the throng. When the tank reached the iron gates, its hatch opened and General Alexei Alexandrov pulled himself up on top of the tank where he could

218

address the crowd through a loudhailer.

'Fellow citizens,' he began, 'for the love of the fatherland! For our fathers and for our children, we take action today to rid our beloved country of the two traitors Balashirov and Makarovna! Right now, the traitor Makarovna is admitting on television her black wickedness! She has betrayed our country and she has betrayed you, dear citizens! She has allowed herself to fall for the vicious lies of the Americans!'

'American warmongers who want to use our precious homeland as a launch site for their infernal unmanned flying bombs!'

'American warmongers who will take the bread from the mouths of our women and children! She has allowed, with her conspirator, the traitor Balashirov, our country to fall into the hands of foreigners! We will not, fellow citizens, have any say in how these flying bombs are to be used or against which friendly peoples! They may even be used against you, my friends!!'

This rabble-rousing peroration had its intended effect and soon the mob was pushing at the railings surrounding the palace. Alexandrov got back inside the tank and ordered it to smash down the gates and drive right up to the main doors. The mob followed behind, surging into the palace gardens. A few nudges from the tank and the big doors fell inward. Alexandrov jumped down from the tank and, with a few of his old colleagues from the Army Staff College, ran over to the presidential private office, where President Balashirov and Prime

Minister Makarovna were waiting.

'Alexandrov,' said the president, 'are you and your mob here to kill us? If so, then do it quickly.'

'Who do you think we are, common murderers? No, we will not kill you. We might put you on trial for crimes against the people! '

'Crimes against the people? You're the one who's committed crimes against the people with this revolt.'

'It is the will of the people. They are sovereign. Didn't you know that? They are kicking you out because Makarovna sold this country to the Americans so that they can use us as a shooting gallery!'

'You know that the prime minister signed the deal with the Americans in good faith. You were there. When she signed, there was no talk of these drones. That came later.'

'She allowed the Americans to fool her. That is not what a prime minister should let happen.'

'So what are you going to do with us?' asked Balashirov.

'Ah,' said Alexandrov, 'it would be so easy to kill you. But we might be creating martyrs and that would never do. On the other hand, a trial would also attract a lot of publicity. Lots of TV coverage. We don't want that either. No, first you will sign these two resignation letters. Then you will take up residence in a foreign country. We have noticed that you seem to like the United States better than your own country. There's a nice retirement villa in Florida we have picked out for you. A plane is waiting at the airport. My car will take you there under armed guard.'

'We can still harm you, Alexandrov. Even from the United States. Maybe we should tell the world about how you got rich?'

'No one will believe you. You would be living like

film stars in the Florida sun! So you won't do that.'

'What do you mean?'

'Ha, ha!' said Alexandrov. 'We will be destroying your reputations as well. Right now, we have uploaded all your bedroom recordings and a video of the two of you beside your swimming pool. Sometime in the next few minutes, they will all 'go viral', as they say on *Facebook* and on *YouTube* and on all the other social media. No one will ever take you seriously again after the whole world has seen you at the pool! You are going to be famous! Porn stars!! A new life is waiting for you! But one word of warning! Don't ever come back here. Next time we might not be so lenient.'

The ex-president and the ex-prime minister were then led to Alexandrov's car where it made its way to the airport through a barrage of angry fists. They never again returned home. Balashirov and Makarovna settled in Florida and merged with the rest of the geriatrics and retirees who live there. They wrote their memoirs and appeared on TV from time to time as minor celebrities or as accessible rent-a-quotes whenever some doings in the Balkans were in the news. Otherwise, after the brief notoriety of the world-wide viewing of their romps by the pool had been forgotten, they disappeared below the media horizon forever.

In the Oval Office, President Bedford was furious. 'Just how did all that happen?' He was pointing at the CNN coverage of the coup.

'They are our people. We paid for them for chrissakes! Bought and paid for! Don't they know that once they're bought they should stay bought?'

'It seems, Mister President,' said Secretary of State Alison Treadwell, 'that there was a little leakage of

221

classified information. Someone got hold of some story about the real Warm Blanket agenda and told the wrong person. Makarovna never knew what we had in mind nor did Ambassador Feldstein. But somehow the story got out and Alexandrov made use of it for his own purposes.'

'Didn't - what's she called? - know that Alexandrov would be a threat if she fired him?'

'Makarovna. No, it seems not. She didn't know he had the info on Warm Blanket. If she had she wouldn't have terminated the old crook.'

'Jeeze! What a mess! Any ideas what we do now? '

'Not a lot we can do, Mister President. The cat's out of the bag. All I can suggest is that we stick to our story and start building a few new bases to reassure the rest that we are good for our word. Then when the fuss has died down in a year or two, we quietly stop the program and start building drone stations as planned. It'll cost us, but I don't see any other way. We'll plant information and disinformation as required to take the heat out of the situation,' said Alison Treadwell.

'Yep,' said President Bedford, 'damage limitation. That's all we have left. Any idea where the leak came from? '

'Norman Bland, the Europe chief at the CIA, is working on that now, sir. It seems that we had two young field guys on the ground there but they got busted. You don't want to know the details. Disciplinary. They got sent home and the CIA didn't have any replacement field officers with the same local knowledge of the country. So we had to use our reserve team.'

'This gets worse!' expostulated Bedford. 'Our reserve team? You mean we used a reserve team for a major operation like this?'

'Yes sir, our reserve team, some local college professor.'

'What, a college professor for a job this important?' said President Bedford incredulously.

'We had no one else, sir.'

'Where is the joker now?'

'I understand that Bland is recalling him in for debriefing,' answered the Secretary of State. 'He's flying out this afternoon on a military flight - non-stop to Andrews and then a car to Langley.'

'Alone?'

'No sir. Two officers will be travelling with him. He will be watched all the way.'

'Good. Let me know what he says.'

'Yes sir.'

Colonel Sieghart called Darius Galpin at AUSB. 'Sorry, Darius,' said the Colonel, 'but it seems that some of our colleagues at HQ think you've got some explaining to do. A car will be there in ten minutes. No need to pack. There'll be clothes and stuff on the plane.'

'Oh, shit,' thought Galpin. He knew the way the official mind worked. The whole situation had gotten out of control and someone had to be blamed. Obviously it couldn't be Alexandrov who had simply exploited an opportunity. Nor could it be Sieghart who hadn't got his hands dirty and was, anyway, Galpin's CIA boss. It obviously couldn't be President O'Brien Bedford, who had come up with the whole flaky plan of trying to fool seventeen governments at the same time and was, so the chain of command argument goes, the ultimate cause of the problem. No, realized Galpin, the buck stops here, with me, with the disposable field operative.

His trip by military plane was just the first part of his ordeal. He was landed at Andrews Airbase and a black car drove him from south-eastern Washington DC around the Capital Beltway to Langley, a suburb of the small town of McLean, Virginia, where the Central Intelligence Agency has its headquarters.

Darius Galpin, Provost of the American University of the Southern Balkans, was in for a rough couple of days. His inquisitors used lie detectors and drugs to loosen his tongue. He was deprived of sleep for forty hours while his questioners asked him the same questions over and over again. It was a relief to be able to tell them everything they asked him to, so that the torture would stop.

At the end of his interrogation, his inquisitors knew of his dealings with Zonkov and the way he had arranged with Zonkov to kill Caradescu and make sure Simonov was arrested for it. They knew everything he had said to Malik the taxi driver and how he had told Malik once, Galpin had thought, he no longer needed to maintain secrecy and he could use the information to stop Malik from killing Joseph Feldstein.

His questioners also knew that he had no personal connection with Alexandrov. After the forty hours were up, they were satisfied that they knew everything about Galpin that they wanted to know.

But the art of interrogation requires more than just a subject willing to tell the whole truth. It also requires that the interrogators ask the right questions. Galpin was not asked whether he talks in his sleep and whom he shares his bed with. The name of the beauteous, promiscuous Annabella Markova-Casillias was never mentioned and her new position as tenured Georgetown professor was never in danger.

The interrogators, at the end of Galpin's ordeal, still had no understanding of the route by which the information had been transferred from Galpin to Alexandrov but they were completely satisfied that Galpin alone had been the cause of the leak and therefore he could be safely blamed for all the diplomatic, economic and strategic damage which it had caused.

'Thank you for all your help, Darius. We appreciate it. You can go home now. North Dakota, isn't it?'

Galpin nodded. 'Jamestown. It's between Bismarck and Fargo.'

'A plane will take you.'

A small executive jet took the tired, emotionally exhausted and utterly depressed Provost Galpin back to his small country home.

The interrogators dutifully reported back to Norman Bland who read their report carefully and made a decision. He asked to see Harry Walbesser, Deputy Head of the CIA.

'Looks dangerous,' said Bland. 'He's a bit of a loose cannon.'

'Yes, I agree,' responded Walbesser.

'He screwed up. He should never have confirmed Warm Blanket to the Taliban taxi driver, even if he had good reasons. That's the only way Alexandrov could have found out. Now Galpin knows too much.'

'Obviously, he can't go back. See to it, Bland.'

'Yes sir.'

Back in his office, he asked his aide 'Who do we have in North Dakota?'

'North Dakota? No one sir.'

'Anyone we can send for a quick in-out removal job?'

'Lemme see, sir. Yep, we have two guys we can use for this sort of thing. They're called Damon Dexter and Charlie Le Moine.'

'Aren't they the two who got busted in the Balkans

225

last year? Is there no one else?'

'I'm afraid not, sir.'

'OK, get them on the phone.'

Darius Galpin was now sick of politics, sick of the CIA. He wanted his old life as a university administrator with its comfortable workload and regular travel. He also wanted rest and quiet. He would, he decided, need to take some leave. He was contemplating these thoughts in his local bar when a young man came up to him and shook his hand vigorously.

'Doctor Galpin! This is great to see you again! You don't remember me?'

'No, er...'

'Chuck Miller,' said Damon Dexter. 'You were my history professor ten years ago at UND! You gave a great class!'

'Miller? I'm sorry. It's been a long time. Do you live in Jamestown?'

'Hell no, sir! I'm just passing through. I work for Chase Manhattan now. I've got a local job to do here. Tell me, what are you doing now, sir? You must be a college president by now. You were one helluva prof!'

Damon Dexter kept Darius Galpin talking just long enough for Charlie Le Moine to fix the accelerator of Galpin's large pickup truck parked outside so that once the speed got up to 60 mph, it would stay there.

'Goodbye, sir,' said Dexter, 'it's been great to see you again.'

'Goodbye, Chuck,' were Galpin's very last mortal words.

Nineteen

With Balashirov and Makarovna gone, Alexandrov immediately set to work following the age-old procedures for a successful military coup. Ever since ancient history, changes of administration have been done according to a standard program. Alexandrov knew it well. He had been one of the junior officers in Balashirov's *coup* when the old man had taken power sixteen years previously. Now it was his turn to go through the hallowed routine. He had learnt much from Balashirov, both from his methods and from his mistakes.

For example, Balashirov had won over the mob by promises, which the former president had kept, of free and fair elections. It had been a very useful ploy at the time, when the country, newly freed from the burden of communism, had needed American money and the respectability of European Union membership.

But Alexandrov could never quite see the point of regularly allowing the peasantry a say in how their country should be run. What do the ordinary people know, thought Alexandrov? They put their crosses on a piece of paper every so often and some feeble idiot is given the keys to the country, unless, that is, there is an Zonkov or two to make sure the keys finish up in the right pocket.

For Alexandrov, democracy was a wasteful way of making sure that the country would always be governed by the weak and the stupid.

His idea of a fair general election was one made by reliable, sound, fair generals in the best interests of the country. It was blindingly obvious to him that only properly trained senior military men would have the necessary experience and ability to able to govern properly. To do the job well, they would certainly not need any unhelpful interference from uninformed civilians. And, naturally, in return for their selfless patriotic service, they should be permitted to create for themselves the cushion of a small personal pension fund before handing over the reins of power to another safe and reliable leader possessed of the essential quality of patriotic military discipline.

Alexandrov's heroes were those who took power for themselves and eliminated anyone who stood in their way. He admired Caesar, Napoleon, Cromwell. Men like that, men not afraid to kill to get power and to hold on to it. Such *coups d'état* as Alexandrov's are commonplace around the world and have been throughout history. So commonplace indeed, that they could be regarded as the standard, the most natural way of transferring ownership of the country. But first, right now, the mob had to be directed. Alexandrov addressed them from the balcony of the palace.

'My friends and fellow citizens, today we have won a historic victory! We have cleansed our country of the wicked and unpatriotic elements who were willing to see our beloved homeland and the lives of you, our glorious citizens, sold into American slavery! Let the traitors depart! Let them go to their precious United States! Free of Balashirov and Makarovna, we can begin the great work of restoring our country to its rightful place as a nation which can, once again, stand tall amongst the nations of the world!'

'Today,' Alexandrov continued, 'I am announcing a new Committee of National Security which will have the task of running the country until new

228

elections can be held. It has just come to light that the traitor Makarovna, in addition to her many other crimes, came to victory in the last election because of her fraudulent corruption of the election. Many forged ballot papers have been found! But, my friends, I promise you that when new elections are held in no more than six months from this date, we will have enacted laws which will make it an offence punishable by death to interfere in the election process.'

'I also announce, the temporary suspension of the National Assembly until after the elections. All military personnel and police will henceforth be responsible to the Committee of National Security. This committee, which will oversee the entire government of the country, will consist of several responsible, patriotic senior military officers. I will be its chairman.'

'Mikhail Simonov, falsely accused of a heinous crime by the traitor Makarovna, will be released from jail immediately and will be invited to serve on the Committee of National Security as Foreign Minister. The Committee of National Security will also employ the services of some of our leading patriotic citizens.'

'Therefore, I am asking one of our most successful businessmen, Konstantin Zonkov, to join the Committee as Minister of Justice. A full list of the new ministers and their portfolios will be published later. Finally, my friends, I am announcing that henceforth Revolution Square will be named Caradescu Square, in honor of

Mehmet Caradescu, one of our most distinguished and far-seeing statesmen, who was so brutally murdered by thugs working for the Makarovna regime!'

The crowd, fifty thousand or more, surged forward, chanting 'ALEXANDROV!', 'ALEXANDROV!'

The general lifted up his hand and pointed outwards. The direction of his arm was vaguely towards the American Embassy. The crowd understood instantly and they were soon on their way to mass around the hi-tech, armed concrete fortress which is the United States Embassy in every country.

'Go now, my friends, and build a new revolution!' shouted Alexandrov.

It was still early morning in Washington DC but already President O'Brien Bedford was in conference with Alison Treadwell, Branwell McFall, George Zymanski and Hubert Tuple. They had all seen Alexei Alexandrov on CNN that morning and had already been issued with transcripts of his speech to the crowds.

'Well, gentlemen, Alison, is that not the biggest load of horse shit you ever heard?' asked the president.

'Text book stuff, if you ask me,' said the Secretary of State.

'That's what they all say. Every time there's a military coup in one of these shit-assed crummy little foreign countries. Elections in six months! Ha! That douche-bag won't hold elections in six years, probably never.'

'The problem is, as far as I see it,' said President Bedford, 'is that this is not one of your shit-assed crummy little foreign countries. This is Europe, NATO. We have

American personnel there.'

'I don't think we need worry about the safety of American lives yet. The embassy is as safe as Fort Knox and the base at Altameda is too far out of the way. I can't see the mob going there,' said Tuple.

'What about other Americans in the country and the American university?'

'Yes sir, AUSB. It has about two hundred or so professors and American students. There is an embassy residential compound out in the suburbs. We could send them there.'

'Can it be defended if necessary?'

'Well, not like the embassy itself, but it is gated and there is a marine detachment there at all times.'

'Get word to the president of the school, president, er..'

'President Spring, sir, Curtley Spring.' answered Tuple.

'Get word to Spring that all US personnel at AUSB can take shelter in the embassy compound if things get out of hand,' ordered President Bedford.

'What about the tourists and Americans who just live in the country?' asked Zymanski.

'What can we do?' asked Bedford. 'They'll just have to take their chances. Let's not worry about American safety. I don't think Alexandrov is stupid enough to threaten American lives. Next item, what do we do about him?'

'We could neutralize him, sir,' answered the Director of the CIA, 'before he gets too settled in.'

'You mean murder?' asked President Bedford.

'That's not a word we like to use, sir,' answered the CIA Director.

'I think the first thing you need to do, sir, is issue a very strong statement, deploring...etc   support for democratic elections…etc …' said Alison Treadwell.

President Bedford pressed a button and an aide with a notebook appeared. Bedford whispered to him and the aide wrote some notes.

'I've just booked the press room for nine am. They've started on the statement right now. After the statement, what then? '

'The way I see it,' said Secretary of State Treadwell, 'is that Alexei Alexandrov may be in place for a while, at least until the next revolution. So we'll have to work with him.'

'But the guy is an anti-American, disloyal, crooked, power-hungry megalomaniac!' retorted George Zymanski.

'And your point is?' asked the president.

'Are we going to work with a guy like that?'

'We usually do,' replied Bedford, 'as long as they don't do anything to harm American interests.'

'But I thought he was promising to halt Operation Warm Blanket and close our base at Altameda?' asked Hubert Tuple.

'Yes,' said Bedford, 'that's what he says. I bet he doesn't intend to follow through. He knows which side he needs to be on. This anti-American shit was just for the mob. Now he's got power, he'll just be like all the rest. He'll take our money, thank us in private and curse us in public.'

'So, we are going to deal with him?' asked Zymanski.

'Of course,' answered Bedford. 'He may be a psychopathic bastard who's looted his country these last sixteen years, but I'm sure he'll see it's in his best interests to be our psychopathic bastard.'

'What about Balashirov and Makarovna?' someone asked. 'Aren't we going to support them? They were our people.'

'Yesterday's folks,' answered Bedford. 'Let them

enjoy a long and happy retirement in the Sunshine State. By the way, did we all see the video of them at the pool on *YouTube* yesterday?'

'It was very good, Mister President.'

'Yeah! The First Lady enjoyed it, too. OK, meeting over. Press conference at nine. Can you be there, Alison?'

'Yes, Mister President.'

The mood at AUSB was gloomy. Curtley Spring had called Mike Mulvaney into his office to tell him the bad news that Provost Darius Galpin had been killed in a motor accident.

'I've just sent a message to all staff and faculty. There will be a memorial service as soon as we can arrange it.'

'We're all shocked, Curtley.'

'He was a good man, a great scholar and a loyal, decent American.'

'He was that indeed.'

'And I got this memo from State, 'said Curtley Spring. He read it out.

'All US citizens working for American institutions are reminded that the US Embassy Residential Community in Sofia Street is available as a safe place to take refuge in the event that the disturbances continue. Please identify yourself at the gate with picture ID.'

'Things seem to have gone quiet,' said Mulvaney.

'Storm in a teacup,' agreed President Spring.

'You have Company clearance, Mike?'

'Yes, of course. Nothing big, just C-4.'

'C-4 should be big enough. I think this place has seen enough action in the last few days. This new man,

Alexandrov, seems to be strong enough. Maybe he can keep a lid on the troublemakers.'

'Why did you ask about my clearance just now? You know I'm Company?'

'Yeah, Mike, that's right. You've been here fifteen years. You're bound to have been recruited in that time. The Agency likes our long-standing local residents to keep an eye on things.'

'And Darius Galpin, was he also CIA?'

'I guess so. He sure spent a lot of time at the embassy.'

'That means that you are with the Company as well.'

'Yes' said Spring. 'So you know about the directive that all Americans working in universities abroad at the level of department chair and higher have to be CIA registered at some level.'

'I was wondering about that,' said Mulvaney. 'We just made Smalley Chair of Business and he's Australian. But he did get an F-3 clearance from Sieghart. Didn't even know he was under the spotlight. We thought it was just a formality. Will we need to fire him and find someone else now that we have trouble?'

'It depends on what Sieghart says. Sieghart's the real boss, not those committee people back at home campus. He is the top CIA desk man in this country and the whole South Balkans region. '

'Well, we now have a vacancy at the top here., ' said Spring. 'Think you can step up to the plate, Mike?'

'Thank you, sir. I'll certainly give it my best shot.'

'Now,' went on President Spring, 'we come to the next difficult decision. Who is going to take over your old job of Dean? I've made a list of who is eligible.' He handed Mulvaney a piece of paper.

'Is this all? We only have these six?'

'We can't choose just who we like, Mike. Our hands

are tied. Must have CIA clearance and must be sufficiently senior to be competent. It's not easy.'

Mike Mulvaney spoke his thoughts out loud. 'Him, no, too abrasive, just like Balfour. Her? No. No academic credibility, PhD from a non-accredited school. Him? No. Thinks he's Einstein so he dresses like a bum because Einstein dressed like a bum. That's where the similarity ends. That one? Oh Christ, no! Him? Always off on conferences. We need someone who can take control. And her? She's never done any management in her life. Making her dean would be a real risk. There's not a lot of choice, Curtley.'

'You'll have to make a choice, Mike. What's your least worst option?'

'It'll have to be her,' said Mulvaney, pointing at a name. 'I do know she's CIA.'

'Yes, long time. Same grade as you, C-4.'

'OK, then,' said Mike Mulvaney, half pleased at his promotion and half fearful at what he had let himself in for by giving the dean's job to Hattie Reilly PhD.

'Ladies and gentlemen of the press,' announced the White House press attaché, 'the President of the United States.'

The president mounted the lectern with the presidential seal on the front. His invisible autocue was already running.

'Yesterday we all witnessed on our TV screens a large public demonstration in Caradescu Square, in the centre of the capital city of one of our oldest NATO allies. The demonstration appeared to be a popular uprising against President Balashirov, the elected prime minister, Anastasia Makarovna and her government. Reports I have seen indicate that

235

extensive electoral fraud had taken place and this had been discovered.'

'Meanwhile, the United States stands ready to offer any support or assistance to the new administration in that country and to continue to promote democratic dialogue with all the people of the region and their elected governments.'

'We are therefore asking the temporary head of the provisional government, General Alexei Alexandrov, to make good on his undertaking to hold full, free and fair elections as soon possible so that his country can continue on the path of progress, with full democratic human rights.'

'President Bedford will now answer questions,' said the press attaché. Several reporters put their hands up.

'Tom Hampson, Associated Press. Sir, would you like to comment on rumors which are going around that the election had been fixed by the CIA for Makarovna to win?'

'There was no CIA involvement. I can assure you of that. The United States does not interfere in the internal affairs of friendly nations. Next?'

'April McGregor, Reuters. Mister President, is the change of government anything to do with opposition resistance to United States plans to impose Operation Warm Blanket.'

'I take issue with Ms McGregor on her use of the word 'impose'. No one is imposing anything on those NATO members who have signed treaties to develop, with us, Operation Warm Blanket. Next?'

'Grant Coverdale, BBC. Sir, is there any connection between this *coup d'état* and last week's assassination of

Ambassador Fernandez in Uzbekistan?'

'We know of no connection although we are following all avenues of inquiry to find the perpetrators of the cowardly attack on our ambassador. All the indications are that it was a terrorist attack for reasons we have yet to determine. One more.'

'Helen O'Grady, Baltimore Sun. Mister President, sir, there are a number of rumors flying around on the Internet and elsewhere to the effect that Operation Warm Blanket is a cover for replacement of manned aircraft in NATO bases by unmanned drones only. This is one of the allegations made by General Alexandrov in his speech yesterday. Can you comment please, sir?'

'You should not believe everything you read on the Internet, or even what you write in your papers. If you took everything on the Internet seriously, you'd believe that Elvis Presley is alive and well and living on the Moon. That's enough, thank you.'

'So,' a lone voice shouted after the president as he turned away, 'you are categorically denying that NATO is preparing to abandon its conventional air force and will be going over to a hundred percent unmanned air force of robotic drones? Can we quote you on that?'

'There are no plans for a sky full of drones!' the president retorted angrily. 'And yes, you can definitely quote me on that.'

Helen O'Grady and April McGregor were comparing notes before filing their copy via their iPads.

'That last answer was very weak, didn't you think? He's definitely hiding something.'

They were joined by Tom Hampson. 'Well, that was a fine performance from our leading comic actor.'

'Ha, ha! Whatever do you mean, Tom?' asked April.

'By the way, good question!'

'Thanks. I have a pal who was there when they counted the votes which got Makarovna elected. Thousands of ballot papers - all photocopied! And all for the exiled video queen! Does that surprise you?'

'What more do you know?'

'According to my informant it appears that the vote-rigging was a bit of an amateur job by local hoods. Rumor has it that it was down to Zonkov, the only local gangster big enough to pull a stunt like fixing a national election. And, my friend believes, Zonkov is getting paid by...? Yes, our friends at Langley! CIA handwriting all over it, he reckons!'

'Wow! Can we confirm this?'

'Regrettably, ladies, no. Confirmation would be rather difficult.'

'Why is that?'

'Well, our nefarious friend Zonkov has just been made Minister of Justice in the Alexandrov government. And our president will not interfere, and I quote O.B. himself, in the internal affairs of friendly countries.'

'Why are you telling us? This is a hot story!'

'Yes, it is hot, if you could get into the country and interview some people, who will certainly not want to be interviewed. Then you would need to accuse the Minister of Justice of a NATO ally of electoral fraud. But the main reason I am giving you such a juicy story is that you two are too good and too beautiful for the reptilian profession of journalist and I would deem it an honor if you would each be so kind to take a small libation with me at Ginny's, a friendly and civilized watering hole located not one hundred yards from here. Do you know it?'

'OK, sweet talker, you've got a deal.'

Twenty

The new order, the Alexandrov regime, now described in the world's media as a 'junta', was settling in. Simultaneously, at the American University of the Southern Balkans, there was also a new order settling in. Even though Mike Mulvaney had accepted Hattie Reilly PhD as Dean, because she was the least worst of the six candidates on the list, he still looked forward with trepidation to her regular temper tantrums. She had a long record of making her strident views felt because it was, she believed, her duty as longest-standing faculty member to speak her mind freely whenever she felt like it.

What she lacked in basic intelligence and scholarly achievement, she was able to make up for in aggressive self-confidence. Mulvaney foresaw regular bruising encounters ahead. All he really wanted was a quiet life, a small house in a temperate American mid-western state, kids in college, then up and married, a placid retirement with a little fishing.

Not much to ask, he told himself. But before he could reach that blissful nirvana, he would need to spend a purgatorial preparation as the punch bag of the avenging angel of the Business Department, now elevated to Dean, a promotion which was, almost certainly, as the Peter Principle has it, to one level above her natural competence.

She presented herself in his office within an hour of the official start of his provostial duties.

'We must make sure,' she told him aggressively, 'that every faculty member submits to regular faculty evaluation as we have in the Business Department.'

'Of course, of course,' replied Mike Mulvaney wearily. It was still only nine thirty but already this harridan was making him feel tired. 'Why don't you write a position paper and we can discuss it at the next executive council meeting.'

'There are one or two people we need to evaluate right away.'

'And who might those be?'

'We have a couple from Computing, three from Journalism, two from Humanities and three from Business.'

'You'll have your work cut out then,' said Mulvaney.

'I am thinking of speeding up the process. Making it more streamlined.'

'In what way?'

'Well, some of these people will go through automatically. Others will need to go through the whole process. I am suggesting that we can just approve those who don't need the formal process and only examine the others.'

'What sort of criteria do you have in mind for letting some folks off the hook?' asked Mulvaney.

'Well,' responded Reilly, 'obviously Company people are too important to put through the wringer, so we can pass them on the nod. Some others, those who have done service for the university, they can also be given the green light. I am suggesting that only the others, about half of them, have to submit to the formal process.'

Mike Mulvaney, for whom conflict avoidance had always been the guiding principle of his life, nodded his assent. 'OK, Hattie, if you think that is best then just do it. I'll square it with the executive council.'

Back in her office, she met with her old friends, Morten Nyborg and Richard Smalley. She saw Nyborg first.

'Morten,' the new Dean began, 'can we talk about your faculty evaluation? I have taken the trouble to make it as easy as possible for you. I have written a checklist of what is required.'

She handed Nyborg a piece of paper with a short list on it.

Nyborg looked at it, horrified.

'But I understood that the FEP would be a shoo-in for me. When we were discussing Balfour, remember? You told me that it would be a mere formality. All this lot, conferences attended, papers published, service to the community, extra-curricular university activities, degrees awarded, honorary degrees! Jeesus! No one in this place ever gets an honorary degree except those politicians who give the speech at Commencement! I have been teaching at AUSB for five years now! You expect me to re-apply for my job?'

Hattie Reilly was adamant. 'I'm sorry, Morten, but it's the same for everyone. The Faculty Evaluation Process is a requirement of your contract.'

'But you know my work, isn't that enough? Doesn't student satisfaction count for anything?'

'It's not enough, I'm afraid, Morten. You also need to show that you are an active scholar. Peer-reviewed papers, attendance at conferences, involvement in university initiatives. You haven't been doing much of that, have you?'

'Nor have you, or Mulvaney or anyone else for that matter.'

'Try to understand, Morten. We don't want to lose you. You're a good teacher. But we can't go against university policy and that means everyone must be evaluated. Sorry, it's not my decision. I would love to just let it go but I've promised the provost that we will be very thorough for everyone.'

'This is unfair! I've already paid my dues to this place. And you promised me! You promised me!'

'That was when I was merely an ordinary prof like you. But now that I am dean, I must follow the rules. Sorry. Look, Morten, it's not much. We only need a short report on your academic development for the committee and then it's all over. No problem. Then you are good for another five years.'

'Short report?' asked Nyborg. 'How short?'

'Nothing much. Ten thousand words should cover it.'

'Ten freakin' thousand words!' shouted Nyborg. 'About my academic development! No way! NO FREAKIN' WAY!'

'I'm sorry, Morten. But rules are rules. If you don't do it, you won't get another contract. Which means you will have to go back to the states and apply for a new job there. Your visa will be cancelled as soon as you no longer have a job in this country. I believe they give you twenty eight days before they deport you.'

'You'll have my resignation letter today. I'll go at the end of semester, as per my contract.'

'We hate to lose you, Morten. Won't you reconsider?'

'No! I am not going through these circus hoops. They don't have them at other places. So, no! I'll take my chances on the open market.'

Hattie Reilly PhD was genuinely shocked by Nyborg's decision. Hadn't he always been a good friend and a loyal faculty member? She was quite dismayed that he had been so rude to her. She had always, after all, considered herself a paragon of sensitivity when it came to working with people. She had even written her doctoral thesis on the subject of compassion in the workplace.

So Nyborg had turned against her, had he? Maybe it's the male midlife crisis, she told herself. What do they call it? Yes, the andropause - that must be why he was being so unreasonable. But, on the other hand, he was not a Company man, so he would probably eventually have had to go anyway, she figured, if she had read correctly the political smoke signals coming from Washington.

Next in was Richard Smalley, newly recruited, without his knowledge, to the ranks of the unofficial spy battalion at AUSB.

'Thank you for coming to see me,' said Hattie Reilly. 'First the bad news. Morten Nyborg has resigned with effect from the end of term.'

'Whatever for?' asked Smalley.

'He refused to undergo the Faculty Evaluation Process. He got abusive and then flounced out. I couldn't stop him.'

'Oh dear,' said Smalley, 'that means we have to find someone to cover his classes from next term.'

'That only gives you seven weeks to get someone interviewed, evaluated and appointed. It's going to be tight.'

'No problem,' said Smalley.

'Oh yes, it's a problem,' answered Dean Reilly. 'It's a big problem. It is going to have to be someone already in the country. If you want an American, then we can't them get a visa in less than eight months. Now after all this trouble with the new government, our own government is clamping down on letting people come to this country. So there are new visa restrictions at each end.'

'So, it's a European then! Europe is full of people wanting to teach here. No problem.'

'But with the experience? Good English? Someone who's ready to move to a new country by the end of the year? A country where there's just been a revolution?'

'What we could do is get a PhD student who wants a university job. We could advertise in business departments across Europe for a temporary. There's bound to be someone willing to come here for a semester. It will look good on their résumé,' replied Richard Smalley.

It will also involve a lot of work for me, he thought, and the final appointee would not have Nyborg's experience. Maybe they could find a European doctoral student in time, or maybe not, in which case he could try to persuade Morten Nyborg to take Reilly's evaluation exercise and to stay on. Worst would be if Nyborg agreed to go through with it, and the evaluation committee failed him.

Smalley knew that Nyborg was not a real academic. He was a hack teacher, who had never done anything remotely scholarly in his life. When he should have been writing academic papers and going to conferences, he was moonlighting as a distance learning adjunct professor at two other colleges.

Now that he had fallen out with Reilly herself, there was little chance of him passing her exam. So his departure was inevitable whether he took the evaluation and passed it or not. Better not even to bother trying to make him stay, he thought. He also thought what a stupid way of doing things was all this reliance on the subjective faculty evaluation procedure. They had lost a good teacher, albeit not a first rate academic. Even if they could find a replacement, whoever it was would be a complete unknown quantity.

'But I have something else to tell you,' said Dean Reilly. 'As a departmental chair, you have far too much to do, so we won't be asking you to go through the evaluation process. Your contract will be automatically extended for another five years.'

244

'Thank you. I'll get on to advertising for a replacement for Morten right away.'

Those countries, NATO and non-NATO alike, who hosted western airbases openly, discreetly or completely secretly and who were signatories to the Operation Warm Blanket treaty had formed their own association. They were, a new treaty declared, The Organization of Pipeline States.

From Italy, down through the Balkans and the newly independent statelets which had once, long ago, been parts of a unified Yugoslavia, through Bulgaria and Turkey, through the disputatious enclaves of shifting allegiance which made up the Caucasus, on to the large new countries of central Asia, the 'Stans' and all the way to the gates of China, governments had come together to present a united front to the might of NATO and its ruling paymaster.

For it was now generally understood that the original plan for Operation Warm Blanket was merely a cover for a devious plan which would have profound implications for each nation's security. Details of the drone plan had also become the subject of much speculation in the world's press following O'Brien Bedford's public denial.

Much was made of it by those who make it their duty to monitor the human rights of those who had been subjected to drone attacks and the random killing of innocent civilians - those unfortunate bystanders whose lives had been ended when they had got in the way of the remote players of the transcontinental arcade game and who had then found themselves translated into mere 'collateral damage'.

The newly-formed OPS was holding its inaugural

conference in Istanbul. Foreign Minister Simonov, recently released from jail, was there as his country's representative. All the other member countries had also sent their foreign ministers or defense ministers. When it came to his turn to speak, Mikhail Simonov made a strong, impassioned speech.

'Fellow ministers,' he began, 'we are at a historic moment! NATO and President O'Brien Bedford promised us a new deal for security. We would, all of us, be granted extra security facilities. In the case of my small country, we expected to get the extra protection of a new base with extra planes and personnel. This would have brought my country economic benefits as well as enhanced protection.'

'Instead we find that the treaty we signed for Operation Warm Blanket was based on false intentions by the United States. Their intention is to remove their present facility, which brings jobs to a very poor region, but also to replace to it with a new station, without personnel! Not only will their new plan not bring the much-needed financial help they promised us but even the small benefit we get from the present arrangement will be taken away!'

'This treaty was signed by the criminals Makaraovna and Balashirov, who were driven from my country for their treachery! My friends, I propose that we demand, immediately, a renegotiation of Operation Warm Blanket!'

The Uzbek representative also made an inflammatory tirade. 'The use of drones is immoral!' he began. 'They are likely to be outlawed by international courts and human rights groups. Those who use them have no control over the incidental killing of civilians. There are countless records of civilian casualties in Pakistan and Afghanistan and the unnecessary deaths of innocent people. Anyone hiding from NATO justice will shelter in civilian areas. Thus these drones will cause more unnecessary suffering among non-combatants.'

The point was taken up by the Kirgizstani foreign minister. 'We in Kirgizstan are hosts to American air force personnel who use our lands as intermediate support. But if we had a drone station instead, we would no longer be neutral and our enemies, and we have many enemies who want to take our rich mineral wealth, would feel that we have moved from being a peaceful, non-aggressive country to a NATO pawn. The presence of drones in my country would increase the likelihood of attacks on our land and people. For that reason we support the motion to cancel the treaty.'

'What is even worse,' said another,' is that the extreme groups and those who want the pipeline to fail, might well launch a pre-emptive attack while the drone stations were being installed. That could be very dangerous!'

'Yes, and if they are going to be controlled electronically from the United States, then we could be playing host to nuclear weapons, without any control. It would make us a target for any terrorist group, not to say wild crazy countries like Iran or North Korea!'

The meeting went on in this way for another couple of hours before they agreed on the wording of a communiqué. Simonov, who had been elected chairman of the meeting, read it to the waiting journalists.

'The Organization of Pipeline States had a very good meeting to discuss new information, now in the public domain, that the original terms of the Operation Warm Blanket Treaty were incomplete. It now seems that some leading NATO countries were intending to use the treaty as a subterfuge to install airbases for unmanned robotic aircraft controlled from within the United States without the operational control of any of our members.'

'We believe the reports to be true and we unanimously condemn them. Furthermore, we contend that the new plan is a major threat to the peace and stability of the pipeline region and will increase our vulnerability to external attacks.'

'We deplore entirely the exclusive reliance on drone technology in conflict situations because of its tendency to increase the risks to innocent civilian life. We are therefore sending a message to Washington that we are no longer bound by Operation Warm Blanket and its provisions.'

The journalists were writing furiously and shouting questions.

'Mister Simonov, will you be tearing up the treaty?'

'Not tearing it up, renegotiating it.'

'What will you do if NATO will not renegotiate? Will you tear it up then?'

'Maybe, who knows? It depends on how the negotiations work out.'

'Mister Simonov, if you tear up the treaty, will that not cause economic problems? Is it not true that ex-Prime Minister Makarovna had promised extra regional aid for the poor areas of your country where the new base would be located.'

'No, that is not true. If we lose the present base then we will lose much-needed American dollars. We were looking forward to a second manned base and the economic benefits it would have brought to a very poor region of my country. But the new form of the plan brings nothing except, maybe, increased risk for our people. My government could not be party to this new plan. It would be irresponsible of us.'

'Mister Simonov, you say 'my government' as if you were legitimate. But isn't it true that General Alexandrov and you are members of an illegal junta, who seized power from the elected government?'

'Do not delude yourself, Mister Reporter, that the Makarovna government was the legitimate government of my country. There was wide-spread electoral fraud and other dirty tricks. General Alexandrov is temporarily head of a government of all the talents which will administer the country until we can hold fresh elections within six months. Then the General and I and my colleagues in the provisional administration will step down and submit ourselves to the will of the people in free, fair and democratic elections.'

No one believed him. Everyone understands that once a government has taken power through a military coup, the rewards of plunder are just too sweet to give up. Alexandrov's next six months would be devoted, not to restoring democracy to his country but to consolidating his own position and that of his little gang of political cronies, the army hard men plus Simonov and Zonkov. The Americans had been hoping that Makarovna might be a prime minister for life they could deal with. Now, they would have the anti-American Alexandrov for a long time. Not their first choice.

They had gone to a lot of trouble and expense on

behalf of Makarovna and they had been wrong-footed when Alexandrov had temporarily outwitted them. No matter, Alexandrov was a politician and surely, a pragmatist who would be open to a deal with his American masters.

If personal bribery, the simplest approach, did not work, then threats of violent overthrow could always be relied on to do the trick. The American observers watched Simonov's grandstanding on behalf of his boss with silent contempt. It would not be too long before the illegal Alexandrov regime would be made to see the light.

The American nose was tweaked even harder when breakdown of the relationship between the United States and its client states in NATO and the Euro-Atlantic Partnership was captured by the world's television industry.

Simultaneously on each's national television stations, the heads of government of the Organization of Pipeline States dramatically, following a short identical announcement, literally tore up the Treaty of Operation Warm Blanket.

No one in the world with access to TV or social media could avoid seeing it. As a universal public rebuke to its original author, President O'Brien Bedford of the United States, it was nothing short of world-wide public humiliation.

At AUSB, Hattie Reilly PhD was also consolidating her power as the new Dean. Two of her old *confrères,* Richard Smalley and Morten Nyborg, had been taken care of. No more would there be rule by departmental internal committee, she was telling herself. Smalley was her creature and he would do as he was told. Nyborg, never a great departmental asset because of his tendency to adolescent displays of temper, would also be no further trouble to her once she had formally accepted his resignation from the university.

That only left Denitsev, a slightly trickier problem. Denis it was who had arranged for Annabella Markova-Casillias to work her charms on the late provost. That was an episode better forgotten, in case its details ever got out.

The stern Baptists and Methodists who sat on the university's Board of Regents of AUSB's stateside home campus might well be offended by reports of such behavior. What Hattie Reilly PhD knew of Denitsev was that he held a superior view of his academic achievements. They were a little above average in a small and unimportant country where only a tiny proportion of the population was formally educated beyond high school level. Unfortunately, his lack of self-awareness did not stop him from dreaming that his rightful milieu would be amid the dreaming spires of Oxford or sharing a common room with the sharp minds of the Princeton Institute of Advanced Studies. He was, like so many second class brains, just not quite bright enough to realize that he was not quite as bright as he thought he was. And, like all second-raters, he was enthusiastic in his mediocrity.

Hattie Reilly PhD realized that if she wanted rid of Denitsev, the easiest way to do it would be to publicly diminish his scholarly record. With luck he would be so affronted that he would storm out, just like Nyborg. She called Denistsev to her office.

'Hello Denis,' she opened. 'What are you doing this term?'

'Oh, the usual. Running the master's degree program and trying to get some decent research done. I am writing a very interesting paper on the relationship between economic well-being and sexual behavior patterns.'

'Wasn't that pretty well covered in the 1960's? I remember the work of Masters and Johnson. They just about closed the book.'

'Ah yes, Masters and Johnson. Their research was very interesting but what happened in California forty years ago is not so relevant anymore, especially here. We've moved on.'

'What I want to talk to you about,' said Dean Reilly, 'is your involvement with the masters degree program. I think you've been doing it long enough. From next semester, I am asking Ashworth from Economics to take over. It is multi-disciplinary, after all. It's time to share the rewards around.'

For a moment, Denitsev was struck dumb. When he got his voice back he was apoplectic.

'You can't do that! I built up that program single-handed. Whatever has Ashworth done? Nothing, that's what! Nothing! He doesn't even teach on the program!'

'I know that Denis, but he is very sound and very keen to do it. He will do a great job. Don't worry. It will give you more time for your research on - what was it? - sex and money and are they related? Isn't that what your paper is supposed to be about?'

'You are aware, are you not,' Denitsev retorted, 'that I was receiving a salary enhancement for running the masters program? I expect that to continue.'

'Yes, it will continue. Right up until the end of the semester when Professor Ashworth takes over. Only fair, after all.'

'You bitch! ' shouted Denitsev into Reilly's face.

'Well, well' said Dean Hattie Reilly PhD, 'I didn't expect to hear that sort of language. It's quite, quite unnecessary. I am deeply offended.'

'Fuck you!' said Denitsev. 'I bet you didn't expect that sort of language either, did you?'

252

Twenty one

Helen O'Grady, April McGregor and Tom Hampson were sitting over cocktails in Ginny's Bar in the shadow of the White House.

'What's it all about? asked Hampson.

'Suppose it is true that the USAF is going to be all electronic. It would make sense.'

'Except that all the human rights people are dead against it,' said Helen O'Grady.

'Especially in places like Pakistan, where our people haven't always been too careful what they hit.'

'If that is the story, then why was Makarovna kicked out? Why was Caradescu killed?'

'That has to be CIA.'

'Caradescu was anti-American. He would be a natural target.'

'Yes, but he stood no chance of winning the election.'

'Neither did that other fellow, Simonov.'

'But if they moved in together in a coalition, they would have defeated Makarovna.'

'Little chance of them doing that. Muslim and Orthodox? In the Balkans?'

'But Alexandrov took over from Makarovna. Why should he do that? He was supposed to be her ally. He was doing very well under sexy Tasha. She let him skim all the arms contracts.'

'But she fired him. Why was that?'

'Obviously she thought she didn't need him anymore. Maybe he got pissed at that. Maybe he thought she would take it further. Throw him in jail or something. He has plenty of form. Maybe she fired him on CIA orders. She would always do as she was told.'

'So he got his retaliation in first?'

'It could be.' Tom Hampson signaled to the waiter for another round of cocktails.

'Look,' said April McGregor, 'this is a big story - all those little countries tearing up a treaty with NATO. Let us suppose there is more to it. Let us suppose that O.B. really was lying about the new airbases and this Operation Warm Blanket. Let us suppose that what Alexandrov was saying was true, that the US really did try to fool all those countries into building new bases only to find that there were no new jobs or NATO payments.'

'Wow!' said Hampson. 'That would explain Alexandrov's takeover. Maybe Makarovna didn't know about the drone plan.'

'Maybe she wanted O.B.'s plan to be true? That would have been a little naive. Naivety is always fatal in her line of work.'

'So, let us work on the assumption that Alexandrov is telling the truth and O.B. is lying. That would be huge! Political assassinations, misleading our NATO allies, interference in another country's internal affairs, election fraud. It goes on and on. It could be bigger than Watergate!'

'I have another question. How much is Zonkov involved?'

'Well,' explained Tom Hampson,' according to my source, it was Zonkov who fixed the election for Makarovna.'

'And now he's working for Alexandrov.'

'I think,' said Tom, 'that our hoodlum friend is a gun for hire.'

'If he's for hire, then why isn't he working for us?'

'Good question,' said Helen. 'Here's another. Look, I've always believed that when two things happen at the same time, especially two unusual things, they are somehow connected. They call it synchronicity.'

'Yes?'

'Yes, why was our ambassador to Uzbekistan assassinated two days before the election? Just coincidence?'

'Possibly, I can't see any connection myself. We'll probably never know.'

'Look, I think we have the makings of a piece. Why don't we write it all up for our editors and see if any of them bites.'

The three of them went back to their homes and offices and sat down in front of their word-processors and wrote the first three articles about the chain of events in that small far-off country which so came to dominate the final year of the Bedford Presidency. Their articles appeared first in the opinion pages of their papers, well down the page. But soon, a trickle of similar articles appeared and the trickle became an unstoppable flood as the story moved from the inside pages to the front. The final year of O'Brien Bedford's Presidency, a Presidency which had hitherto been so carefully stage managed, came to be known, for the rest of American history, as the year of 'Dronegate' .

O'Brien Bedford was in conference with Secretary of State Treadwell, Defense Secretary George Zymanski and CIA Director Branwell McFall. The president was not happy, not happy at all.

'This leak has been very expensive. Did we get the guy who did it?'

'It's all been taken care of, Mister President. He has been neutralized,' answered McFall.

'Good. I don't need to know the details. Now, where do we go from here? Alison?'

'Well, sir,' replied the Secretary of State, 'it's time for Plan B.'

'Which is?'

'Well, sir, we could go ahead with the original plan of building a second wave of regular airbases and then gradually withdraw our forces as we replaced them with drones. It will take longer and there may be some problems on the way but in eight to ten years, all this TV drama will be forgotten,' explained Alison Treadwell.

'Will they trust us now?'

'Of course not, sir,' the Secretary of State went on. 'They don't trust us now and they didn't trust us before. So what's changed?'

'Good point,' conceded President Bedford. 'Do you have a plan?'

'Well, Mister President, we have a plan of sorts. It needs a little polishing.'

'Go on.'

'We've made a list of the seventeen countries in this so-called Organization of Pipeline States. We've divided them into three groups. First - those countries which will be difficult. They are the ones who are going to be more suspicious and are likely to hold out. Then, second, we have a group of countries who might be open to negotiation. Finally, there's group of four, no, five, countries who should be a pushover.' Alison Treadwell passed the list to the president who looked at it and asked

'Tell us about the third group first. Why do you and your clever people at State, why do you think these five are going to be a pushover?'

'They all have presidents or kings or heads of government on our payroll to some degree. A couple of them are getting two million a month from our funds, courtesy of our good friend Mister McFall here.'

'Is this true, McFall?'

256

'Yes indeed, sir. It is much easier to deal with one single strong man. They all take dollars – always in cash.'

'How many countries do we pay off like this? How much are we spending on these bribes?'

'Oh, around the world, I don't have the exact figure, but ballpark, not too much, little over a billion, maybe a billion and a half. Remember, we are keeping the world free for democracy. Money well spent, in my view. I think we have forty some countries on our payroll. Well, not the whole country, of course, aid comes under State, but wherever there's a one-man government, we can usually cut a deal.'

'And all those five countries on the list are getting dollars direct from us? Then why the hell did they go in for all that TV treaty ripping?'

'No sir, not quite. All the top men from those five are getting dollars from us. The countries themselves get regular aid. As for the reason they acted like jerks on TV was probably because they didn't want to be seen to be out of step with all the others.'

'Right,' said President Bedford, 'so we have five in the bag. That leaves twelve. Who's next, Alison?'

'Well, this group,' she pointed to a short list of four countries. 'We think they may be made to see sense.'

'Don't we bribe their presidents?'

'Yes, we do, sir,' said Branwell McFall of the CIA. 'But all four of them are sort of, well, democracies, which means that we have to give payola to the leading opposition boys as well as the main man. It's an expensive business.'

'You're telling me,' said the president. 'Just out of interest, because I've forgotten, what was the intelligence budget last year?'

'Total intelligence programs about a hundred and ten billion, give or take,' said Tuple.

257

'I'm not surprised, 'said Bedford drily. 'What do we do about these countries where they have an opposition?'

'Sir,' began Alison Treadwell, 'we offer a deal to the sitting government. If they don't bite, we find someone from the opposition who feels ambitious, or lucky, and we do a deal with him. Then, come election time, McFall's little helpers make sure he wins. We've done it before. With these four, it'll just be SOP.'

'SOP?'

'That's Standard Operating Procedure, sir.'

'That leaves half, lemme see, eight, who will be difficult. How do we get them to see sense?' asked Bedford.

'We have to take those on a case by case basis,' put in McFall. 'There are some anti-American fanatics amongst them.'

'Anti-American fanatics!' expostulated Bedford. 'Then just how the hell did we get them to sign up the first place? Alison?'

'Yeah,' answered the Secretary of State, 'it's the US umbrella they are looking for. They may hate us like poison but they hate some other countries even more. You know how it goes, one Sunni country with a Shia neighbor next door. Better to be looked after by us good Christian guys.'

'Or Jewish,' said George Zymanski, speaking for the first time.

'I see our old friend Alexandrov is on the list. I never took him for anti-American,' said Bedford.

'He's the one we will need to, er, 'convert' first.'

'And why is that?' asked the president.

'Well, sir, he's a newbie to the dictatorship business. He won't have his feet under that table yet. He'll still be looking over his shoulder at who might be trouble. Agency thinking is that a new man like Alexandrov needs a year to find his feet, dispose of possible enemies, get his own people in place. It takes time before he'll start to feel secure.'

'A year?' asked O'Brien Bedford. 'I thought he was promising elections in six months?'

'Maybe, sir, maybe. Then again, pigs might fly,' replied Branwell McFall. 'Better to be sure, before he gets too comfortable in the presidential palace.'

'OK,' said President Bedford, 'as I see it, we can probably do deals with nine of these countries and then pick off the other eight, one by one. Alexandrov first. I will get a speech written about how we are committed to Operation Warm Blanket as per the original treaty and we are sorry that some of our oldest allies have chosen to reject the treaty which was negotiated in good faith *etc.* Branwell, what sort of time scale are we talking before we're back on track?'

'I think we can do the simple deals and get to Alexandrov within, say, one year,' said McFall. 'The other seven, in maybe two, three years before we have them tied up. If we can show that we're building bases in these other countries, they might come around. It's going to take two years for work to get started.'

'By which time,' said the president, 'my term will be up anyway. Next item.'

The only other item on the agenda was more contentious. Everyone could be in complete agreement about the importance of keeping foreign governments under sensible American control, while, of course, maintaining vital democratic values. Nevertheless, when it came to internal political matters, dissent between loyal government officials would be inevitable.

The matter now on the table was the very important issue of just which United States department or agency would be in overall control of the new robotic air force when it was up and running.

O'Brien Bedford opened the debate. 'Next we come to a very sensitive matter, the overall command structure for the future electronic air force. As you know, up until now, drones have mainly been used for surveillance and unarmed patrols. But as we move to the new air force, with a much enhanced electronic component, drones will also eventually come to replace manned aircraft in regular combat and offensive roles.'

' While they are still mainly our eyes in the sky, it is proper that their control and operation should be a matter for the Central Intelligence Agency. But a case can be made for moving the entire command structure to the United States Air Force. I have to make the decision whether to do that or to leave things as they are before my successor is elected in thirteen months time.'

'I know you two gentlemen have strong views,' he nodded to Branwell McFall and George Zymanski, 'and I need to hear them. I have read your position papers. George, would you start.'

'Sir,' began the Secretary of State for Defense, 'you would not expect me to say anything other than I think the overall control of the new electronic air force should rest with the United States Air Force. The reasons are obvious.'

'First, it is the Air Force which has the longest record of successful combat experience. We have fought and won air battles whenever the USAF has been called upon. Learning the art of air warfare is not something which can be done overnight. It takes years, decades before one understands the strategies for deployment and operation of airborne weapons. The new all-electronic air force is a big step up from where we are at now. It will need proper professional air force control and management.'

'Branwell,' asked President Bedford, 'would you like to comment?'

'Thank you, Mister President,' said the Director of the CIA.

'What Mister Zymanski says is partly true. It will take professionalism and experience to make the new drone force work. That is why its control should stay with us, the Agency. We have been operating drones over all sorts of terrains for at least fifteen years. Not only spy drones but also operational drones under combat conditions. We have the necessary experience. If control were to pass to another department or agency, then that fifteen years of successful experience would need to be rebuilt from the ground up.'

'Mister President sir,' cut in Zymanski, 'that fifteen years experience includes numerous negative incidents which have been brought to the attention of both friendly and unfriendly governments, not to say human rights organizations around the world. The CIA record on drones includes an awful lot of civilian casualties which do not look good on their record.'

'We understand that our safety record is not so good,' answered McFall, 'but we do have the experience of operating drones in a war situation. If the USAF ever get their hands on the triggers, they will find that it isn't so easy to avoid loss of innocent life, regrettable as that is.'

'That is why we use a lot of surveillance satellites which can identify when civilians are least likely to be within target range. I hope, sir, you are not suggesting that the CIA might also lose its surveillance mission?'

'I don't think anyone has any criticism of the CIA expertise when it comes to intelligence gathering,' the president smoothly assured Branwell McFall.

'Do you want to come back, George?'

'Yes sir, just to say one thing. Our air force has a

hundred years experience of aerial warfare. Moving from manned to unmanned will be a big step forward. It will mean that American lives will be made safer. We have made these big changes before. For example, the move from turboprops to jets or the development of a carrier based force. We are accustomed to change and we will embrace drone warfare just like we embraced all those necessary changes in the past.'

'Do you have anything to add, Branwell?'

'Yes sir. Can I just remind everyone of our success with taking out Osama Bin Laden? That was a classic CIA operation, with minimum collateral damage.'

'That was small potatoes compared with...' George Zymanski got no further before President Bedford cut him off.

'I'll take on board both your comments. Thank you, gentlemen. Final decision by December of this year. That just about wraps it up. Thank you all for attending. Good morning.'

General Alexandrov, who now styled himself 'President', was installed in the presidential palace and Mikhail Simonov had been promoted to prime minister. Alexandrov did not trust Simonov, his long-time political opponent, but he knew, as a new dictator, just how important it was to keep his enemies close.

Simonov could always be executed later. It might even become convenient, at some future date, to curry favor with the mob by having Simonov stand trial for the murder of Caradescu. New evidence could always be invented.

Right now though, Alexandrov had the slightly tricky task of a meeting with the American Ambassador, Joseph Feldstein.

'Mister Ambassador, you are very welcome. How can we help?'

'General,' began Feldstein.

'President,' corrected Alexandrov.

Feldstein accepted the correction with good grace.

'Mister President, as you will know, my government is most concerned that you, together with all the other members of the Organization of Pipeline States, have abrogated, unilaterally, the Treaty for Operation Warm Blanket as signed by your predecessor only a few months ago.'

'Yes, that is true,' agreed Alexandrov. 'We acquired information that the famous Operation Warm Blanket was little more than an attempt to remove proper air cover from our defenses and replace them with robotically controlled unmanned machines, the reason being that the United States would save money and, as a result we would also lose much needed revenue. Added to which, Mister Ambassador, we and my fellow members of OPS would not have any control over your flying bombs which would be entirely controlled from within the United States. This would present us, the members of OPS, with numerous security problems.'

'That is correct, as far as it goes, Mister President, but in fact, your information is not quite complete. We are intending to go ahead with the original plan for Operation Warm Blanket at least until the year twenty thirty when the treaty provisions expire. Then, and only then, will we consider a change of plan from manned to unmanned planes. Meanwhile, the building of the second base at Nyo Brutske will proceed as planned and the promised economic benefits will be delivered, especially to you personally.'

'What do you mean,' Alexandrov's eyes narrowed, 'especially to me personally?'

'Well, I don't know if Ms Makarovna told you this but it is normal to assist the heads of friendly governments with certain expenses to enable them to run their private offices.'

'And how big a bribe did you have in mind?' asked Alexandrov.

'Not a bribe, Mister President, an honorarium to a friendly country.'

'How much is your 'honorarium'?'

'I understand the figure is about two million a month, US dollars.'

Alexandrov laughed. 'I cannot see Makarovna taking two million a month. When it came to you Americans, she was an amateur whore. She would do it for nothing.'

'Well, that's the going rate. Let us say that it's a gesture of friendship between two friendly nations.'

'No, Mister Ambassador, let us say that it's a stupid attempt to bribe the head of state of a sovereign country. And let us also say that you screwed it up. Two million a month! Ha, ha! Don't make me laugh, Ambassador. I make more than that in one week! Without selling my country! Thank you Ambassador. We will talk again when you have learnt to show us some respect.'

The American University of the Southern Balkans had been used to employing itinerant American professors to meet its teaching obligations as an anglophone liberal arts college on the American model. Suddenly, visas were difficult to obtain – the local immigration bureaucracy, never streamlined, had moved from slow to glacial and US citizens in need of a work permit found themselves waiting for up to a year before approval would be granted.

Naturally, this made it impossible to find suitable candidates willing to wait that long before they could even start to go through the Reilly-designed convoluted faculty recruitment process. More and more local professors were brought in as Americans came to the end of their contracts and went back home, never to return. Gradually, imperceptibly but inexorably, AUSB metamorphosed from being an American university for local students to being a local university with some American faculty members.   The turning point occurred the following academic year, when President Spring announced that classes need no longer be delivered in English but could instead be given in the local language. As the numbers of English-speaking teachers fell, it became obvious that within a few years, nothing much would remain of the American liberal arts college, so confidently inaugurated by President Bill Clinton all those years before.

There was much urging that the university accept the new situation and abandon its pretensions as a centre of American culture. Perhaps a name change would be appropriate, now that English was disappearing and even the university's computer systems now operated in Cyrillic script. When the idea was suggested to Alexei Alexandrov, he was, surprisingly, unenthusiastic.

'No,' he said, 'let them keep the name. Maybe the Americans will continue to pay. But most of the Amerikanski will soon be gone anyway. All except those who won't go because they are really working for the CIA. If we let them stay, we will know who they are and we can keep an eye on them.'

Denis Denitsev seethed with fury at his removal from running the prestigious masters program and the loss of income that had meant. He had not accepted Hattie Reilly PhD's assurance that she was no more than the passive tool of the AUSB management. He was now sure that she was the real problem. Was it not her who had begun the witch hunt against Balfour? Wasn't it Reilly who had provoked Nyborg into resigning? And wasn't Smalley, now elevated to the chair of the department, hadn't he always been Hattie Reilly PhD's blue-eyed boy?

Denitsev wondered how he had been so gullible, to be taken in by her continual protestations that what she had been doing was always in the best interests of the department and the university. He had supported her throughout the campaign against Balfour and now he had been rewarded by this humiliation! He! Professor Doctor Denis Denitsev with his brilliant academic record!

He knew what he had to do. Had he not been very good for General Alexandrov? Had he not brought the General the charms of the sweet, perfumed Annabella Markova-Casillias? She, he now realized, had passed on the information from Galpin's nocturnal ramblings which had been so useful for the success of Alexandrov's seizure of power. The whole picture was suddenly clear to him. What Galpin had revealed to Annabella in his sleep was the real secret plan for Warm Blanket and it was he himself, Denitsev, who had been instrumental in passing on to Alexandrov the information which had enabled the General to take his revenge on Makarovna.

That could only mean that Galpin had known the details about Operation Warm Blanket before they had got out into the public domain. So Galpin had been an employee of the CIA and it must have been Galpin and the CIA who had fixed the election and arranged for the murder of Caradescu. A little more logic brought Denitsev to the conclusion that all the other senior people at AUSB were also CIA, including Spring, Reilly, Mulvaney and Smalley. If that were the case, then his demotion, which was, in effect, an invitation to resign, was because the new professor in charge of the master's program, Ashworth, was also a Company man. So, Denitsev realized with sudden clarity, by not being CIA himself, he would have no future career at the American University of the Southern Balkans.

The best he could ever hope for would be a middle-ranking faculty position. He would serve out his days as a tenured professor with no possible hope of preferment. That was the only deal on the table.

Or, he could call in the favor which, he now realized, he was owed by President Alexei Alexandrov. He phoned the president's secretary, the redoubtable and pragmatic Irina, who had changed sides quite effortlessly, and asked for a meeting.

Alexandrov greeted Denitsev warmly. 'My old friend,' said the General. 'I expected to see you before now. How are things at your university? What news of the beautiful Annabella?'

Denitsev told Alexandrov of his conclusions about the goings-on with Galpin and the others but Alexandrov was ahead of him.

'Denis! We know all this! Spring and Mulvaney and the others. All CIA! Spies to spy on us! But tell me what we don't yet know.' Denitsev then told Alexandrov about Nyborg and how he had been driven to resign and he told the president of how Galpin had been killed in a car accident.

'If I know the CIA, that was no accident,' said Alexandrov. 'We knew that Galpin was a CIA agent and he must have been killed because he'd leaked the information about Warm Blanket. Still, Denis, my good friend, you will not be very welcome there yourself anymore, if they are never going to promote you. Only the American spies will be safe at AUSB.'

'You're not going to close it down, if it's full of

Amerikanski?'

'No, no. The spies are all second class. They are all old or fat women. They all get their orders from that asshole Sieghart at the American Embassy. No problem. Let the Americans pay for the education of our children. It is better if we know where the spies are for now. We can always take it off them any time we like. But Denis, what about you, my old friend? If you hadn't brought me the lovely Annabella, I would not now be sitting here in this palace. You deserve something for your trouble. And now that you have no career with the Americans, you should come and work for me as a good patriotic son of our fine country. We will pay you ten times what the Americans were paying you, maybe more. What about it, Denis?'

Denitsev thought for a moment. He was aware that he would be stepping into a minefield by working for a man who would certainly never allow his closest aides to live to enjoy a ripe old age and a sedate retirement. The lifetime of the coup would probably be very short anyway. The Americans had been publicly insulted and that was an act of impertinence from a small country which they certainly would not allow to go unpunished, if only to discourage those others of the OPS who might also be contemplating a similar adolescent outburst of self-assertive independence. It would be necessary to deliver a swift and decisive counter-blow to the General's fit of *lèse majesté*. On the other hand though, if Denitsev allowed himself to become Alexandrov's creature, he might be able to make a little money quickly and await his chance to escape with it before the inevitable American riposte.

'Yes, General, thank you, I will take it.'

'Good man! You will not regret it. You will be rich!'

Twenty two

That evening, General Alexandrov made a TV broadcast. Standing beside him was Denis Denitsev.

'Fellow citizens, I speak to you tonight as your president. I have to announce that I am asking our Committee of National Security to approve a new member of the government. I am certain that they will recognize, as I do, one of the finest public servants our country has produced. I have the great pleasure of asking Professor Denis Denitsev, a leading professor at the American University of the Southern Balkans and one of our most famous academics, to assume the duties and responsibilities of Director of State Security. Professor Denitsev will take immediate control of our fine security forces, including all branches of the police and the SSP, in whose safe hands the country's safety and peaceful wellbeing is entrusted. I congratulate Professor Denitsev on his new appointment which will ensure the continuing stability of the homeland at this critical point in our history.'

'I also have another announcement to make, my dear friends. Today I spoke with the United States Secretary of State, Alison Treadwell, and informed her that our country will no longer consider itself a member of NATO. I have today signed an order which separates our country from that organization and I have also asked our American friends and allies to close their airbase at Altameda within twelve months from today.

Madame Secretary Treadwell accepted our decision on behalf of the president and people of our great ally across the Atlantic and she wished us well.'

Secretary of State Treadwell had not wished the General well. Quite the contrary, their long phone conversation had been extremely ill-tempered on both sides. There had been much shouting and argument. The General had accused the Americans of trying to fool the OPS states into accepting a Trojan Horse of a deal. In return Alison Treadwell accused Alexandrov of betraying his country by abandoning the shelter of NATO and leaving it defenseless.

'How can you be so stupid? ' demanded Ms Treadwell. 'If you leave NATO, you will be giving up a vital part of your defenses for nothing! You will also be losing all the benefits of the NATO base at Altameda! Can't you see how dangerous that will be?'

'But it is your plan to close Altameda anyway! Even if you do build a second base here, it will only be temporary. You will still go ahead with your plan to replace all your planes with unmanned drones! Then where will we be? The drones will bring us no financial benefits and will make us a target for every crazy terrorist group in the Middle East!'

This loud bitter exchange went on for the best part of an hour before, in exasperation, the United States Secretary of State slammed down the phone.

'Fuck the crooked little bastard!' she shouted at the State Department office wall. Then she called Branwell McFall of the CIA.

'Come round, Branwell,' she ordered.

'Now,' she asked, 'who do we have down there that we can rely on?'

'Local man is John Sieghart, old Vietnam vet. Good man.'

'Is he an operations or desk?'

'Desk, I'm sorry. He doesn't see too much action these days.'

'Do we have anybody there who can carry out a small covert operation?'

'There are some people at the local American university. But they are all low-grade intelligence gatherers.'

'What I had in mind was a little regime change - in the best interests of democracy, of course. Before Alexandrov can consolidate his power and become another president-for-life dictator. The world has enough of them.'

'True. Given time, they all start to bite the hand that feeds them.'

'So, Branwell, better to remove this one ASAP, don't you think, before he settles in?'

'What did you have in mind, Madame Secretary? Not an all-out military action?'

'No, Branwell. Boots on the ground is out. It looks too crude. Anyway, we are supposed to be drawing down all our troops. No, it will have to be covert. A very small team smuggled into the country. Do you have any people who could do that?'

'We have no one in that part of the world anymore. We do have a couple of guys who were busted from there last year.'

'Tell me about them. What were they busted for?'

'Big scandal but we managed to keep it quiet. They went over the border into Bulgaria for a night out. Got drunk and screwed a couple of underage schoolgirl hookers. They also beat up a Bulgarian colonel and wrecked a hotel room. The Bulgarians made a big, big fuss

271

and kicked them out. Joe Feldstein won't have them back.'

'They sound perfect. They won't be going to Bulgaria, so no problem there. Feldstein doesn't need to know. Are they up to it, do you think? What are they doing now? '

'Right now, they're doing squat - just small internal odd jobs within the US. That's all.'

'But could they complete a covert mission like this?'

'They should be OK. They've both got over ten years in the field. They have all the local languages and familiarity with the country.'

'What about the local connection? Do they have someone there?'

'Yes, but that could be a problem. They usually used Konstantin Zonkov for local operations. He's used to be one of the biggest gangsters in the region before Alexandrov made him Minister of Justice.'

'Is he still on the Company payroll?'

'Yes, he is. We, that is, the Drug Enforcement Agency and the FBI, turn a blind eye to his shipments from South America. Zonkov is also the region's biggest wholesaler.'

'Sounds excellent, so what's the problem?'

'The problem, Alison, is that he just might have a conflict of interest. He might not play ball if he's doing well enough out of Alexandrov.'

'How long is the shipment agreement for?'

'It was for six months, two months to run. But obviously, in the circumstances, we have just put the word out that it's canceled.'

'You're not thinking creatively, Branwell. This Zonkov has worked for us before. I'm sure he will work for us again. Does he work for anyone else?'

'Just about anyone who'll pay him.'

'Even better. Why don't we ask him to come back home to Uncle Sam and there is no reason, if he is a good boy and does as he's told, why the DEA shouldn't be turning a blind eye to his Colombian imports for many years to come? All he needs to do is one little favor for the two brave boys who will shortly be turning up in his country.'

'But, Madame Secretary, won't it look a bit obvious if Alexandrov announces he's pulling out of NATO and soon afterwards he meets with a nasty accident? It will have CIA written all over it.'

'Yes it will, and that will be a clear message to every other tin-pot little Hitler who thinks he can go it alone without us. Don't worry, the other sixteen so-called OPS countries will get the message.'

Branwell McFall called his two best Balkan field operatives to his office. Charlie Le Moine and Damon Dexter were surprised by the unexpected recall to favor. Since the previous spring they had been employed on tedious low-level operations inside the United States.

Only the trip to North Dakota, to fix the car of the late provost of AUSB, had been anything like real work. For the most part they had hung out with possible subversive groups, picked up gossip, mostly irrelevant, and they had written reports from behind desks in suburban Virginia. It was a waste of their talents, they both knew, but they had a penance to pay and, boy, were they paying it. Now, though, it looked as if their moment of redemption had arrived.

'Sit down, gentlemen,' invited Branwell McFall. 'Let me be frank. The agency is still unhappy about your little pranks last March, but we are prepared to give you a second chance. Screw up again and you are out.'

'Thank you, sir.'

'This job is highly classified, which means that it is

highly dangerous. It could go wrong, in which case, you, me and everyone right up there will feel the chill. Do I make myself clear?'

'Yes sir!'

'Now you may have heard that there has been a small disagreement between Alison Treadwell and General, or President as he calls himself now, Alexei Alexandrov? Yes?'

'Yes sir!'

'Good! Well it seems that Alexei is getting a little bit above himself. He thinks he can run his little piece of God's green Earth without reference to his friends and protectors here in the United States. Well, we don't take too kindly to that sort of arrogance, so it looks like it is time for the General to be replaced by a more co-operative personality.'

'Are you asking us to depose the General, sir?'

'Depose, yes, that's a very nice word. Yes, I am asking you to 'depose' him.'

'But I thought regime change was no longer United States policy?' asked Damon Dexter.

'And quite right too,' answered McFall. 'The United States cannot, under international law, be seen to be involved in regime change under any circumstances. So you have to be very, very, careful not to get caught. It has to look like a local job.'

'The locals all report to a man called Konstantin Zonkov. He was the top hood before he was made Justice Minister,' said Damon.

'Reports are that he is still the *numero uno*. It's just that these days he appoints the judges instead of bribing them,' McFall told them.

'But he is still doing his bad things?' asked Charlie.

'Oh yes. The government job is just a favor from his old friend Alexei. You two know Zonkov, according to your files. Isn't that right?'

'Yes sir, we've had dealings.'

'So, it should be straightforward. What we want you to do is get into the country quietly, meet Zonkov and put a simple proposition to him.'

'Which is, sir?'

'If he will take over from Alexandrov as president, then we will support him as long as he remains in the top job. We will turn a blind eye to all his shipments for as long as he wants us to - forever, if he likes. In return, he will not raise any awkward questions about our military presence in his country. Oh, and he will come out as even more pro-American than the famous poolside porn star. If he's for sale then let's buy him ! Do you have any questions?'

'Will we be working with John Sieghart and Joe Feldstein, sir?'

'No! Absolutely not! You are to have no contact with them at all! This is to be an entirely covert operation. Don't go within a mile of the embassy.'

'Right sir!'

'Now, what I suggest is that you take a couple of EU passports and drive into the country from the Greek side. Some disguise like itinerant workers. Fly to Athens and an old car will be waiting for you. You'll get the details via your iPhones. No official communications until it's all over and we have a nice safe President Zonkov in power for a long while.'

'Yes sir.'

'Thank you, sir.'

'So, let's go!'

Charlie Le Moine and Damon Dexter knew when they were lucky to have been given one final chance and this time there would be no screw-ups. On that they were determined. They had been kicking their heels in suburban Virginia and taking various internal trips within the United States for nearly a year after they had so disgraced themselves. They were glad that they would not be seeing John Sieghart or even visiting the US Embassy just off Caradescu Square in the newly-named city of Caradescugrad.

They were glad that Sieghart and Feldstein would not even know of their mission to meet Konstantin Zonkov and to cut a deal with him on behalf of the US government. Without Sieghart being in on the operation, it would mean that there would be no backup if things went wrong. But they shouldn't go wrong, they convinced themselves. Both of them knew Zonkov well. They had dealt with him many times and they both admired his amoral single-mindedness.

Twenty three

The two of them took a business class flight from Baltimore Washington International Airport to Frankfurt where they met a CIA staffer who provided them with a change of clothes to make them look like just any other pair of migrant workers. Armed with a few hundred euros and two false EU passports they boarded the Athens flight in cattle class. At Athens airport they were met by another Company colleague who handed over a ten-year-old Toyota which they drove over the back mountain roads to Caradescugrad. There they checked into the cheap, basic, 'Patriot' hotel. When they guessed that Zonkov would be in his office at the Ministry of Justice the next morning, they phoned him on the private direct number which the CIA, ever efficient and all-knowing, had already provided.

They were surprised when Zonkov answered immediately.

'Hello, who is this?' asked the Minister of Justice.

'You know us,' said Charlie Le Moine. 'We have helped you before. Remember Bezaki Steel when I and some of my colleagues helped you with the strike? About three years ago?'

'So, can you be more specific?'

'OK, the Company was very grateful for the help you gave us during last year's elections. Does that ring a bell?'

'Not now. I am in a meeting. Phone again in one hour.'

The two CIA men waited an hour and phoned again.

'Amerikanski! Is that Charlie? I recognize your voice. You speak our language well! What do you want this time?'

'It's a bit difficult to explain on the phone,' said

Charlie. 'Can we meet privately?'

'For you, my old friend, I'll make time for a meeting. Are you alone in Caradescugrad?'

'No, I have a colleague with me. You will know him. We want to make you an offer.'

'This colleague, he's not Sieghart from the embassy?'

'No, Sieghart doesn't know about this.'

Good, thought Zonkov, the less the US Embassy knows the better. It must be big.

'Can we meet?' asked Charlie Le Moine.

'Two pm this afternoon. My car is a black Mercedes. I'll be outside the main gates of the Winter Park.'

Damon and Charlie were waiting, sitting on a bench and looking for all the world like two unemployed workmen. The large black Mercedes drew up. Zonkov opened the door just enough to beckon the two CIA men inside. Zonkov greeted them warmly.

'Charlie! Damon! My old friends! It is good to see you!'

'You too, Konstantin! You've become respectable! You look good!'

Justice Minister Konstantin Zonkov did indeed look the part. He had lost much of his old peasant appearance. In his new incarnation, the apparel really did proclaim the man. His suit was Savile Row, his loafers were Gucci and his watch was a heavy, vulgar, diamond-encrusted lump of gold.

'Thank you. Not bad for a peasant boy from Nako Grodski who never learned to read and write properly! Now I am so rich I can employ graduates from the very best universities to do my reading and writing for me! Do you know, they have asked me to be the Chancellor of the American University? I think they need some of my money.'

'You've certainly done well for yourself, Konstantin.'

'So what are you two boys doing here? Maybe you want to come and work for me? I pay better than the CIA. You could have a good life here. Become citizens. Get rich. But no, I understand. It is too difficult to leave your CIA. If you come to work for me, then they will come after you to shut you up. Then that gives me a big problem. So, boys, what do you want?'

'What we want, Konstantin, is to make you the richest man in the Balkans. Maybe even the richest man west of the Urals.'

'That makes me very interested.'

'Konstantin, who is the richest man in this country right now?'

'Well, Alexei Alexandrov, of course. He has more money than everyone else. He is worth billions. He took everything Balashirov and Makarovna left behind when he threw them out. Plus he has all his other business activities.'

'But Konstantin, if you were president then the richest man would be you, wouldn't it?'

'Are you suggesting what I think you are suggesting?'

'Just think how rich you would be if you took over Alexandrov's position. Not bad for a peasant boy from Nako Grodski who never learned to read or write properly.'

'So, you want me to kill Alexandrov?'

'If it's necessary to kill him, then kill him.'

'What do I get in return?'

'In return, the US government will give your government its full support. If you want to run the country on your own without an opposition then that is fine with us, whatever President Bedford says in his speeches. What you do with all that money is your own business. We will not interfere, just as long as you are seen to be strongly pro-American. Not just in private but in public as well.'

'I love Uncle Sam, no problem.'

'Well, Konstantin, there's a bit more to it than that.'

'More?'

'Look, Konstantin, if you are president, then we will stay out of your way. But we don't like the way Alexandrov is doing things. We want to close the base at Altameda and build a couple of small, discrete drone bases out of the way somewhere, very well hidden.'

'Alexandrov thinks that would be bad for the country. It would leave us undefended and open to terrorist attacks.'

'No, Konstantin, what Alexandrov has done is to weaken your country's links with NATO and the West. That is where the real danger lies. If you are attacked you need the United States to back you up. We think it is your patriotic duty to replace Alexandrov with you, yourself.'

'And if I refuse? I have sworn an oath of allegiance to the president. He has been good to me.'

'Sure, good to you but bad for the country. I think your duty to protect your fatherland comes higher than your oath to Alexandrov. He is not going to be here for long anyway. The CIA will find a way to get rid of him, with you or without you. If you are still Minister of Justice when we neutralize Alexandrov, then you will not be safe either. We will be sure to remember if you refused to help us when we asked you. But if you do the necessary work yourself, you will be safe, Konstantin. Not only safe, but rich as well!'

'So the Amerikanski are planning a coup against my country?'

'Not against your country, Konstantin. Against just one bad and stupid man! '

'If I agree to do it, is there anything else in it for me?'

'I'm glad you asked that, Konstantin. You should know that our organization, the Central Intelligence Agency, makes regular, er, disbursements to friendly presidents and prime ministers, to help with the expenses of their offices.'

'What do you mean, disbursements?'

'It's the standard fee. Only for our friends, of course.'

'How much is it?'

'Not much. We pay two million US dollars a month.'

'You mean that Alexandrov is getting two million a month and still he pretends to be anti-American?'

They did not mention that Alexandrov had refused the monthly two million.

'The CIA does not appreciate his ingratitude.'

'You would have no problems with me,' said Konstantin Zonkov, 'if you were paying me that sort of money. And what about my shipments?'

'No problems there, either. You could continue to get your shipments inspection-free. For as long as you are president.'

'My American friends,' said Minister of Justice Konstantin Zonkov, holding out his hand, 'you just got yourself a deal! Where are you two boys staying?'

'The Patriot Hotel.'

'Good name!'

Charlie and Damon went back to the Patriot Hotel, ate a late lunch and waited. At five pm, the manager brought a large package up to their room. They ran their portable scanner across it and when it did not appear to be metallic, they opened it cautiously. Inside were lots of hundred dollar bills. There was a short note, hand-written in babyish Cyrillic characters, as if by someone who had never learnt to write properly. It read '*Thank. This to yous*'.

281

The phone rang. It was Zonkov. 'You got my little gift? I am going to be the richest man in Europe, so I am sending you a little token of my appreciation. I suggest you leave the country right away and watch tomorrow's news on TV.'

Within ten minutes, Charlie and Damon were packed and in the old Toyota and driving over the back roads into Greece.

Zonkov spent some time debating with himself what to do about Dexter and LeMoine.. Would be a good idea to have them killed to cover his involvement with them? No, he decided, although the Americans would stick to their bargain whatever happened to two low-ranking CIA goons because the stakes were already too high for them to go back on the deal.

Better to let the two try to hide the million dollars. They will never be able to tell anyone where the money came from. If they are caught with all that cash, they could go to jail for attempted money laundering, and no one will ever believe their story about Konstantin Zonkov. Or 'President' Konstantin Zonkov, as would be tomorrow morning.

He picked up the phone and asked Alexei Alexandrov for a private meeting late that night.

At the presidential office, Zonkov was greeted warmly by President Alexandrov.

'My dear Konstantin, it is always a pleasure to see you. '

'Mister President. Thank you so much for seeing me so late.'

'My dear friend, what can I do for you?'

'I'm sorry, Alexei. Your time is up.'

Zonkov, a powerful man, grabbed Alexandrov's arm

282

and twisted it up his back. Zonkov then put his other arm around the president's neck forcing his mouth shut so that Alexandrov could not call for his guards.

Alexandrov struggled but Zonkov, a veteran of many a dirty street fight, was heavier and fitter and younger than President Alexandrov. The president was pushed face-down into a cushion, where Zonkov held him until Alexei Alexandrov stopped struggling and all life had gone out of him. Zonkov let go and pulled the presidential body on to the floor. He tested the pulse and after satisfying himself that Alexandrov really was dead, he removed all signs of the struggle, walked over to the door of the office and called the guard.

'Quickly! Fetch a doctor! I think our president has had a heart attack!'

The palace doctor was called and examined the body.

'It is a heart attack, isn't it, doctor?' Zonkov fixed the doctor with a cold stare.

'No, it's a... Yes, it's a heart attack.' He changed his mind when he noticed Zonkov's stare.

'I'll write out the death certificate now.'

'Thank you, doctor.' A small packet of money was discreetly put into the doctor's bag.

Zonkov's little army quickly surrounded the presidential palace, the state broadcaster, the State Bank and the main airport. By dawn, after the summary executions, or plain old-fashioned score-settling, of political unreliables like the Chief of Police, Justice Minister Zonkov had complete control of the country. He made a live early morning TV broadcast.

'It is with very grave regret that I announce to you all the sudden death last night of President Alexei Alexandrov. The cause of death was a massive heart attack brought on by the enormous workload undertaken by the late president during his brief but important term of office. He will be greatly missed by all our citizens and by all freedom-loving people around the world. But his work will continue and I have been persuaded by the Committee of National Security to assume, myself, the onerous duties and responsibilities of the presidency of our great country.'

'President Alexandrov, distinguished servant of the state and gallant, heroic veteran of our armed forces will receive a state funeral as soon as arrangements can be made. A week of official mourning will be observed, beginning today. '

'In my first duty as your new president, I am pleased to be able to announce that our country will henceforth seek to restore its traditional good relations with our friends in NATO and across the Atlantic and we will proceed forthwith to the implementation of Operation Warm Blanket, which is so important for our own security and for the security of our friends and allies in Southeastern Europe. '

'As from now, the name of our fair and beloved capital city will be changed from Caradescugrad to Alexandrovgrad in honor of our dear departed president. God bless you all and God bless our precious homeland.'

Thus it was that Konstantin Zonkov, gangster, thug, murderer, wholesale drug dealer and semi-literate peasant boy from Nako Grodski became the third president of his country. After a few more years in business as the Americans' favorite son and blue-eyed local boy, he ascended to the coveted position of being the richest man west of the Urals.

President O'Brien Bedford had had a good presidency for the most part. Even though he had presided over the continuing decline of the United States as a world power compared with the rising stars in the East, he was not reviled for recognizing the end of empire and adjusting his country's self-image to a vision smaller than that of some of his predecessors. He had carefully scheduled the ending of America's military adventures when he had tacitly given up the US's traditional role as the world's policeman.

He was preparing his country for a future with a smaller world-view than its citizens had been used to. Mostly, save for a minority on the lunatic right, his constituents had appreciated the way that O.B. had read the national mood correctly - that the United States was getting tired of sorting out the problems and failures of other countries far away.

The ghost of isolationism was reappearing and the average American in the street was beginning to see the wisdom of leaving the rest of the world to stand on its own two feet.

President Bedford, after seven years in the world's top job, was winding down a calm and constructive presidency. He had been expecting a year of gradual easing up of his duties and a gentle smoothing of the way for his anointed successor, Secretary of State Alison Treadwell, who would be able to build on Bedford's popularity and continue the management of the slow expiration of the American imperial dream.

But, without being truly aware of how it had happened, O'Brien Bedford had succumbed to hubris. His final year in office became, not a peaceful transition to a new golden age, but a year of vicious internal Washington infighting which would destroy much of the good work and the goodwill which he had so carefully built up in his seven years as incumbent of the highest office in the world.

His last, unhappy year began with investigation by the Senate Foreign Affairs Standing Committee into the 'Dronegate' crisis. It was watched on TV by millions of people around the world. Secretary of State Treadwell would appear before it several times.

'Madame Secretary, is it true that you deliberately misled our NATO allies when you met them in Brussels last year? Is it not true that you hid from them the true nature of our new involvement in their countries by not telling them of the projected cutbacks in our regular air force personnel and the building of drone stations on their territories?' asked Senator Rupert O'Malley .

'No, Senator,' answered the Secretary of State, 'we presented to our NATO allies and to the Euro-Atlantic Partnership countries a plan for Operation Warm Blanket which is a doubling up of regular air bases across a line going through a number of countries and roughly following the central Asian oil pipeline. There was no misleading.'

'But isn't it true, Madame Secretary, that Operation Warm Blanket was intended as a front for a plan to replace, eventually, all manned US military aircraft with unmanned drones?'

'The president and I were certainly not intending to mislead...'

'Yes or no, Madame Secretary? Yes or no?'

'American military technology is proceeding at a ...'

'Yes or no, Madame Secretary? Yes or no?'

286

'We cannot give a definite answer to that question until...'

'So the answer is yes, is it not? It is the policy of the US government to close all USAF NATO air bases and replace them with drone stations?'

'Certainly not! The fully manned USAF bases will stay in place for the foreseeable future, certainly until the technology has made unmanned airborne vehicles safe and reliable.'

The chairman cut in. 'Thank you Madame Secretary. Senator Rafinez, you have a question?'

'Thank you Mister Chairman. Can I ask the Secretary of State if she is in favor of drone warfare in view of the many protests against their use which have been made around the world by human rights groups?'

'Senator Rafinez is correct to say that there have been numerous protests which we believe to be misguided. Drones are no more lethal than conventional military aircraft,' replied the Secretary of State.

'Surely', continued Senator Rafinez, 'the argument made by these protesters is that the balance of weaponry is too one-sided. The operator of the drone can inflict numerous casualties on the ground and yet can stay completely safe himself. So a drone will be used with less respect for human life.'

'Yes, sir,' said Alison Treadwell, 'that is true. There is, unfortunately, collateral damage in all forms of warfare. If the casualty rate is higher with drones it is because the enemies of our country are aware of the value of the anti-American propaganda caused by a high casualty rate and therefore our enemies will put their offensive material in centers of human population. Remember also, Senator, that drone warfare will save valuable American service lives.'

'Before you go on, Senator,' broke in the Chairman,

287

'I have some news you might like to hear before the press get hold of it. I have just been handed a note which is not entirely irrelevant to the discussion of this committee. It says that General Alexandrov has died of a heart attack in his sleep. His replacement is Justice Minister Konstantin Zonkov. That is all I have right now. I believe you might like to consult with your office over this new development, Madame Secretary?'

'Yes, I would, Mister Chairman. Thank you.'

'Hearing adjourned until ten am tomorrow. All rise.'

President Bedford called his Secretary of State the moment she got back to her office.

'What's the story, Alison?'

'Yes, we did it.'

'Well, that's one down - only sixteen to go.'

'No, sir, it's better than that, sir. Alexandrov was the leader of their OPS thing. If he can be rubbed out for taking an independent line, a few of the others will start to regret tearing up the treaty.'

'So, Operation Warm Blanket is still alive and well?'

'Yes sir.'

'Is there anything we should be worrying about? Our hands are completely clean?

'Not too much, sir. To all appearances, it looks like a genuine heart attack. Difficult to prove the CIA did it. But the bad news is that two CIA operatives have been arrested by the Athens police. It seems they'd been in contact with Konstantin Zonkov only a few days ago.'

'So, tell me the worst, why were they arrested?'

'Well, sir, it seems that they tried to deposit a large amount of money, believed to be a million dollars, in a Greek bank account. It seems that the bank became suspicious of the large amount and checked the serial numbers on the bills. The money came from a large cash payment received last year by one Mehmet Caradescu, who was assassinated last year before the elections.'

'Rubbed out, yes? By Simonov, wasn't it?'

'Simonov got the blame, sir. But everyone knows it was Zonkov who stuck the bomb on to his car.'

'And Zonkov took over Caradescu's empire? Who was paying him? Was it us?'

'Seems likely. You'd need to ask McFall for the full details. But it looks like Company work.'

'Have you any idea how some of Caradescu's money finished up with two of our men?'

'Well, sir, it seems that the two of them were on some kind of mission to talk to Zonkov. Oh, and another thing, they were on false EU passports. The Greek police are not letting them go. It appears they were trying to open bank accounts in false names.'

'We need to get them out of Athens.'

'Yes sir! Our embassy people are talking to the Greek Foreign Ministry right now.'

'If they were going to keep the money, then it's embezzlement of US government funds. Ten to twenty, if I remember my criminal law class.'

'It won't stick, sir. Their defense will be that they were just storing the money temporarily because they had nowhere else to park it and they were intending to turn it in.'

'So, who owns the money anyway?'

'Unless we can prove otherwise, then they do, I guess.'

'Right then, Alison, get them out. Bring 'em back and debrief them. It's up to McFall what he does with them. Don't worry! It'll work out, Alison. This Dronegate thing will blow over.'

289

'I'm sure you can handle it, sir. It's just a matter of keeping a lid on things until the election. No third term to worry about.'

'But I thought you had your ambitions, Alison? Dronegate is not going to help you.'

'Oh, I don't know, O.B. It could work out. I'll run on the patriotic ticket and the continuation of a quiet presidency. I'll say Dronegate is down to unpatriotic people who don't want to support our service personnel by making war safer for them. Anything sticking after I win and I will write some presidential pardons like Ford did for Nixon.'

'And it you don't win, Alison? What then?'

'Well sir, if I don't win then I guess we can both write our memoirs from jail.'

Also by
Christopher Worrad Payne

ERASED!

Ken and Sonia are lecturers in a further education college whose principal, Morton Scregg, is a lecherous tyrant. One day, after a drunken lunch, Principal Scregg falls down the college stairs to his death. As the last to speak to him, Ken is accused of his murder.

The death of Scregg and the injustice of being blamed for it, is a turning point in Ken's life. He and Sonia come to realize that there is a market for an assassination business dedicated to erasing all the evil Scregg's of this world as a public service. At first the business goes well, and they get a steady supply of clients who are victims of everyday bullies, cheats and psychopaths.

But Ken and Sonia soon find out that the 'conflict deletion' profession is far more crowded than they had expected as they get drawn into a parallel universe of assassins and hitmen.

In a tense climax to this comedy thriller, Ken and Sonia are forced to commit the execution of the century, which they must complete satisfactorily and escape, or be 'erased' themselves.

ISBN   978-971-9578-02-4 (Paperback)
           978-971-9578-06-2 (eBook)

The Descent of Gustave K

Gustave K had everything. Born to a wealthy titled German family, he had risen to the top of international financial and political life when he was made Managing Director of the World Development Fund. He was expected to go even further – many thought he would go on to become president of his country.

The Descent of Gustave K is the story of a principled and brilliant man whose prediction of a forthcoming world financial catastrophe and how it could be prevented, made him some very powerful enemies who were determined to silence him at any price.

The weapon they chose to bring about Gustave K's descent was his well-known weakness as a sexual libertine. For their plan to succceed, they also needed to destroy the life of Estella, the Mexican chambermaid they had used to entrap him.

Both Gustave K and Estella find themselves unwitting victims of the arbitrary immorality and cruelty of big government power when it balances injustices to the individual against what it perceives as the greater public good. The humanity of the two is what gives them the strength to survive the forces set against them and find a means to rebuild their shattered lives.

ISBN   978-971-9678-08-3 (Paperback)
        978-971-9678-09-0 (eBook)

ISBN 978-971-95780-3-1

9 789719 578031 >